Allusions of Innocence

Edited by

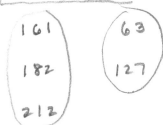

READ ORDER Jax Goss

161	63	28	3
182	127	75	41
212		219 (13)	85
		167	139
		111 (16)	188
		257	232
			274

Solarwyrm Press

Published by Solarwyrm Press, 2014
www.solarwyrm.com
Cover Design by Luke Spooner
ISBN 978-0-473-27721-5

TABLE OF CONTENTS

INTRODUCTION

JAX GOSS

I have long been fascinated by childhood, and the various perceptions of it that exist. The concept of childhood is a newer one than most people realise. It was only really in the 17th century that childhood as a concept emerged, and the notions of innocence and purity often associated with children began to appear.

Over time, there have been various shifts in this perception, and horror and fantasy writers have begun to realise the power of subverting those notions of innocence to very creepy effect.

Children see the world very differently to adults, which can be frightening, or enlightening, or funny. When I picked the theme for this anthology I had no idea just how wide this particular aspect could be.

I've always loved stories about smart children, kids who were a bit more perceptive than their peers, children who were often outcasts or sidelined despite (or maybe because) of their precocity. Characters like Mary from *The Secret Garden* and Bastian from *The NeverEnding Story* were my companions as a child, characters I related to perhaps more than I liked to admit.

And so I created a brief that the stories should involve these smart child protagonists, but be stories aimed at an adult audience.

I probably should have predicted how dark many

of these stories would go, but they ended up often being darker than I anticipated. Many of these stories are not for the faint of heart. Some are downright disturbing. Some are hopeful and funny. All of them are, in my not-so-humble opinion, exceptional.

I hope you enjoy reading them as much as I enjoyed compiling them. Welcome to the rabbit-hole.

Jax Goss
Dunedin, 2014

MR. HARRIS' DOOR
A.P. SESSLER

Greg stood just past the dune line, watching the breaking waves grow larger by the moment. The few surfers bold enough to brave the angry Atlantic looked like cutout felt figures on a flannel board of gray. Tiny red flags flapped madly in the September wind, warning beach goers of possible riptides.

A handful of locals lazed the Sunday away walking up and down the beach, playing a game of Frisbee, or just enjoying a picnic for their last fix of summer.

As the small boy turned to walk up the bald path, a gust of wind blew locks of brown hair and sand in his face. He turned his head and brushed his eyes free of sand and continued down the path when the giant sea oats on either side began to thrash at him. He ran past them until he reached the other side of the dune line and saw the cul-de-sac.

Mitchell entertained himself by scribbling strange symbols in the sand with a damp piece of driftwood. He and Noland sat adjacent to each other on two of the six black, creosoted pylons laid end to end in a circle, forming the border of a large bonfire pit.

For the boys it served as their water cooler before school, their watering hole after school, and their round table when discussing more serious matters. They dubbed it a variety of monikers including home, base, home base, the circle, headquarters or just HQ.

When Noland heard Greg coming down the path he stood up.

"What's it look like?" Noland asked.

"The red flags are still up," answered Greg.

"That stinks. Last day of summer and we can't even swim," said Noland as he and Greg took their respective places at the circle.

"And we won't be able to hang out at school for a whole 'nother year."

"It's just half a year. We can hang out during lunch and after school."

"Not with all the homework we'll have."

"You're only in the fourth grade—you won't have as much as Cliff and me."

"You and Clifton won't have as much as me," said Mitchell, a grade higher and a foot taller than all of the friends.

"Where is Clifton?" asked Greg.

"He's home," answered Noland. "Why don't you go get him?"

"Why? There's nothing to do," Greg complained.

"We could light a fire," Mitchell proposed.

"It's too windy. My mom won't let us," said Noland.

"What about your parents?" Mitchell asked Greg.

"If one parent says no it doesn't matter what the rest of our folks say," Greg answered.

"That's not fair. Your dad made this for us," said Mitchell.

"No, he made it for our parents," said Noland.

"But they don't ever use it," said Greg.

"That's because—" Mitchell started when Noland's eyes flashed in his direction. "Sorry."

"Anyways, it's cool your dad made it," said Greg. "He'd be happy it's our home base."

Noland turned his head and remained silent.

"Your dad was cool," added Greg.

"Yeah," Noland managed to agree.

"You still miss him?" asked Mitchell.

"Of course I do," said Noland as he grabbed the stick from Mitchell. "What kind of stupid question is that?"

"Sorry, Nol," said Mitchell.

Noland scribbled over Mitchell's runes until they became nothing but wavy lines.

"Hey," Mitchell objected. "You didn't have to do that. I said I was sorry."

"Everybody's sorry. Stop being sorry and start being careful," Noland huffed as tossed the stick in the pile of ashes in the circle's centre.

"You got it all dirty," whined Mitchell as he retrieved the ash-powdered piece of driftwood and wiped it on his long swimming trunks.

Noland stood up and brushed the dirt and sand from his hands. "All right," he said. "Greg, you go get Cliff. We're going to Peach Shores."

"What are we gonna do?" asked Greg.

"We're gonna go nigger-knocking," Noland exclaimed.

"My mom says you shouldn't say that word," said Mitchell.

"We won't," said Noland. "Not in front of Cliff."

"How do you play it?" Greg asked.

"You go to someone's door, knock, then run like crazy. When they open the door there's no-one there. It drives them crazy," said Noland with a devilish grin.

"That sounds fun. I'll go tell Clifton what we're playing."

"Don't tell him what it's *called*!"

"What do I tell him we're playing?"

"Just tell him we're going knocking on people's doors and running."

"Okay."

"And hurry up. I'll tell my mom we're gonna play hide and seek. I'll meet you guys back here."

"I'll go tell your mom and mine," said Mitchell. He ran up his porch stairs and entered the side door with the piece of driftwood in his hands. He and Greg's mothers sat at the kitchen table talking.

"Mitchell, leave that outside. It might have sea lice," his mother instructed. He stepped outside and looked for a secure place to store his treasure. On the wooden, railed porch were three folding canvas chairs by a round, wicker table. He laid the piece of driftwood in a chair and returned to the kitchen to ask permission to play.

Greg stepped on Clifton's porch and knocked on the front door through the screen door's mesh. The painted white door opened inward and Clifton poked his head out from behind it.

His skin was the colour of hot cocoa, and when he smiled his brilliant teeth looked like a mouthful of marshmallows. When he saw Greg he opened the screen door halfway.

"What's going on?" asked Clifton.

"We're going ni—knocking on people's doors at Peach Shores then running off," answered Greg softly as he looked for any sign of Clifton's mother. "You wanna come?"

"Yeah. Let me ask my mama," he said and instantly released the screen door which banged shut like a firecracker behind him.

"Clifton!" his mother's voice boomed, resonating throughout the house. "How many times have I told you not to let that screen door slam!"

Greg looked back toward Mitchell's porch in time to see him step off into the boys' mutual sandy yard.

"She said yes," said Clifton, catching Greg off guard.

"You didn't tell her what we were going to do, did you?"

"Of course not. I ain't dumb."

"All right. Let's go back to base," said Greg.

The four boys reunited at home base and within seconds found themselves at the foot of the concrete titan next to the cul-de-sac. The entire complex was a peach colour, hence its name, with doors in contrasting leafy green.

The boys went past the outer courts of the complex into the hallowed inner sanctum, far from their parents' sight, where the building formed an angular C-shape, rotated 90 degrees clockwise with its open side facing the highway. It offered plenty of room (and rooms) to carry out their mischief.

After walking along the concrete path a short distance, the four collectively chose a single door as their first target. The three boys stood behind Noland and waited for the signal to run, which sounded remarkably like knock, knock, knock. That was the extent of their plan.

Just before the neighbour opened the door, the boys split into two groups. Noland and Clifton ran in one direction and Greg and Mitchell in the opposite. They were perfectly quiet until they heard their first victim speak.

"Hello?" said the weak, shaky voice.

Though the boys didn't see the skinny, old man with glasses or the bathrobe he wore over his plaid trousers, his confused voice was enough to elicit an outburst of laughter until each group found their next door.

It was the same basic procedure: silence, knock, run, and laugh. Each time the victim was heard, not seen, but their vocal response provided a thorough if inaccurate description.

There was the fat, hairy man in a tank top, the crazy lady with the cat in her arms, the military man with the crew cut who cussed like a sailor, and the long-haired, bare-chested man with funny eyes who smoked a cigarette that smelled like burnt chicken.

The two groups divided again as each went his separate way.

As the boys ran up and down stairwells and around corners, footsteps reverberated on concrete above and beneath and laughter echoed all around. It was contagious. Each would burst out loud in front of a door just as he was about to knock, even when the aim of the game was stealth.

Noland turned a corner on the second floor and

ran down a hall on the side facing the cul-de-sac. He nonchalantly passed a door and was about to knock on its neighbour when he stopped mid-motion. He lowered his hand and looked back down the concrete walk and slowly approached the bypassed door.

There was something about it. Maybe it was the layers of peeling paint, one colour laid on top of another like a confused chameleon unable to hide itself or shed its skin—peach over red over green. And like a chameleon the flaking and bubbled layer of peach seemed to indicate the camouflaged door was meant to remain concealed.

Perhaps it was the sound of the wind whistling through the cracks between the door and its frame. Whatever it was, it wasn't going to stop Noland from pranking some jerk.

He turned his feet leftward and bent his knees slightly, ready to spring into full sprint. As he lifted his right hand to knock on the door, a dark hand wrapped tightly around his wrist.

"Not that one," said Clifton.

Noland looked at the hand angrily then past it to Clifton. Clifton slowly opened his hand and spread his fingers out like a crossing guard's stop signal.

"Why not?" asked Noland.

"This is where Mr. Harris lived," answered Clifton, lowering his hand.

Noland lowered his hand as well. "Who's that?" he asked.

"He hung his self."

"Who lives here now?"

"No-one."

"Liar," said Noland. He went to knock on the door

a second time but his wrist was intercepted again by Clifton's intense grip.

"Let go," Noland warned.

"No," defied Clifton.

Noland used his free hand to knock on the door.

Clifton released Noland's arm and ran around the corner to hide. "Why are you doing that?" asked Clifton in a loud whisper.

Noland knocked again.

"That's disrespectful," said Clifton.

Noland knocked again.

"I'm telling your mama," Clifton threatened.

"Why?" asked Noland. "'cause you're a scaredy nigger?"

None of the boys had ever called Clifton that, not even behind his back. He was one of them. Instinctively, as any child would, Clifton returned the favour, though he never would have in any other circumstance.

"Stupid honky!"

Noland ignored Clifton's volley and knocked, harder, slower, staring at Clifton with the most contemptible look he could muster.

"I bet you walk on your daddy's grave, too!" yelled Clifton.

Noland stopped knocking as the pain of a singular nerve was struck. "Don't you talk about my dad," he said.

"If you disrespect the dead you disrespect your daddy."

"That's bull crap. At least I know who my dad was!"

"I know who my daddy is!"

"How come I never see him around then?"

"At least my daddy can still come around."

The two boys breathed deep, slow breaths as heavily as they had when exhausted from running. They were emptied of all the hateful things they could stand to say. As they stared at each other, the door continued to whistle its haunting melody. It caught Clifton's ear and drew his eyes to the door.

He swallowed the lump in his throat. "I'm going to find Greg and Mitchell," he said nervously as he stepped backward out of Noland's view.

Noland listened to the sound of footsteps growing hollow. He wiped the tears from his eyes with the butt of his palms and left in the opposite direction.

After searching both floors at length, the two boys happened upon another at either end of a stairwell.

"Did you see them?" asked Noland as he glanced quickly up at Clifton then away.

"No," answered Clifton as he looked down on Noland.

"I'm going back to base," said Noland and left.

Clifton descended the stairs and followed Noland from a distance. When they exited the first floor breezeway they saw Greg and Mitchell seated on the jetty logs.

Noland stopped to look back when he no longer heard the echo of Clifton's shoes on concrete. When Clifton saw Noland waiting for him to catch up he intentionally slowed his pace.

Noland looked down at the sand and stalled as if he lost something. He waited until Clifton was a few steps behind him then pulled up a blade of sea grass. As the two walked silently side by side to base, Noland tore the sea grass into pieces and tossed them along the path.

When the two boys reached the circle they took a seat.

"That was fun," said Mitchell.

"Yeah it was," agreed Noland.

"Who's door did y'all knock on?" asked Greg.

"Some coloured man's," answered Noland.

"Don't you mean *nigger*?" retorted Clifton.

Greg and Mitchell were surprised to hear the word come out of Clifton's mouth. Mitchell would have corrected him but Clifton seemed to be the only one qualified to use it.

"Who was the coloured man?" Mitchell inquired.

"Mr. Harris," answered Clifton.

"Did he come outside?" asked Greg.

"No. He's dead," said Noland coldly.

"That's disrespectful," rebuked Clifton.

"How did he die?" Mitchell asked.

"He hung his self, a long time ago. Even before any of us were born," answered Clifton.

"Why did he do that?" Greg asked.

"He was the only black man at Peach Shores. All the white people hated him, so he killed his self," explained Clifton as he looked intentionally at Noland.

Greg stared at the sand as he visualised the gruesome scene. "That's so mean," he said.

"We were the first black people to move here after him," said Clifton.

"How come we never heard of him, then?" asked Noland.

"I told you. It was before we was born, maybe

even our folks."

"My mom never told me about that," said Noland.

"Mine either," "Or mine," added Greg and Mitchell.

"I bet they didn't," said Clifton indignantly.

"Why did you knock on his door, Noland?" asked Mitchell.

"Clifton says his place is haunted," Noland answered.

"No I didn't," said Clifton. "I just said that's where Mr. Harris killed his self."

"Maybe we shouldn't knock on his door," suggested Mitchell.

"Y'all are a bunch of scaredy cats!" insulted Noland.

"Just 'cause we don't wanna do what you wanna do doesn't mean we're scared!" objected Clifton.

From all around in turn, the voice of their mothers called their names. "Clifton... Noland... Gregory... Mitchell."

"I better go," said Clifton. "My mama's calling."

"Yeah, me too," said Noland.

"See you guys later," said Greg.

"After a while, crocodile," said Mitchell.

Noland and Clifton threw up a one-hand wave as they walked home. Clifton walked quickly ahead of Noland. Mitchell and Greg waited on Mitchell's porch until their mothers said goodnight to each other, and turned in for the evening.

**

During that first chaotic week back at school

there wasn't much time for play during or after. Only at the bus stop and ride did they have time to discuss their big plans for the gullible residents of Peach Shores the following weekend.

After Saturday morning cereal and cartoons, the boys arrived one by one at the jetty log circle. They discussed the week's events, such as the funny-looking teachers and good-looking girls, and held a brief convention, at which time they came to the conclusion another game of Nigger Knocking was in order on such a beautiful day, minus its true title in the presence of Clifton.

Like the previous game the pranksters started off in a group of four, but before the first neighbour answered the door, Clifton ran off with Greg and Mitchell, while Noland was left to fend for himself. When the three boys went to knock on another door, the spurned Noland rejoined them.

Just before the second neighbour answered the door, Noland nabbed Greg and dragged him down the hall. When Noland saw that Greg didn't put up much resistance, he released Greg's arm. The two hid around the corner to decide their next move.

When the two groups went to their next intended target, it was again every man for himself. The boys laughed hysterically that their previous targets fell victim again to the same trick. After a few more doors the exhausted boys rejoined in one of the breezeways to take a break.

When they caught their breath they went for another round. They turned the next corner and a moment later Greg and Mitchell walked past the old door with the peeling paint. Noland stopped as soon as he heard its familiar whistle.

When Clifton saw Noland at the door he stayed behind at the corner. Greg and Mitchell turned back to see why the others weren't following suit.

Noland stared at the door.

"Go ahead, Noland," said Greg. "Knock on it." He and Mitchell were ready to run.

"Come on! Let's get someone else!" Clifton appealed. After a moment of inaction he tried again, enthusiastically this time. "Come on! I know someone we can really get!"

"Knock on the door, Noland!" insisted Greg.

"No!" yelled Clifton. "That's the door I told y'all about!"

Mitchell and Greg approached the door and looked it up and down.

"You hear that?" asked Mitchell. "What's that sound?"

Greg held his hand an inch from the crack of the door frame. He felt the life of summer being sucked into that dark, hairline abyss. "I'm not knocking on it," he said as he pulled his hand away.

"Scaredy cats," sneered Noland and knocked on the door. "See. I told you," he said when no-one answered. "Clifton's a liar."

"Am not!" objected Clifton from around the corner. "I never said it was haunted."

"No-one's answering!" mocked Noland as he knocked on the door again.

"Then let's go already!" said Greg impatiently.

"Yeah!" agreed Mitchell. "This is dumb."

"Noland, you're so disrespectful. I hope somebody spits on your grave!" said Clifton.

"Scaredy nigger!" taunted Noland.

Greg and Mitchell stared at each other, then at Noland in disbelief. They shook their heads in disapproval as they walked past Noland to offer Clifton their support.

"Bring him here!" insisted Noland.

Greg faced Noland. "What?" he asked.

"Bring him over here. Show him there's nothing to be afraid of," said Noland.

"Why?" asked Mitchell.

"Just do it!" ordered Noland.

Greg and Mitchell reluctantly took Clifton by the arms and dragged him toward the door.

"No, don't," pleaded Clifton.

He tried to no avail to dig his heels into the solid concrete as if it were mere earth.

"You said it wasn't haunted!" reminded Noland. "What are you afraid of?"

"It ain't right! It's disrespectful!" said Clifton.

"No it's not!"

"Please, guys, let me go. I don't wanna be here."

The four stood in front of the door. Clifton struggled to break free, but his growing fear soon rendered him docile.

"We're not letting you go until you knock on the door," said Noland.

"I won't do it," said Clifton in tears.

"You're going to, or I'm gonna punch you," Noland shook his fist in Clifton's face.

"No, Noland!" said Mitchell.

"Shut up or I'll punch you, too!" Noland warned the larger Mitchell, who could have easily taken him.

"Go ahead and punch me, 'cause I ain't gonna do it," said Clifton.

"Just knock on the door," urged Greg.

"You'll have to hit me first!" cried Clifton.

Noland's lips pursed and nostrils flared as he gritted his teeth.

He swung.

Noland punched poor, weeping Clifton right in the nose. Greg and Mitchell looked away.

A red stream trickled from Clifton's nose. It ran into his mouth and onto his yellow Fat Albert t-shirt. It was a mess of blood, snot and tears.

"Knock on the door!" demanded Noland.

"Okay," said Clifton between hyper-ventilated breaths. "I'll do it."

The boys lessened the tension of their grip on Clifton's arms when they were sure he wouldn't run or fight back.

With a trembling lip and hand, Clifton raised his fist to the door. All eyes were fixed on him. He faced Greg on his right, then Mitchell on his left, but refused to look at Noland.

"Go ahead," said Greg, "it's all right."

"We're right here, Clifton. We won't let anything happen to you," said Mitchell.

Clifton's trembling fingers tightened into an angry fist. He looked down at his bloodied shirt. He heard each drop from his bleeding nose as they hit the concrete beneath him, that and the cold, harsh whistling. He gave a hard snuff to suck the string of bloody snot down his throat. He quickly reached out and knocked on the door.

There was a long silence, almost loud enough of a silence to drown out the whistling. Nobody answered.

"See," said Noland as his scowl turned into a smile. "Nothing to be afraid of."

The boys patted Clifton on the back. His tears and trembling ceased. He smiled at Greg and Mitchell and used an arm to wipe his running nose. He snorted, spit the blood and snot out of his mouth, and laughed at himself.

He looked at Noland, who extended a hand.

"Friends?" asked Noland.

A sense of pride rose in Clifton's heart as he looked in Noland's eyes. He had conquered his childish fear. There was no bogeyman—or Mr. Harris. He extended his open hand toward Noland's when the creaking door interrupted their reconciliation.

The boys stared with wide eyes and gaping mouths as the door opened fully. A tall, black man stood towering before them.

Noland, Greg and Mitchell were too breathless to scream as they ran. Noland hid in the breezeway just to the left while Greg and Mitchell ran to the opposite breezeway to the far right. Noland curled up into a ball with his head between his knees and his arms around his legs. Greg and Mitchell lay on the floor as they repeatedly peeked around the corner and waited for Clifton to join them, but he didn't budge.

Clifton slowly looked up at the man—from the brown, leather dress shoes to his red, polyester, bell-bottomed pants a generation old to the tight, button-up, purple-striped shirt with elbow-length sleeves. Clifton's eyes stopped just above the shirt's collar, where a dark, purple bruise ran round the man's neck.

"Clifton!" shouted Greg. "What are you doing?"

"Run, Clifton!" yelled Mitchell.

Noland mumbled incoherently as he rocked back and forth like a Weeble Wobble.

Clifton looked into the man's unblinking gaze. The grimace he wore turned into a white, toothy smile. Though Greg and Mitchell continued to call his name, Clifton could only hear the voice of the man.

"Now I'll finally have some company," he said.

With a welcoming arm extended, he placed his other hand on Clifton's shoulder.

"Don't go in there!" yelled Mitchell.

"Noland!" called Greg. "Stop him!"

Noland was much too afraid to do anything.

The wind picked up, blowing along the railed path outside Mr. Harris' room and through the breezeways where the boys were hidden.

Clifton entered the room alongside the man. The walls were painted a shade of orange reminiscent of the '70s. The shag carpet had thin, horizontal, sun-bleached lines from the permanently closed window shades, while the remainder had aged from eggshell white to sepia tone.

The only furnishing in the long-vacant room was a worn, dark-brown sofa bed, a rectangular coffee table, and a rope fashioned into a simple noose fastened around a ceiling fan.

As the door slowly closed of its own accord, the whistling swelled from silence to a scream. The terrified boys nearly stumbled down the stairs and over one another as each ran straight home to hide from the incessant whistling that continued to scream in their ears.

**

Noland opened his eyes and slowly pulled his hands from his ears. The otherworldly whistling was now replaced by the equally deafening sound of silence. He was nearly accustomed to the quiet when it was broken by a single knock on his door.

He fumbled with the nightstand lamp, only pushing it away when the door began to open. In the thin shaft of light from the hallway, a dark hand reached inside and felt along the wall, intently searching.

"Who's there?" Noland asked.

The blinding light forced him to turn away from the figure that stepped into the room.

"Clifton's mother is out here," said Noland's mother by the bedroom light switch. "She wants to know if you've seen him."

When Noland's eyes adjusted to the 100-watt ceiling bulb he sat up in bed. His mother pushed the lamp on his nightstand back to the centre of it.

"Mom," was all Noland could say before bursting into tears. His mother sat on the bed to comfort him when Clifton's mother entered the room.

"What is it?" she asked.

Noland jumped from his bed and ran into her arms. He buried his head in her chest and wept.

"What happened? Where is he?" she said, now weeping herself.

"Mr. Harris," he answered.

**

Within the hour the cul-de-sac was filled with police cars and emergency vehicles parked on the sea grass median beside the Peach Shores complex. The brick building and beach houses were splashed with pounding waves of red and blue light.

The lifeless body of Clifton hung like a rag doll from the same spot Mr. Harris had hanged himself. After the EMTs pulled Clifton's body from the ceiling, the forensics team placed the noose in a plastic bag marked "Evidence" and sealed it.

"There's no sign of forced entry," noted the detective. "The boys couldn't have gotten in here without that key."

"Maybe they jimmied the lock," suggested an officer.

"I don't think so. Looks like the landlord wanted to make this room impossible to break into. He even nailed the windows shut."

"Then how did the victim get up there?" asked the officer, giving the ceiling fan another unwanted glance.

"Don't know. There's no shoe prints on the coffee table. Even a grown man could give himself a hernia trying to move that hide-a-bed. There's no way any of these boys are responsible for this, including the victim."

"What about the landlord?"

"All three boys described the perp as a tall, black male. Obviously the landlord is neither tall nor black."

"This is just too bizarre."

"You're telling me."

Officers restrained Clifton's mother until his body was placed on the stretcher. From their safe porches the boys witnessed the wailing lament of a mother's soul as she ran to hold her little boy to her breast one last time. Her groaning echoed through the brick and concrete hall so much like laughter and footsteps had just hours earlier. The unnerving sound visibly shook the seasoned officers and emergency crew.

Mitchell looked across the cul-de-sac to Noland on his left, then across to Greg on his right. The silent admission of guilt was written on their faces. When Clifton's body was forcefully pulled from his mother by the police, the boys were escorted by their parents back into their homes.

**

That Monday the boys prepared for school as usual, with the exception they couldn't wait at the cul-de-sac bus stop unattended by a parent. Their mothers took turns that week, sometimes even waiting together to comfort one another when releasing their little boys into the harsh, cruel world that lay atop those few small steps onto the school bus.

A suspicious eye was cast on any man that dared slow his car down even to brake for traffic or pedestrians, and even more suspicious were the occasional passersby on foot or bike. Every man was the child-killer who took Clifton's life.

On the ride to school the three boys hardly spoke a word to one another or anyone else. They gazed out windows at coloured blurs, indifferent to what the shapes were that went speeding past them. Everything and every word and every action were all meaningless.

That Sunday the three families attended Clifton's funeral and during the weeks that followed the boys only saw each other in passing. Their schoolwork suffered for some time, understandably, and being aware of the situation, their teachers gave them more time to finish their work and more grace when their conduct was less than exemplary.

But as time healed their open wounds, the boys found themselves again talking to one another, staying the night over at each others' houses, going to movies and birthday parties and shopping malls. They even returned to the jetty log circle for round table discussions.

But no matter how well the surgeon of time stitched together their wounds, the living things that had been cut out from them could never be replaced. Though they were chronologically not much older, they were grownups now, and would never know the innocence of childhood or the joy of games again.

Expensive videogame consoles collected dust, leather gloves grew mould, and balls lost air. Any activity that held the semblance of a game instantly became a nightmare of introversion or violent tantrums. Beneath every mask, behind every curtain, inside every prize box, was a potential spectre in the form of Mr. Harris.

It was a cold fall evening that year when the three friends sat around a warm bonfire in the jetty log circle to reminisce about good ol' Clifton, whose empty seat served as a gnawing reminder of their betrayal.

They had hardly mentioned his name since the event, but knowing they would soon be called home for dinner, it was time to adjourn their meeting. Noland proposed the motion with his hand extended, seconded by Greg's hand over his, and passed by Mitchell's hand over Greg's. It was unanimous.

The three friends walked to the Peach Shores complex, up the stairs, and straight to Mr. Harris' door. It was agreed Noland should be the one to knock. Greg and Mitchell stood on either side of him.

As soon as it was quiet enough for them to notice the door's horrid whistling Noland turned to leave. Greg and Mitchell each placed a firm hand on Noland's shoulders to assure he stick to the agreement.

The two lowered their hands when Noland reluctantly lifted his to the door. He looked at them for one last chance to stop him. They did not intervene.

Noland knocked on the door. The whistling seemed suddenly louder. He would have run to hide but the boys agreed by binding vote not to move a muscle no matter what manner of deserving evil should befall them all.

The door didn't open a sliver. Noland again looked to his associates for a last-minute reprieve. With a single nod they signalled he try again.

Noland knocked on the door once more. Still nothing happened.

The boys sighed in relief, though something seemed unfinished. Moved by the same unknown compulsion, Noland pressed his left cheek hard against the cold door and spoke.

"Clifton, we're sorry." He paused to reconsider his words. "Mostly, *I'm* sorry. I was the one who put you up to it. I was wrong. I just want you to know we miss you, and we're sorry. Forgive us—me especially. And tell Mr. Harris we're sorry too, and we won't ever bother you or him again."

The three waited until it seemed right to leave. When they walked a few steps away the door slowly creaked open.

They turned back to see a shaft of light coming from the room which widened as the door turned on its hinges.

"Noland," said a voice at once recognisable as Clifton's. "It's all right."

The three boys returned to the door fearfully. They saw Clifton standing at the threshold and seated behind him on the old sofa bed was Mr. Harris, who whittled a piece of wood with a pocket knife as he leaned over the coffee table. On the table lay a towel and a whetting stone.

"I forgive you," said Clifton. "And so does Mr. Harris."

When Clifton spoke his name, Mr. Harris looked at the boys with a blank stare. A moment later he returned to the piece of wood he was carving.

"Will you stay here forever?" asked Greg.

"Yeah, can we come and see you whenever we want?" Mitchell asked.

In the distance, three mothers called from dark porches to their baby boys standing at the open door.

Clifton turned his attention to the far away voices.

"Boy," said Mr. Harris.

His voice startled the three. Clifton looked back at Mr. Harris, who tilted his head slightly and raised a brow.

"We better get going," said Noland when he saw Mr. Harris' expression. "Our moms are calling."

Clifton looked back one more time at the man, who was again intent on whittling away. Clifton turned to the boys and said softly, so Mr. Harris wouldn't hear, "So is mine."

The three boys listened, but heard nothing.

"Don't you hear her?" Clifton asked with a most sorrowful voice. "I wish I could go to her."

The boys were speechless.

"Boy, it's getting late," said Mr. Harris. "Tell your friends to go home, or else come in and stay."

"Stay?" asked Noland.

Clifton didn't say a word. As he turned his head and looked upward, the boys' eyes followed. In the centre of the room, fastened to the ceiling fan, was a rope fashioned into a simple noose. It started to swing gently as the wind picked up along the railed path and rushed inside the room.

The boys' eyes were fixated on the hypnotic motion of the swinging noose. Moving left to right and right to left and back again, their eyes followed its rhythm as their resolves were put to sleep by a silent lullaby. The wide shaft of light coming from inside the room narrowed as Clifton started to push the door shut.

"Go home," warned Clifton. "Your mothers are calling."

As the door closed completely, the trance that held the three boys mesmerized was broken. Their attention was immediately drawn to the single lit window of Clifton's house. There they saw his mother with her head bowed in silent prayer. They listened for the mournful voice that called out to Clifton, but all they heard were their own worried mothers and the whistling wind through the cracks of Mr. Harris' door.

About A. P. Sessler

A resident of North Carolina's Outer Banks, A.P. searches for that unique element that twists the everyday commonplace into the weird. When he's not writing fiction he composes music, dabbles in animation, and muses about theology and mind-hacking, all while watching way too many online movies.

His short stories have appeared in *Zippered Flesh 2*, *Dandelions of Mars*, *SQ Magazine*, and *Strangely Funny*.

WHITE HAIRS
RECLE E. VIBAL

"Hey Grandpa, whatcha doin'?"

Ban smiled at Pido, his best friend, and continued drawing.

"Are you deaf now too, Grandpa?" Pido asked.

"Are you blind or just can't understand what I'm doing?"

"Ah I see. Doodles. Nice lines there, Grandpa."

"This is not a doodle. This is the school's mango tree."

"Oh," Pido looked at Ban's paper, then to the tree beside the principal's office. "I was going to say nice dog, but yeah, nice tree."

"You just don't appreciate art." Ban finished his drawing's shadings.

"I can give a critique though. Seems like your art gives tribute to your hair because of the dominant black and mostly white, in it."

"I draw using charcoal. It's natural to see black and white only."

"Yeah whatever, Grandpa. If you're done we can grab some *isaw* before going home."

"Sure," Ban squeezed the sketchbook and the charcoal pencil in the remaining space of his bag. He hunched forward to support its weight and to avoid falling backward. He waved and smiled at the school's caretaker. "Bye, Mang Temyo. Take care of that tree."

The caretaker smiled and nodded at Ban.

"We could race you know?" Pido said.

"I don't want a broken nose, a chipped tooth, and a split lip," Ban replied.

"C'mon, Grandpa. Tata ran and tripped on his own foot. We will just brisk walk, no danger of tripping."

"No. Race on your own if you want."

"Geez, Grandpa. You've turned into a kill joy, too."

The boys laughed. Without knowing it, Ban was brisk walking with Pido, a step ahead, then a step behind. They raced to Ninya's store.

Ban got there first, but Pido insisted his friend cheated with an illegal blockade. Nonetheless, Pido paid for one of Ban's *isaw*, the universal wager for all their competitions.

"You have any news about Lana? She's been absent for a week," Ban ate his *isaw* before Pido could start with his first.

"Nope. Even Ma'am Santos doesn't know. No excuse letter from Lana's parents, it could be chicken pox or typhoid fever." Pido held an *isaw* in each hand. He bit the ends and chewed the chicken intestine as it went in his mouth.

Pido's technique left smudges of sauce on his face. Ban resisted the urge to imitate his best friend. He took his three remaining sticks of *isaw* and dipped it in chili sauce. Pido was about to finish his first two *isaw*. Ban bit the bottom end, took the *isaw* off the stick in one sweep, and repeated the strategy with the other two. He felt the chili burn his lips and tongue. His best friend was halfway through his third and fourth grilled chicken intestine. With their mouths full, they took a gulp of *gulaman* to wash down their throat and remove the burn in their mouth.

"Done!' The boys shouted. Both showed their tongue as proof. Ninya inspected the two mouths and declared it a draw. Pido, failing to redeem his previous loss, paid for five chicken intestines, Ban for three.

"Hey. Why don't we visit Lana to see how she's doing?" Pido said.

"Do you know where she lives?"

"Nope. I saw her once when my mother brought me to the public market. The vendors knew Lana. They were even giving her money as she passed by. They should know where she lives."

"Public market huh? Sure, why not?"

"Hey I know, Grandpa. We can buy some *proben* on the way," Pido rubbed his stomach and licked his lips.

**

The vendors shouted the different meat cuts for a pig and a chicken, the different kinds of fish, and the different ways one can cook each. The customers bargained for even an extra gram or a peso saving. The tricycle motors roared outside the wet market.

"You better start asking for directions, Grandpa," Pido said.

"Why me? This was your idea."

"That's the point. It's my idea. I've given my share. Now you give yours," Pido grinned.

Ban saw the logic in Pido's argument and the sauce stains on his best friend's teeth. He went first to the milkfish vendor.

"Excuse me. Can I ask a question?"

The vendor stopped cleaning the scales off the fish and looked at Ban. Then the vendor cut the belly and removed the fish's internal organs. Four milkfish got their scales cleaned off, their bellies cut, and their bodies chopped into three pieces. The vendor slid the cuts into a plastic bag, gave it to his customer, and then wiped his hands on his bloodstained apron. He sat down and hid behind the counter.

"I think he's busy," Pido said. Ban shrugged and went to the next vendor.

Five vendors, either busy or pretending to be busy, ignored them. The vendor on the end of that lane also hid behind the counter. The children turned the corner and came face to face with the woman.

"I just want to—"

"No. I won't give any protection money," The woman said.

Ban and Pido looked at each other.

"I said I won't, okay? We just got a breather here. We won't bow down to any gang yet. Not until we are sure the leader approves of it or is unable to."

"But we don't know anything about gangs or payments," Ban said.

"Really?" The woman raised an eyebrow and looked at the boys from head to foot. "Then what are you doing here?"

"We just want to ask if you know where Lana lives," Ban said.

"Who is Lana?"

"That would be Lana Gomez," Pido said.

"Is she a girl with short hair and about this height?" The woman raised her hand somewhere at Ban's eye level.

"Yeah, I think that would be her," Ban nodded.

"Oh. So you're looking for the retriever."

"Retriever? You mean Lana?"

"Yeah," the woman still had her right eyebrow raised.

"Do you know where we can find her?" Ban continued.

"You just follow the alley behind that rice store. Then turn left at the first corner. Her house is at the end. She should be there, if she's still alive."

Pido's eyes widened. Ban swallowed. He was getting scared of the woman; the sooner they leave, the better.

"Okay. Uhm. Thank you," Ban's voice trembled. The boys turned around, a small step after another, and ran when they felt the vendor's eyes following them.

**

The alley, bounded by the public market's wall and the residential walls and gates, allowed two children to walk abreast. Pido walked behind Ban to give way for the outgoing people. Ban watched his step to avoid the scattered dog shit.

Houses made of scrap metal and wood sandwiched the next alley. A naked boy covered with soil or charcoal cried for his mommy. Three women ignored the boy's cry and continued their card game.

The dog shit mines had increased in number. Litter covered some of the shit. Pido almost stepped on one.

"I can't believe Lana lives in this kind of

neighbourhood," Pido said.

"Why not?" Ban asked.

"Well, her stuff is always new. Never saw her wore the same shoes in the same week."

"You look at her shoes?"

"Yeah. Only to verify what Mel said to me. I also heard Lana's father donated a lot of money to the PTA. Some of that money went to the library's repainting."

"Where do you get all these things?"

"From my mother, she's a gossip magnet," Pido said.

"We're about to confirm all of those. I think that's Lana's house."

The alley's dead end was a gate. Beyond that was the door of a two-story house. The front porch was a heap of soil elevated from the concrete alley. Patches of paint and plywood ornamented the facade. A curtain blocked light and curious eyes from reaching inside the house. The second floor overhung the entrance.

"Well? Should we call out for Lana?" Ban asked.

"I don't know," Pido leaned on the gate. It swung open. The hinges creaked. "I guess we better knock. You go first, Grandpa."

"Why me?"

"Because I opened the gate."

"Okay, but you'll knock."

"You'll call out for Lana."

"Fine. Let's just do this," Ban took a deep breath, sucked his stomach in, and puffed his chest out. The weight of his bag straightened his back. He walked to the door. Pido crouched behind Ban. Pido knocked three times.

"Lana! Are you home?" Ban blushed when he realised he might have called louder than he wanted to. They heard footsteps descending a stair inside the house.

"What do you want?" A girl's voice called out.

"Lana it's me, Pido. I'm here with Grandpa Ban."

"We just want to know why you've been absent for a week," Ban said.

"Go away. I don't want any of my classmates nosing around," Lana said.

"But... We're not just your classmates. We're your friends," Pido made his voice sound as if he was about to cry. Ban still felt his best friend's sincerity.

"Yeah. Come on Lana. You played with us, and you saw us cry after Ma'am Santos spanked us," Ban said.

"You don't have to remind that," Pido whispered.

Locks and chains rattled behind the door. Half of Lana's face peered through the opening. She hid the rest of her and the house's interior behind the door. "Come in quick before somebody sees me."

The two boys squeezed through the gap that Lana kept as narrow as possible. Dust and heat greeted them inside. Lana shut the door, replaced the locks, padlocks and chains, and pushed the sofa against the door.

"Are you expecting monsters to—" Lana's blood-soaked shirt surprised Ban. Pido fainted. Ban took his best friend on the shoulders and shook him. "Wake up. This is not the time to sleep."

Pido's eyes opened and almost popped out. "Buh-buh-blood on Lana's shirt."

"What's happening Lana?" Ban asked. "Is that your blood?"

"No. It's my Papa's," Lana replied. "Let's go upstairs."

Ban followed Lana, but Pido remained seated on the floor.

"I thought you wanted to know why Lana isn't going to school," Ban said.

"I'm hesitant now that life and death might be involved," Pido replied.

Ban sighed and dragged his best friend all the way upstairs.

The air on the second floor irritated Ban's nose. Light slipped through the gaps and holes on the wall. A pitcher of water, sachets of milk, a pot of cooked rice, and a plate with white liquid and grains of rice occupied one corner of the room. Pieces of cloth soaked in blood surrounded a man on the mattress.

"This is my Papa," Lana said. She took the plate of white liquid, mixed in some rice grains, took a spoonful of the mixture, and placed it on her father's lips. The mouth stayed closed. Lana withdrew the spoon and started to cry.

"He hasn't eaten since last night. I've been feeding him milk and rice for a week now. He can't eat anything else." Lana's tears created ripples on the plate of milk.

Pido stood and pressed his back on the corner farthest from the man. Ban checked the pulse of Lana's father and felt nothing. The man held a picture in his other hand. It was Lana's family picture when she was just a baby.

"I showed that to him when Uncle Kiko brought him here. I was hoping it would give him at least the heart to continue living. Mama was always an inspiration to Papa. She made our home back in the province as happy as it could possibly be. When she died, things were just not the same, but her love remains in my heart. It keeps me alive. Papa was different; revenge kept him alive."

Pido left the corner, sat beside Lana, and held her in an embrace.

"Papa was the best policeman in our town. He protected everyone, but no-one protected him against the Drug Lords. Nobody protected us. A group of men gunned down our house one night. Papa covered me with his body. Mama was near the kitchen window. At least twenty bullets pierced her body. All I could hear was gunfire, Papa's curses, and then the sound of a vehicle speeding away.

"I had no wounds, but I spent more than a month in the hospital. After a week, I saw Papa for the first time after Mama's death. He stood at the doorway of my room. Blood ran from a hole on his left shoulder to the tips of his finger. Drop by drop, I saw the pool of blood grow on the hospital floor.

"Papa said Mama is already in heaven, and her killers are already in hell. He cried. I stared at his wounds and the blood on the floor. I was amazed Papa was still alive after he lost that much blood.

"The police took Papa away. I cried every night, shouting for my Mama and Papa. I don't know how long I waited for Papa. He took me one night from the hospital. Uncle Felix drove us to the bus terminal. We found home here.

"Papa didn't return to the police force. He said

they think he's crazy, and they deny the justice Mama deserves. I don't think Papa's crazy.

"He formed a group to serve the people and to protect this town from Drug Lords and gangs. I have to collect the vendors' donations while Papa focused on leading his Peace Corps.

"His last mission went badly, though. Uncle Kiko brought him here. Papa's head was bleeding from a lead pipe blow on his head, and there were knife stabs on his arms and stomach. Uncle helped me wrapped Papa's wounds. After two days, Uncle left me here with Papa. He said Papa's group is finished; the remaining members were going to other groups. Uncle said he wanted to leave town and bring me with him. I don't want to leave Papa alone."

"You've been here for a week now, and you never asked for help?" Pido asked.

"I can't leave Papa for more than a minute. There's a lot of food downstairs so I don't need to worry about starving. I'm having a harder time feeding Papa," Lana hugged her knees and rocked on her heels. She stared at her father's corpse.

"What would make you happy Lana?" Ban asked.

"Grandpa?" Ban saw the disgust on Pido's face.

"Lana," Ban knelt in front of the girl and held her shoulders. Lana kept her eyes on her Papa's corpse. "Lana, tell me what will make you happy? Tell me what your wish is."

"What's my wish?" Lana took a deep breath. She cried and took gasps between words. "I wish Mama, Papa, and I can live peacefully and happily for all our lives like the days before Mama died."

"Your wish is granted," Ban's hair began to glow. Pido covered his eyes from the light. Lana hugged her father's corpse. Another strand of hair was turning white.

**

"What are we doing here again?" Pido asked.

"You said you wanted some *proben*, only available at the public market," Ban replied.

"So why are we here in this neighbourhood?"

"We can't find it. We got lost. We entered an alley and found a dead end."

"Okay," Pido looked at the concrete wall covered with moss, crinkled his nose, and scratched his head. "I really can't remember, but whatever."

"Come on, don't worry. The public market is just at the other end of this alley. Sun's about to go down, there would be no *proben* anymore."

"Why are you holding your sketchpad?"

"Oh, this is nothing."

"Come on, Grandpa. Show me your ugly drawing."

Ban kept his sketchpad away from Pido, but his best friend used size and speed to snatch it from Ban's hands.

"Wow. I don't believe you drew this, Grandpa," Pido said. "Who's this girl anyway?"

"Just a childhood friend, she lives in the province, so I don't see her anymore. Her name's Lana."

"Hmmm. She's your crush, isn't she? Huh? Huh?" Pido poked Ban's arms and sides.

"No. Stop that. She's just a friend."

"I guess this is her mother and father. They look

38

so happy together," Pido returned the sketchpad.

"Yeah. They are happy now," Lana's father carried her in his arms, and her mother hugged both of them. "I wish everyone could be this happy."

"Too bad your wish can't come true," Pido said.

"I know," Ban placed the sketchbook in his bag. "Do you know how much hair we have on our head?"

"Nope. Why do you ask, Grandpa?"

"Grandma said all her hair was white before she reached 35."

"Now I get you. You're worried your hair will be all white before you reach high school. You can colour it if you're ashamed of your white hairs."

"I'm not ashamed."

"Stop worrying, Grandpa. You're just aggravating your condition," Pido placed his arms over his best friend's shoulder.

Ban felt happy for his new strand of white hair.

About Recle E. Vibal

Recle Etino Vibal (born in the Pispis, Maasin, Iloilo, Philippines) spent his childhood and currently lives in Mayondon, Los Baños, Laguna, Philippines. A son of an Ilongga and a Bikolano, he is proudly Filipino. He obtained a Bachelor of Science in Chemical Engineering at the University of the Philippines Los Baños, but works with numbers that are zero percent chemical and 100% financial engineering. He balances reading, writing, and living, a daily juggling act on a high tension wire a hundred metres above the ground. He manages to survive such a stunt, read, learn, write, and live for another day. Learn more about him at ibongtikling.wordpress.com and @ibongtikling on Twitter.

THE CHANGING OF THE SEASONS
FRIDA STAVENOW

The breakfast room at Hotel Krabbklon had only just started to fill with the smell of fresh rolls when Fru Gyllenhammar walked in and stopped all conversation. Granted, not much conversation had been going on between the four young seasonal workers that, at seven thirty in the morning, made up the room's full populace—they had all stayed up enjoying their staff discounts the night before, and only two of them had had time to brush their teeth—but what little dialogue there had been was brought to a halt at the appearance of their manager's wife and two small daughters. It was the first time anybody had seen Fru Gyllenhammar before noon, discounting the time when, three years earlier, she had silently observed her father-in-law's burial from behind large, black sunglasses.

**

"Good morning, ma'am," said Fredrik, the only returner among the staff, as he reported at Fru Gyllenhammar's habitual beach-facing table. "All set for tonight, are we?"

"Well, *I* am," Fru Gyllenhammar said and refused a menu held out by the stocky young man, "but these two have all of ten hours to catch more cuts, bites and bone-breaking blows than they ever dreamed of." She looked at the older of the two girls, distinguishable as such not so much by her size as by her hair, into which she had accepted the application of two strawberry-shaped hairclips. Her sister, whose hair was more like that of a troll doll, had agreed to no such inanity. "In fact this one," Fru Gyllenhammar said and stroked the shiny blonde hair of her firstborn, "has already caught herself a nasty cold. Haven't you, dear?"

"Hmph," Line said and snivelled, "why else would I be *here*?"

"That's true," Fru Gyllenhammar said and withdrew her hand. For a moment her face wavered, but she quickly regained composure and looked back at Fredrik. "She was supposed to go with her father to fetch the oysters," she said and rolled her eyes. Done with this, she tried to catch her daughter's gaze, but was beaten to it by a salt shaker. Still, she put on a nursery teacher's exaggerated inflection as she continued. "But sun and wind and salty sprays," she said to the girl's downturned eyes, "is no recipe for recuperation, now is it?"

"That'll be two bowls of porridge, then," Fredrik said and tried not to look at the two buttons left unbuttoned on Fru Gyllenhammar's dress. He looked instead at the redundant menus in his hands. "Am I correct?"

"That's right," Fru Gyllenhammar said and smiled, the sweet, reserved smile she used towards all her husband's staff.

"Very good, ma'am," Fredrik said and looked at the redhead's pretty face, until he realised she'd only put mascara on the lashes of her left eye. He gave a quick bow and left the table.

"Those ferries better be as crowded as your

father thinks they'll be," Fru Gyllenhammar said as Fredrik disappeared into the kitchen. She looked out across the empty dining room. "Or there will be an awful lot of oysters for us to finish."

"*Of course* they will," the older girl said and sighed. "You said the same thing last year, and just about a billion people turned up. In fact you say the same thing *every* year."

The woman smiled, but did not take her eyes off the empty chairs around them. She did not speak as Fredrik came with the children's porridge bowls, and Fredrik—unlike the children—knew better than to ask Fru Gyllenhammar again before midday if indeed she did not want another look at the menu. And so they sat, Line in her hairclips eating the porridge and Grete with her troll hair moving it around in the bowl, until the first guest showed up at the breakfast buffet and Fru Gyllenhammar finally sat back in her chair. She looked at her daughters.

"Why are you not eating, Grete?" she asked and frowned at the smaller girl. Her tone made it clear this was a reprimand, not a question.

"She doesn't *like* porridge," Line replied.

Fru Gyllenhammar looked at Grete, her face a blend of disappointment and surprise. Grete looked at the porridge. "Well it's good for you," Fru Gyllenhammar said after a couple of seconds. "There is no alternative on the cards. You'll learn to like it in time."

"Daddy lets me eat cereal," Grete said without looking up from the sticky spoon in her hand, going round and round. "Ouch," she said then, feeling her sister's sandal hit her shin.

"Oh *does he?*" replied her mother and raised a theatrical eyebrow. Keeping her eyes on the face of her youngest daughter, she seemed to be considering this new piece of intelligence. "Well," she said then, "you won't be eating from that buffet so long as I'm in the room. People grab those bread rolls with their *fingers*."

"Can I go then?" prompted Grete.

"Not until you've finished. As you would have," Fru Gyllenhammar said and reached a long, slim arm across the table to loosen a linen napkin, once eggshell and now covered in blue and green crayon, from underneath Grete's elbow , "if you hadn't spent your time converting your father's investment into, now what is this, a... cow?"

"It's Uncle Klas' *motor*-bike."

"Where's the sketchbook I gave you?" Fru Gyllenhammar asked, a wrinkle appearing between her two shapely eyebrows.

"In our room."

"Well you better hurry back and put this in with the others," she said and nodded to the napkin between her thumb and forefinger. "You know you'll never make it through first grade unless you become more organised."

Without a word, Grete snatched the napkin back from her mother. She put it on top of the clear plastic crayon suitcase next to her bowl, and carefully folded it to the same shape and size. Then she pulled her legs out from beneath her scrawny body, grabbed her artist's materials, and left the table.

**

Down in the harbour a few more people had

woken up, but Grete paid no mind to the bath-robed couples having coffee on the decks of their sailing boats who, at the sudden sound of footsteps, turned their sleepy heads to look at the barefooted girl as she thundered down the jetty. Grete really did make an awful lot of sound for a girl of such slight build, never having learned to run as graciously as her sister or the other girls at gymnastics, but she couldn't care about grace when the fishing boats would be tying up any minute. In fact, she noticed as she turned the corner behind the last of the rust-red fishermen's huts, they had already come in. Her mother had kept her past seven-fifteen. She stopped in her tracks, wild-eyedly scanning the tall figures unloading cages and untangling nets around her. *He wasn't there.* She took a deep breath, and was just about to ask Jörgen, who had a glass eye, when something big and cold nudged her from behind. She spun around to find an empty red wheelbarrow, wheeled by a pale-faced boy of slim build, a good six feet, twenty-and-some years and spectacularly bad posture. Grete broke out into a wide grin, unashamedly displaying the gap left by her recently fallen-out left canine tooth.

"So what did you *think*?" she asked enthusiastically.

The boy glanced over at Jörgen, who was combing through a piece of sun-bleached-green net. "You shouldn't have come to my house," he said lowly. "I've told you that already."

Grete turned her head to the fishing-boat on her right and lowered her eyes. "Nobody saw me," she said flatly.

"That's not the point," said the boy and stepped

from the jetty into the turquoise-bottomed boat. He grabbed the sides of a tank no bigger than an average suitcase, and began edging it out from a row of four identical containers. Some water splashed over the edges, and he bit his lower, already chafed lip. Then, in a feat that seemed to require the boyish frame's maximum strength, he hoisted the tank onto his knee and wobbled it onto the jetty.

Grete stared down into the dark clouds of claws and antennae that scraped about the bottom of the tank. Her eyes widened. "There's a crab in there with just one claw," she said and squinted at Nikolai's flushed face. "You have to take it out, or it won't get any mussel when you feed them."

"I'll make sure to tell Jörgen," Nikolai said and wiped his brow with the back of a surprisingly large hand. He let it drop to his side and looked at the child in front of him. Grete was watching him intently, albeit with one eye only, the other shut to prevent sneezing from morning sun. When no command came, she dug her hand into the belly pocket of the red-and-white cotton dress her mother had sewn for her first day of school, and which she was intent on wearing every day until then. Tenderly she took out a small packet wrapped in the crayoned napkin. She looked at it for a second, a bit like one would look at a hamster before passing it to the vet, then held it out towards Nikolai.

The boy looked at the packet, not taking his hands off his sides. "What's this?"

"Open it," prompted Grete.

"It better not be pancakes again."

Grete said nothing. The boy sighed loudly, and it

was with considerable grudge—facial, if not vocal—that he took the packet off the girl's hands. But he took it nonetheless, and his face softened a fair bit as he unfolded the moist pieces of cloth. He looked at the limp yellowy slabs, and then he looked at the blue and green lines surrounding it.

Grete, noticing immediately the shift of focus, quickly snatched the napkin back. The pancakes flopped onto the wooden planks below. "It's not *finished* yet."

"*Easy*," Nikolai hissed, realising too late the sharpness of his tone. Grete looked down at her feet. For a moment the boy said nothing, looking at the sun-burnt line that zigzagged through Grete's white-blonde hair and thinking of a way to repair the damage. He crouched down to attain a matching height. "Hey," he said softly, putting a finger underneath Grete's chin. He began pushing it upwards, seeking the eyes of the child. "Oh don't *cry* now," he said as he saw Grete's tearing eyes. "I'm not angry. See?" He stretched the corners of his mouth as wide as he could. "See that? I'm *happy*."

Grete closed her eyes and sniveled loudly. "I'm not *crying*."

"Oh no?"

"I don't mean to be so ag—"—she gasped, not very successfully, for air—"a-gu-gu..." The girl paused, swallowed loudly, and used her final bit of air to get the end of the word out: "—guh-*ressive*."

A little uncertainly, Nikolai looked around the jetty. The other fishermen were still going about their business, taking no interest in the little girl who had come down to greet the boats every morning for more than two months. He turned back to the girl. She was looking pointedly away, breath held and lower lip out. The lip, however, was not moving. Gingerly, Nikolai reached out and tugged at the hem of the red-and-white dress. Having regained the child's attention, he dug his hand into the freezing water of the tank and snatched out the one-clawed crab. He held it in front of Grete just long enough so she could recognise the cripple, and then, with a Frisbee-thrower's flick of the wrist, tossed it across the jetty and into the glittering water.

"Well come *on*, then," he said to the breathless and, by now, certainly snivel-less child as he got to his feet. "This won't wheel itself to the fish-shop. You gonna be any help this morning or what?"

**

"So did you *like* them?" Grete asked after they'd wheeled the crabs into the shop, and were walking up the peeling white steps that lead to the seasonal staff huts.

"Oh yes," Nikolai said and looked down at the eager face climbing next to him. "You must really like your Uncle Klas, huh?"

"He's the best sailor I know," Grete said, nearly out of breath from trying to keep up with Nikolai's much longer legs. "Mom can't even run the Flipper."

Nikolai smiled. "Bet you can't wait 'til tonight, can you?" he said. "What time's your uncle getting here?"

"Uncle Klas doesn't come here anymore," Grete said and ran over to the door, number nine, at the end of the balcony. "Which one was your favourite?" she called back.

"What's that?"

"Of the *drawings*."

"Oh. They're all very nice."

"I know they're all *nice*," Grete said as Nikolai caught up with her. "I'm very good in art."

The boy pushed the door with his hip to click the lock open, then disappeared into the shade of the room. "Don't come *in* here," he said without looking back. Grete, with much dignity, walked backwards out onto the porch.

"But which one did you like *best*?" she called a little uncertainly, aiming for the point of darkness where she guessed Nikolai was to be found.

"Tough call," the boy said as he reappeared and held out an A4 notepad in Grete's direction. When she did not take it he moved his pupils to the top left of his eyes, scratched his head and made loud signs of thinking. "Hmm," he said and frowned. "The one where Uncle Klas teaches you to swim?" Right then, the hip pocket of his jeans began vibrating. He pulled out a scratched silver flip phone and looked at the caller ID. "I have to take this," he said and looked at Grete, his face betraying no emotion. "I'll see you in the morning, ok?"

He dropped the notepad onto the ground before Grete and shut the thin wooden door. Grete heard the lock turn. "I'll see you at the *party*, silly," she yelled at the closed door, bending down to admire the galloping chestnut pony on the cover of her sketchbook.

**

Since their mother had been asked to manage the hotel gardening team until their father came back from North Koster, the responsibility of the two children's behaviour, at least until their baths at four o'clock, had to fall onto the inconveniently ailed Line. Promising to keep in the shade and away from water, she had accepted this task gravely and confidently. After all, she was already nine and a half, and had taken Grete cycling to the stables on the other side of the island an *innumerable* number of times. And she was doing a good job, too, perching in the shade of the big lookout stone beneath the Southern veranda as her sister ran about the beach. Grete was fishing for crabs among the barnacled cliffs, putting them into a big blue bucket, racing them down the sandy beach into the water and catching them again with the crushed blue mussel attached with a clothes peg to her very own piece of string. Green, importantly. Not pink like Line's. Doing a good job wasn't actually that hard—in fact, Grete was by far the more reliable of the two girls when it came to dealing with all things marine, and the older sister's task was mainly to keep an eye on the younger one's occasionally bolting audacity. A few times during the course of the day she had to remind Grete of their mother's forewarnings of what happened to little girls who interrupted the preparations for big parties, but generally Grete busied herself with little games of her own. She did already read, having learned with her sister two years earlier, yet displayed no interest in the copies of pony comics which her sister had taken with her to the beach as pastime. There was really only one occasion, when Grete had again filled her bright blue bikini bottoms with so much sand they nearly fell down, at which Line needed to use her big sister authority to keep these games, as she said, 'in check.' In Grete's opinion the bottoms served for nothing, as she would always get sand in there anyway, but Line, who already wore a two-piece, just sighed and said that Grete would get it as she

50

got older. All in all the day with no parental supervision passed rather splendidly, and by the time their mother came and collected her daughters for cleansing, her second-born had contracted only two cuts, right below her left knee ("from a barnacle, of course," Line was quick to inform), and no jellyfish stings at all.

**

"'You know I think it's stupid," Grete said as she climbed the wooden steps that lead from the beach up to the veranda, one hand in her mother's and the other in her sister's, and encountered for the first time that day the newly amassed crowd of long-legged city visitors. "They call it the end-of-summer ball but really it isn't. The end was already last week when these people all left the *first* time."

"Nothing ever really ends, sweetheart," said the mother and squeezed Grete's hand. "We just made this thing called seasons so it would feel like things are changing."

In the evening the two sisters, now dressed in identical sailor dresses and with attempts at identical hairstyles (failing as much due to the largely inferior quality of Grete's hair, as to the largely superior quality of her resistance towards the mother's threats), were allowed to stay up longer than usual on account of the special occasion. In Grete's eyes it did not count for much, however, so long as she was expected to sit down together with the other children at the somewhat obscured children's table, separated from the real party by an upside-down *dinghy* of all things. To make matters worse yet, the table was hosted by a clown who did not even speak Swedish, but was lost, he said, from a circus that had travelled around the fiords of Norway since before his own *mother* had been born. Aside from not believing him, obviously, Grete felt a great aversion towards speakers of her mother's native tongue, not having mastered herself the transition into clear Swedish that came so easily to Line after two years in the island's primary school. And so she refrained from speaking throughout—even as the clown squirted water from the flower in his buttonhole onto the lapel of her sailor dress—limiting her frivolity to making more drawings in her sketchbook. She kept an eye at the increasing number of guests who had loosened themselves from the long white-clothed tables, now making their way either to the veranda, where an accordion player was entertaining and couples were dancing, or down towards the beach, where lanterns had been lit and the sky was ablaze with what had to be a bonfire. Around eleven, when the clown did that old trick with the dog on the wire leash and even Line, who definitely ought to have known better, laughed so hard that she nearly fell over, Grete saw her chance to quietly slip away from the awed group of lesser-discerning party-goers. She knew she needn't worry about the clown, who was more entertained by his trick than anyone, and so it was at Line's back that she threw her careful glances as she grabbed her crayons and sketchbook, snuck back into the row of folded-up sun-chairs and made her sortie.

**

She ran out of the garden and towards the tennis courts, and as soon as she was sure to be out of party sight, protected by the tall rusty railings that wrapped the courts, she untied the white ballet shoes her mother had forced her to wear and threw them into a hazelnut bush. Instantaneously, she felt a great deal better, and she had skipped a fair bit down the darkened path from the courts towards the beach, enjoying the sensation of soft and dewy soil against the her feet, before she stopped, turned, and walked back to brush the soil off the silky fabric. She had just put the shoes down on a large flat rock, rather fabulously fit, in Grete's opinion, for shoe-holding purposes, when she heard the rapid and heavy steps of an adult come running across the gravel court behind her. She froze mid-step, and was just about to dive into the hazelnut bush, when she recognised the tall silhouette that elegantly straddled the fence on its way to her.

**

"I *knew* you'd come back!" she called out as she threw herself at Uncle Klas' legs. "I never doubted you a *second.*"

"Shhhh," Uncle Klas said and, having put his glass of champagne on the gravel, gripped the girl by her small, bare thighs. He twirled her some laps around the deserted court, sending the troll hair flying and the girl into a near fit of delight. "No-one knows yet," he whispered, a half-smoked cigarette dangling from his lips and turning his s' into sh's. "You're going to ruin the surprise for your mother if you aren't quiet."

Grete exerted a delighted laugh, but caught herself halfway through. She put a hand against her mouth. Instead of speaking, she nodded vigorously to show her understanding of the deal. Uncle Klas put her back down onto the ground and retrieved the champagne glass.

"Still drawing?" he said and looked towards the shoe rock, where Grete, in her excitement, had left her pad and crayons. Grete gave another nod, turned and ran to fetch her work.

"Mother took the best ones out already," she said in as low a voice as she could, still not quite able to curb her excitement, as Uncle Klas flipped through the pages. "She says she'll send them to that competition in the magazine."

Uncle Klas nodded gravely. "Good. Your mother always knew a lot about art."

"My teacher in school says I'm much better than Line, and Line's already in third grade."

"You show these to your teacher?"

"Uh-uh." Grete shook her head. "In class we've only drawn our houses so far."

"You don't forget our deal," Uncle Klas said and took a drag off his cigarette, "do you?"

Grete's eyes widened. "*No*," she said with emphasis, as if this was the most obvious answer in the world.

"A lot of people would want to get rich from these drawings you know. But competition people can't steal."

"Because it's against the *rules*."

"Exactly." Uncle Klas looked back towards the assembly of lights and music at the top of the hill. "Now, Grete, I have to get back. You be a good girl and not go ruin your mother's surprise, all right?" He looked Grete in the eye, very seriously, but in the end he couldn't fight the smile. "All right," he said and tapped her on the black and white striped shoulder. "Just say I promise, and tomorrow we'll go crab-fishing."

"I promise," Grete said, and as she watched the silhouette of her mother's little brother get smaller and smaller, until eventually it was swallowed by the darkness of the hill, she felt more compelled to make the perfect drawing than she had all summer.

**

The sea was already lit orange when she woke up, and it took a few panicked moments before she realised that this, in August, did not necessarily mean that the party would be over. Her mouth was dry and her shoulders ached from the pose in which she had been sleeping, crouched over the notepad and the crayon-box in-between the two supportive pillars beneath the fishing boat jetty. It was her favourite place on the whole of the island, and she did not unusually spend several hours listening to the conversations of the people passing overhead, herself unseen and unheard. But she had never before dozed off on the ledge against her will, and she felt more than a little annoyed at her lack of self-control as she stretched her arms and legs and crawled out into the early morning light. She looked back at the hotel, less crowded now of course, but not empty. *Her* parents would still be dancing. Then she saw the bonfire on the beach below the veranda, burning big and bright and beautiful, and without further hesitation jumped down into the shallow morning tide and began making her way towards the light. She was so excited she even forgot about her fear of crabs, feet pushing forth among weeds and critters alike.

**

As she reached the shore she could make out the faces of the dozen people assembled around the bonfire, and she forgot all about the pain in her newly-awakened legs as she ran the last bit up towards Nikolai. He had been sitting quietly, a little aloof from the rest of the group, flicking pieces of broken-up driftwood into the flames. At the sight of the young girl running towards him, Nikolai first flinched but then, observing her overjoyed face, broke out into a sleepy smile. As she stopped in front of him, however, he lost his smile and took on a nearly mock-concerned expression.

"Do you know what time it is, young lady?" he asked.

Grete looked over towards the rising sun. "Five-forty," she said.

Nikolai raised his eyebrows. "Well it was a question, I suppose."

Grete poured herself down onto the sand next to him. The air was chilly now and it felt good being close to the fire. It smelled like the beginning of spring, when the hotel gardeners burnt the leaves that had come out of the thawing snow, and not at all like the end of all the warm seasons. She closed her eyes and inhaled deeply, bothered only when the undeniably summery smell of mosquito repellent arrived to break her fantasy. She turned again towards Nikolai. "Was that your girlfriend on the phone?"

"Huh?"

"Why did you lie to her?"

Nikolai frowned and looked back at the fire. "I don't have a girlfriend," he mumbled. "Isn't it past your bedtime?"

"I can stay up longer on Saturdays," Grete said, looking where Nikolai was looking. The fire was reflected in her eyes, a pale face of freckles and burning red mirrors. "Why'd you say I was a tourist?" she prompted. "You know I was *born* here."

Nikolai frowned, looking at Grete's fingers cleaning sand off a cigarette butt. "You've no business listening to my calls," he said and grabbed the cigarette butt. "That's garbage. Don't touch it."

Grete's left eye began twitching, not significantly, but enough for Nikolai to see that she had picked up his tensing tone of voice. Spotting the notepad, he quickly changed the subject. "I've had a think," he said rapidly. "And actually the one where you ride the bike is the best. The one by the lake. *Excellent* colouring."

Grete's eyes brightened, and she reached for her drawings. "I've made more," she said shoved the sketchbook onto Nikolai's lap. "They're much, much better."

She studied intently the face of the boy as he began looking through her latest oeuvres. She paid careful attention and, a natural born mime of the people she adored, froze no more than a blink of an eye later than Nikolai. He dropped the pad and got to his feet. A little unsteadily he began walking backwards and away from Grete.

"Why are you doing this to me?" he asked and put his hands across his eyes. Grete was still sitting on the sand, her mouth fallen open. "Go away," he prompted. Grete stood up and began walking towards him. "I've told you enough times now," he said, voice rising, as Grete grabbed hold of one of his denim legs. "Let me go, I can't *be* your friend, I'm—"

At that moment, a shriek was heard from the boardwalk above. Nikolai and Grete looked up. The shriek had come from a pretty brunette, wearing a lavender crepe-de-chine gown and holding onto the elbow of Uncle Klas.

"That's the one," she said and dug her fingernails deeper into her cavalier's shirted arm. "Over by the child. That's the boy I told you about."

Uncle Klas looked at the childish figure of Nikolai, shrouded in an oversized black t-shirt with the Krabbklon logo, and then at the wild-eyed child tugging at his grass-stained jeans. "Surely that can't be true," he said mechanically.

"You think I'd forget that face?" prompted the brunette, worked up now, not just gripping but shaking Uncle Klas' arm. "He used to live down my *street* before they took him away."

"But that was almost eight years ago," stammered Uncle Klas. His eyes were a little bloodshot, and he'd spilled red wine onto his white shirt. "Surely eight years do a lot to a face." He glanced nervously at the notepad, sitting not an arm's length from the bonfire.

"*Hey,*" the brunette shouted down towards the beach. "*City boy.* I know who you are, you *monster*—"

Uncle Klas put up a hand across the brunette's mouth. "Karin," he said, trying to keep his voice down but speaking too fast to succeed. "Karin, you've made a mistake. That's not the guy."

In addition to bringing the stoned teens around the fire back to life, the commotion had served to attract the still standing party-goers within reasonable earshot of the beach. The crowd of spectators was large enough to conceal at first the arrival of the mother, and you could hear Fru Gyllenhammar's voice long before her figure, make-up smudged and shoes in hand, emerged to run the last few steps up to her daughter. She lifted Grete by her armpits and began scolding through tears, all the while planting little kisses on her face and head, and then she saw Uncle Klas.

"What the *hell* are you doing here?" she said and put her daughter back down on the sand. Fru Gyllenhammar looked from the well-dressed image of her brother to the tousled Grete and back. Uncle Klas said nothing. Grete made a motion to start walking in Uncle Klas' direction, but was stopped by her mother's hand on her head. She twitched at the sudden touch, stumbling at the pile of driftwood that Nikolai had been picking from earlier. A few sticks rolled down towards the edge of the bonfire. "What have you done to my daughter?" Fru Gyllenhammar asked slowly, her hand not letting go of Grete's scalp.

Nikolai, who had been keeping his hands across his eyes for the duration of the exchange, now looked for the first time between his fingers at the tall man in the suit. Uncle Klas kept biting his upper lip, his torso awkwardly angled in-between the smear-eyed redhead and the child. Just next to him, but quite without the affectionate hand on the lower arm that, before the appearance of the mother, had been so solid as to appear sewn-on, stood the brunette with her eyebrows wrinkled. She was moving her gaze from the face of the mother to that of Klas, to Nikolai and back.

"Nothing," began Uncle Klas, "I swear this time…"

With a final look at the brunette, Nikolai began to walk along the edge of the crowd towards the harbour. The brunette said nothing.

"Just go away," Fru Gyllenhammar said and shut her eyes. "Just leave, right now, and don't ever go near my child again."

"Mom," Grete called from below.

Fru Gyllenhammar hushed. "I know what you think sweetie," she said and ruffled Grete's hair, "but Uncle Klas has to go back to the city. It doesn't mean he doesn't love you anymore."

"But *Mom*," Grete called again, tugging at her mother's hand. Fru Gyllenhammar looked down and, seeing the distorted face of the child, loosened her grip. But it was too late to rescue the notepad, and together they watched it disappear into the flames that had crept over on the fallen driftwood. Grete didn't even throw sand on it. When she looked back up, Uncle Klas was walking away.

"Mom you have to stop him," she called and began tugging at the mother's dress. Fru Gyllenhammar grabbed the tugging hand and squeezed it tightly. "But mom," continued Grete, "he still hasn't taken me crab-fishing."

"Crab-fishing," Fru Gyllenhammar echoed.

"He promised he would do that," Grete prompted. "And school starts already next *week*."

Fru Gyllenhammar looked away at the

diminishing figure of her brother, the brunette walking next to him with gesticulating hands. Then she looked down at the burned notepad.

"Oh dear," she said, "look what happened to your sketchbook."

Grete looked at the blackened pad and shrugged. "It doesn't matter," she said. "I made the perfect drawing already."

The mother smiled. "What you gonna do all day then? Fish crabs?"

"No, *silly*," Grete said and rolled her eyes. "Don't you know crabs *hibernate* in the fall."

"All right then, sweetie," the mother said and bent down to lift her child. She secured the girl in her arms, and shivered as she felt her take a deep breath against her neck. "Don't you worry," she said and put a protective hand on her wispy hair. "You'll get your crab trip before the season closes. Jörgen's boys still have to finish the week."

About Frida Stavenow

Frida Stavenow was born in Stockholm, Sweden, but quickly exchanged the offensively pure snow for some more relatable East London fumes. She studied Media & Modern Literature at Goldsmiths College, then spent a couple of years teaching English and sucking inspiration out of dirty Saigon backstreets, filthy Bangkok rivers and rather nice Spanish plazas. She also tamed wild horses in Mexico for a bit, a fleeting escape from life she has since been trying to recreate. At the moment of writing she is based in Barcelona, but a safer bet would be to look for her at huvudstupidity.tumblr.com, where she tries to improve the world by sharing things and thoughts that have made her a nicer, smarter or more interesting person. She follows other people's tweets @fridastavenow, and who knows, one day might even share an original thought in 140 characters or less.

STEP RIGHT UP

GERRI LEEN

As *Styx*'s "Grand Illusion" blared in the background, the lights of the midway lit Gray's face eerily, making his expression of grim determination look like something out of a nightmare. Phil found herself drawing back.

"Philippa, what is it?" He reached for her hand even as he scanned the area.

"These lights... they make you look—"

"Utterly handsome? Irresistible, perhaps?" Gray pulled her into his arms, and she didn't fight him even though they were working—they were trying to look like ordinary young-in-love carnival goers, after all, not magical repossessors.

"Sense anything?" Phil asked him.

"Other than the woman who in a few short months will make an honest man out of me? No." He let go of her. "And I find that troubling. Where the hell are they?"

"I thought I got a surge from over by *The Zipper*, but now it's gone."

They both looked over at the hellish little ride, guaranteed to make you throw up any cotton candy or candy apples you'd spent your hard-earned money on, while whatever loose change you had left was conveniently shaken loose from pockets and purses to the carnies waiting below. Carnies who appeared devoid of magic—totally normal.

The person they were looking for was definitely not normal. He, or possibly she—Phil was having a hard time getting a "taste" of their quarry—was using magic for evil and their own gain, and the Universe was tired of it. And when the Universe called, repossessors like Phil and Gray answered.

On the plus side, the Universe paid well. On the not-so-plus side, it was dangerous work. Repossessors tended to live fast between jobs—no-one knew when a repo would be his or her last. It was why she was marrying Gray. She wasn't sure she was the settling-down kind, but she loved him and he was traditional and wanted to put a ring on her finger. And she wanted to wear it. For now.

"What are you thinking about?" he asked as they strolled down the midway, dodging people who by their outfits didn't realise they were a decade too late for the Summer of Love.

"Our job. Us. The future."

He smiled as he pulled her closer, their magic blending, amplifying their individual power. She'd melded power with others before, but this was different; love made it different. Love made it stronger in a way that she was only learning to master—probably because both she and Gray were control freaks and in magic, as in dancing, someone had to lead. It didn't always have to be the same person, but they needed to stop fighting each other and concentrate on the mission.

"There." Gray pulled her to a stop. "Over by the balloon pop."

She glanced over and saw no-one but a little girl

holding an older man's hand... her grandfather? The old man peeled off some bills, handed them to the huckster, then wandered away. The huckster gestured for the girl to pick up some darts—from the look of it, Gramps had paid for a lot of games. The little girl shook her head, blonde curls bouncing, then she held out her hand.

The huckster said something; Phil imagined it was along the lines of: "Play or get lost, kid."

The girl didn't stamp her feet. She didn't pout. She didn't raise her voice. She raised a column of power so big and bright Phil worried even the normals could see it.

The huckster handed the money over, his face expressionless.

"Gray."

"I see it. And her. Good Lord, that much power in that little body." He sounded almost envious.

Phil felt sick. She hated repossessing children. She'd learned the hard way not to let them off easy just because they were cute and small. She had a long, ugly scar down her forearm thanks to another cherub who turned out to be more impish than angelic.

"I would like a daughter," Gray said, and smiled at her look. "Without the evil overtones, of course. But a little girl, our child."

"Given our colouring, love"—she brushed her long, dark brown hair off her shoulders—"blonde is probably not an option."

"As long as they look like you, I'll be ecstatic."

"They? We just went from one to a houseful?"

"As the Universe wills, my dearest. The next generation of repossessors and all that."

Phil was starting to feel a little claustrophobic. "Let's just get this done. That little brat may put you off spawning altogether."

He laughed softly and followed—for once—as she led them after the girl.

**

The girl was busy riding the Ferris wheel—for free from what Phil could tell. More magic had roiled out from her as she used it to convince the carnies that she was holding a ticket when, in fact, her hand had been empty. Phil saw the old man who'd been with the girl; he walked by slowly, was checking his wallet as if he'd lost something.

"Sir?" Phil asked, stopping him. "Do you need some help?" She turned on the charm that had never needed magic to work, just warm brown eyes and a sweet smile.

"Well, they tell you not to bring much money with you to these things. I've misplaced forty dollars."

"Maybe your granddaughter has it?"

"My what?" He shook his head. "I'm a bachelor. Have been all my life, missy. Don't even like kids." He looked around at the many children packing the carnival, distaste clear on his face.

"I'm sorry. I thought I saw you with a little girl."

He shot her an annoyed glance and walked away, muttering about his money.

"Not much of a shock that she used him, Phil." Gray was watching the girl discreetly, leaning up against the side of the booth that sold ride tickets. He looked elegant, even in casual clothes, standing in this field with litter around him. "What?"

"You really are quite handsome."

He smiled gently. He kidded her about his appeal, but at heart, he was a little insecure. "Thank you, my dear." He turned his attention back to the girl. "So far, what we've seen hasn't been anything the Universe would normally take notice of. I think that—" He stood up straight, his smile fading. "What the hell?"

She looked up at the Ferris wheel, saw that the man in the car just above the little girl's had managed to swing his legs out from under the safety bar and was standing on his seat, which was rocking.

"Hey! Sit down. I mean it. Sit down now!" the carnie operating the ride yelled. He seemed at a loss as to whether to stop the ride or not, but opted not to— probably to avoid jerking the man when he was perched so precariously.

The man began to sing the theme song of *Welcome Back Kotter*, dancing along with it. He got to the edge of his seat and sang louder as the car tipped backward. He fell, still singing, the notes ending abruptly as he hit a spoke of the wheel, then another. His final impact on the ground was silent other than the dull thud of flesh hitting packed earth.

Screams erupted, but Phil could hear the tinkle of little laughter as if it were right next to her. She realised she wasn't hearing the girl's enjoyment; her magic was hearing the child's power laughing. "Now we know why the Universe cares," she said.

"Indeed." Gray took a deep breath. "We can't have a magical shoot-out right here, in front of everyone."

"I know." Phil stared up. "But maybe we can

make her come to us." She grabbed Gray's hand, trying to wrestle the power between them.

"Philippa, what—"

"Just work with me." She pulled at his power, finally felt him let her have control. "Hey, kid," she muttered, as she sent a stream of stinging energy the little girl's way. "Mommy's home and she's not happy."

The girl peered over the side of the ride, and as soon as her car got to the base, she stepped out. She stared at Phil and Gray, and then smiled serenely. "Go away."

Power blasted them. Gray pulled their shields up, and grabbed for their combined power. Phil let him have control; he was as angry as she'd ever felt him.

The little girl should have gone flying backward from the strike he launched. She should have been twisted into the metal of the Ferris wheel. She barely staggered back, then took off running toward the games.

"Well, at least we've got her on the run," Gray said, letting go of Phil's hand and taking off after the girl.

"Do we?" Phil muttered, as she followed him, power building inside her—power that didn't rival that of a little girl.

**

The hucksters cried out their sing-song siren calls. Three darts for a quarter. Three rings for the same. Phil ignored them, trying to ride the trail of power that was rapidly dissipating.

"She can't have gone far," Gray said, as he pulled her toward the hall of mirrors.

"No. It's stupid to chase her in there." Phil hated

funhouses. Hated the sense of being out of control, of nothing being what it seemed.

"I cannot believe you're afraid of a few distorted mirrors," Gray said as he pulled her into the tent.

The light disappeared, replaced by a darkness far deeper than just the gloom of a black tent on a sunlit day. This was magic. This was—

"Two by two, they come for you." The little girl's sweet, high voice rang through the space. "Run and hide, they'll still find you."

"I'll take what's behind door number three: stand and fight," Gray murmured, holding more tightly to Phil's hand. "She wants us to hide, to be scared."

Power buffeted them, a dark miasma crawling up Phil's legs, and she almost told Gray she was scared. This kid creeped her out. Not least because the power she used was so utterly lacking in anything... human.

"Let me have it, Phil," Gray said, and she gave him control.

Their combined power filled the room, sending the tendrils of ick scuttling away. The space started to lighten.

"Who are you?" The child stepped into view, a sickly, green light surrounding her. "Where did you get that power?"

Phil could feel the girl's confusion. "Where did you get yours?"

"Born this way." For a moment, she was just a little girl. For a moment, her eyes were the eyes of a frightened, lonely child.

"Us, too." Phil let go of Gray's hand, held it out to the girl. "You're alone. All alone. But you don't have to be.

You could use your power for something good. You could be with us."

"Phil... " Gray was pawing at her, always pawing at her. Couldn't he let her have a moment's free time. "Philippa, she's using you... "

The blast of the girl's power sent her into the nearest mirror, silvered glass shattering around her, pieces picked up by the whirlwind of the girl's power.

"Now, who's alone?" The tinkle of the girl's laughter sounded again and she began to suck energy from the air around them. "Now, who's all alone?"

Phil felt Gray reaching for her, his magical reach much longer than any physical one. There was love in his touch. Love and desperation and anger—boiling rage that this child would do this to her.

Holy God, how much did he love Phil?

She let that thought go and grabbed onto his power, holding on tight. And then was thrown out of the tent when Gray let loose, the magic exploding out of him like a nuclear blast. The little girl lay on the other side of where the tent had been.

Phil forced herself to her knees, realised she was bleeding from the mirror and from Gray's power play. She tried to walk, but dizziness overcame her, so she crawled over to where Gray stood watching the girl, who amazingly wasn't hurt.

"You're evil," he was saying over and over, and he looked at Phil, his expression guilty. He'd never hurt her before. Never lost control this way.

"Letting go feels good," the child said, then she held her hand out to Phil. "Help me. He's going to hurt me."

Phil could feel the child pulling power in, waiting for Phil to either cave to some maternal feelings she was surprised to realise she had for the kid, or try to take her out with power.

The child smiled, and Phil felt that smile all the way to her gut.

"I like you. We could be together forever."

It sounded good. This little angel, blonde and sweet.

"Help me?" The girl pushed again, too hard this time.

"I'll help you, you little brat," Phil said, as she decked the child.

"Philippa!"

"Well, she's out." Phil cast a quick blinding spell, ensuring any passersby would just keep walking. "Let's get her out of here."

Gray stopped her, took out a handkerchief and dabbed at the blood on her face. "I'm sorry."

"You took her down."

"I lost control. I was angry."

"She hurt me." But inside... inside she felt something shift and shiver. Doubt. It was doubt.

"I couldn't stand it if you were hurt." He hugged her quickly, and she realised he was trembling badly.

"It's all right. This isn't you." She kissed him and pulled away, grabbing the child and slinging her over her shoulder.

"I can take her."

"I've got her." She wasn't sure why, but she felt that it was important that Gray not carry her.

As they walked back to his car, Phil felt the girl's

magic whispering to her.

"Could make you so much more powerful."

"Nothing we couldn't do together."

"Give in to me and I will make you a goddess."

She ignored the call as best she could, finally whispered a binding spell to block it as she shoved the child into the back seat and crawled in after her.

The magic was alive even when the child was out. That usually meant possession, not inherent evil. The little girl might be salvageable. That was important. She was just a kid. Kids should be innocent of this darkness Phil and Gray lived in.

The ride to Thomas Repossessions was short; Phil kept her eyes on the girl and her mind safely tuned away.

"Here," Gray said, as he parked the car and got out. "I don't want her screaming all the way in." Power that Phil barely recognised as his bore down on the child, binding her in ways more secure than any ropes or chains.

The girl struggled, but the magic inside her was contained. Gray pulled her out and carried her into the building; to anyone watching, she would look like a large package, not a little girl about to be repossessed.

Phil could feel the girl's panic—no, not the girl's. There was barely anything of her left. This was the thing inside her panicking. As they neared the vault, as Gray opened it and they slipped into the power-filled space, the girl began to scream—the sound not audible, but resounding in Phil's mind like a gunshot in a small, metal room.

Gray set her down on the ancient carpet and

backed away. There was the sound of an oncoming train and oily black smoke covered the child. The mental scream turned into a wail, then a whimper.

Finally, the smoke cleared. The little girl was gone.

"No." Phil sank to her knees at the edge of the carpet. No, this wasn't fair. She was just a kid. She hadn't asked for evil to take over. And she hadn't been equipped to say no to power like that. What kind of Universe did this to a child?

"Phil. Phil, come on. It's over." Gray sounded like he always did. Like this child had been nothing more than a magical knife or urn.

"She was a human being."

"I know." But there was something in his voice that told her he didn't understand. That he would never understand.

"I thought it would leave her."

"There must not have been enough to leave once the evil was scrubbed." He sighed. "Phil, as sad as this is, this isn't the first time or the last time we'll see someone who might have once been innocent taken. If you can't deal with it, you might be in the wrong line of work."

"And if you can deal with it too easily, *you* might be in the wrong line of work."

Something flared in his eyes, then he pulled her close and took a deep breath. "You're right as usual, my dearest."

She let him hold her, let him whisper words that sounded more like misdirection than capitulation. And all the while, the empty spot on the carpet mocked her.

About Gerri Leen

Gerri Leen lives in Northern Virginia and originally hails from Seattle. She has a collection of short stories, *Life Without Crows*, out from Hadley Rille Books, and stories and poems published in such places as: *Sword and Sorceress XXIII*, *Spinetinglers*, *Entrances and Exits*, *She Nailed a Stake Through His Head*, *Dia de los Muertos*, *Return to Luna*, *Triangulation: Dark Glass*, *Sails & Sorcery*, and *Paper Crow*. Visit http://www.gerrileen.com to see what else she's been up to.

SUMMER'S END

MERIAH L. CRAWFORD

One night when we were both five, James and I stood on the porch at Gramma's house on a hot July night, staring in awe at the lightning bugs flashing in the darkness. When we asked Gramma how she made them glow like that, she just smiled and told us the magic only worked if we didn't know the secret.

That was the first of many summers I spent at the farm in Pennsylvania with my cousin James. They were days filled with water-gun battles, fishing in Keller's Creek, shared secrets and dreams, and Gramma's constant benevolent presence. They were blissful times, at least according to my memories.

But then in my fourteenth year, without warning, our refuge was invaded—by death, and by a horde of strangers come to pay their respects. Grampa, who rarely figures prominently in my memories but who had always been there, had a heart attack and died.

It happened just two days before our annual drive to the farm. My usual rushed packing became more complicated as dresses, stockings, and stiff black shoes were added to swim suits, fishing gear, and the biggest, baddest water canon money could buy. Mom cried, Dad comforted her, and I wondered, more than once, why I didn't feel sadder. Why I didn't, in fact, feel much more than inconvenienced and annoyed.

During the drive, I found myself thinking about

how things would be different this year. Was Gramma okay? Would it be sad all summer long? How many days would James and I need to wait before beginning our long-planned water gun battle in the woods? But nothing at all prepared me for what I found when we arrived. The wide yard was overflowing with cars, pickups, a couple of motorcycles, and the square black buggy belonging to the lone Amish family in the county. Their big bay gelding, Thomas, watched us from a window in the barn while he chewed a handful of hay. He was a beautiful horse, but I knew from experience that he liked to bite, so I always gave him a wide berth.

"All those people parked on the lawn," I said, frowning, as Dad looked for an open place to park the car. "They're going to make a mess of it. And what are they doing here?"

"They're here for the funeral, hon," my dad answered. "Anyway, the grass'll grow back."

"Grampa would be furious," I said.

Mom laughed sadly. "Lizzie's right, you know. I can just see him standing out on the front porch, waving his arms, yelling 'Dammit, look what you've done! Do you know how much work it takes to keep that grass looking nice? Now get those cars moved!' And he'd get out there himself and tell each one of them exactly where to park."

Dad grimaced as he pulled into a narrow, grassy space near the barn, his memories of being harangued by Grampa probably still fresh in his mind. Grampa didn't like many people, as far as I could tell, and my dad wasn't one of them.

Mom and Dad climbed stiffly out of the car and we walked up to the house. Gramma would normally be on the porch by now. She always heard us driving up, and she'd come out and wait for me to leap from the car and run right into her arms. A big hug from Gramma was my official start of summer. This time, though, there was no-one waiting for us.

As we got closer, we could hear the rumble of voices inside. And then we went in, and found the house teeming with an endless crowd of black-clad strangers. I scanned the herd quickly for signs of a friendly face as Mom and Dad began greeting people they recognised.

I slipped past them, moving through the rooms as fast as I could, looking for Gramma or James. Finally, I spotted Gramma in a corner of the formal parlour that she almost never used. She had her arm around a young girl I didn't know, and I felt a sharp stab of jealousy. Who was this trespasser, and when would she be leaving?

Just then, Gramma spotted me. She smiled and moved toward me, arms opening and then enveloping me, holding me tight. "Elizabeth! How wonderful to see you."

"I'm so sorry, Gramma," I whispered. "Are you okay?"

"I'll be fine, honey. Don't you worry about me." She leaned back and looked at me. "Well, don't you look beautiful. You get lovelier every time I see you. And have you seen James yet?"

"No. He's here?"

"He got here just about an hour ago. I sent him off to the stream with some sandwiches—he was going to try to catch some fish for dinner. Why don't you see if you can give him a hand?"

We smiled at each other, both of us well aware

she was rescuing me, as she had James.

"You go on ahead," she said, squeezing me tight again. "We'll have more time to talk after this bunch is gone."

So off I went, walking casually to the nearest door, slipping outside, and then racing through the field to where I knew James would be: our favourite fishing spot. We liked it more for the big, smooth rocks that made good seats, and the old gnarled oak that protected the spot from the worst of the heat, than for the fish. There were better spots for that further downstream.

"James!" I yelled as I got closer. "James, are you here?"

Just before I reached our oak, he stepped out from behind it, a serious look on his face. I came to a stop in front of him and straightened, putting a similarly serious look on my face, and we stood facing each other.

"I'm James," he said, putting his hand out.

"I'm Elizabeth," I said, shaking his hand.

And then he threw his arms around me and spun me around as we laughed at our joke. We had greeted each other this way every summer after that first one. It seems odd now that James and I didn't meet until the year we both turned five, but our parents had always visited the farm at different times. They said it was because they didn't want to overburden Gramma and Grampa, didn't want to tire them out with all the noise and chaos of kids and comings and goings. But the truth was, my mom and James' mom didn't get along. The reasons why were unclear to us—something about a stolen boyfriend and cheating to earn a Girl Scout sewing badge. The details were never discussed, and honestly, we didn't really care.

When we arrived that first year, our moms stared at each other for a moment, and then hugged stiffly and began chatting about things like the weather, the traffic, and why their husbands hadn't been able to get away from work. James and I, meanwhile, were looking each other over, trying to figure each other out. Finally he walked up to me, stuck out his hand, and said, "I'm James."

I took his hand and shook it firmly, like my dad had taught me to ("Nothing more important than a good handshake, Lizzie") and introduced myself: "I'm Elizabeth." At this critical juncture, both our moms had burst out laughing.

"Well, aren't they just *darling!*" James' mother exclaimed.

"Oh, they are *adorable*," mine agreed, and they laughed even harder.

James and I scowled at each other with nearly identical looks of disgust and anger. And in that moment of shared humiliation, we recognised each other as friends and allies.

Nine years later, we were closer than ever, and each knew how the other felt about this invasion. Grateful we'd escaped and knowing there was nothing to be done about it, we headed to the water to fish. I picked up the rod James had brought for me, we baited and cast our lines, and then settled down on our favourite rocks to stare idly at the bobbers swaying in the gentle current.

"It's about time you got here," James said with a contented smile.

"Yeah, Dad took forever packing the car, as usual.

Any bites?"

"Not unless mosquitoes count." He sighed. "The house still crammed with people?"

"Yup. Wonder when they'll leave."

James shook his head. We both knew it would be hours. Most of the time, we could happily fish for half a day or more, but knowing we had no choice made it irksome. We filled the time by telling each other about the last nine months: school, friends, his aikido lessons (the girls thought it was really cool) and my horseback riding lessons (the girls thought that was really cool, too). Finally, I asked what had been on my mind off and on all day.

"James... do you miss him?"

He was silent for so long I didn't think he was going to answer, but finally he shook his head, no. He didn't look any happier about it than I was.

"Do you know many of those people?" I asked, trying to change the subject.

"Nah, not really. Great Aunt Helen and her lot are there. And Mom's cousins from California flew in with their kids. That and tons of neighbours and friends. Plus, of course, Grampa's spy buddies," he added with a grin.

During our third summer together, James had tried to convince me that Grampa was a spy. "That's why he doesn't talk to us much," James explained. "Too many secrets. He has to watch every word and make sure nothin' secret slips out." But even though I was only eight, I knew James was full of it, and I told him so.

"Full of what?" James demanded, shoving me. "C'mon, full of *what?*" Always hoping I'd say it—what James was full of—so he could run off and tell Gramma and get me in trouble. But I wasn't falling for it.

Not that there was much trouble to get into with Gramma. She was the kindest grownup we knew. The embodiment of fun and presents, cookies and laughter, stories at bedtime, and comfort when we were sad. But when she scolded you, though it was gentle, it was with such a look of disappointment that you wanted more than anything to avoid doing it—whatever it was—ever again.

Getting in trouble with Grampa was another thing altogether. He didn't seem to have much interest in us most of the time. When we did catch his attention, the results were never pleasant. Luckily, Gramma was always around to intercede on our behalf.

There was the time James and I went running into the house to show Gramma the snake we'd found, and tracked mud all over the carpet. We were rushing down the hall toward the kitchen, where we knew Gramma would be cleaning the fish we'd caught that morning. We were almost to the kitchen when Grampa stepped out of the bathroom and stopped in front of us, blocking our way. He opened his mouth, probably to yell at us for being noisy or bothering Gramma, when our trail of mud caught his eye. He gaped at the mess, then looked down at us, his face twisting in anger.

"*Damn* you kids!" he roared, waving his arms at us. "Your grandmother and I work hard to keep this house clean and decent, and all you do is tramp through here making a mess. If I acted this way when I was your age, my father would've had me out to the barn for a whipping faster than—"

"Frank!" Gramma called to him, as she stood in

the kitchen doorway frowning. "It's just a little mud, and they'll help me clean it up."

He turned to face her, still glaring. "These kids have got to be taught respect!"

Gramma paused for a moment, then gently sent us outside to clean up. As the door closed behind us, we heard Gramma telling him to come into the kitchen for a cup of cocoa. James and I released the snake, cleaned up, and then hurried back to the house to help Gramma with the mud. Grampa didn't reappear until we were finished, and then he pretty much pretended we weren't there for the next week.

James and I had an unspoken agreement after that incident never to take chances and risk his anger again. Not that we always behaved—we just made sure to stay well away from the house when we were being "wicked, filthy creatures," as he called us, and to clean up with the hose behind the barn before going inside. And, at Gramma's request, we kept the snakes outside too.

"Best to leave animals where you find them, undisturbed," she told me one time, as she wiped a fresh garter snake bite on my arm with iodine. "Imagine how frightened you'd be if a giant snatched you up and carried you home."

And I couldn't argue with that.

**

James and I had been fishing for over three hours before the first cars drove off, leaving long clouds of dust hanging in the air behind them.

"If Grampa was here," James said as we watched them go, "he'd yell at us to get back to the house and hose down the drive to keep the dust down."

"Gramma would tell him to let us be, but we'd go anyway to keep him from scowling at us at dinner." We smiled at each other and then looked away as the smiles faded.

**

Over the next two days, dozens of people came and went, paying their respects, laughing, crying, bringing and eating mounds of food. James and I washed a vast quantity of dishes, which we were grateful to do as it kept us away from the visitors. Every so often, one of us would go tell Gramma we needed help in the kitchen, and she'd come sit out on the back porch with us, drinking lemonade and resting her feet. We talked about the things we'd do that summer, and about summers past. Anything but what was going on inside, and why.

Finally, the whole herd was gone, including our parents. A peaceful, friendly silence descended, and we eased gently into the routine of summertime. Much was the same, especially at first, but as the days and weeks passed, the haze of disapproval that hung around Grampa's chair in the living room gradually dissipated.

On rainy days, there would be marathon sessions of Monopoly that went on so long we'd have to use money from all the other board games. Gramma liked to buy utilities and railroads, and did pretty well with them. James used the reverse strategy and aimed for building hotels on a few expensive properties. That approach either succeeded or failed dramatically. I took the middle path and collected the lower-rent properties. In the end, I think we all won an almost equal number of times. It was just fun to sit and play together, and listen to the rain rattling on the metal roof over the porch.

When the sun came out, James and I would take part in a water-gun campaign with eight neighbouring kids that lasted for days. We had one every year, each more elaborate and water-soaked than the last. This year, James and I used walkie-talkies he'd gotten for Christmas, and the compass I'd learned to use just for this purpose. We broke up into four teams, set the rules, and the battle began. James and I, paired of course, got very wet. But in the end, we were victorious. To celebrate, Gramma made cookies.

Cookies are one of the things I always associated with Gramma. She made all the usual kinds, of course, but there was this one type, called Forgotten Cookies, that I was convinced only she could make. James and I would lean on the long wood-topped counter in the kitchen and watch, transfixed, as she made them. First, she separated two egg whites, in itself a fascinating operation. Her gnarled fingers tipped the yolk back and forth from one half-shell to the next, the slimy whites oozing into the bowl below. Why didn't the yolks ever break? They always broke when I tried to do it, and there'd be bits of eggshell to fish out, too.

Next, she'd beat the whites in her ancient stand mixer until they were creamy white—a thing I couldn't believe quivering, gelatinous egg whites would do for anyone else. Next, she'd add two scoops of sugar with her peeling wooden third-cup measure. She'd run the mixer some more until the whites were stiff. Impossible! And then, two critical ingredients would go in: an entire bag of chocolate chips (minus a handful or two for snacking), and a teaspoon of vanilla. Last, the most important ingredient of all: green food colouring. I'm not sure why, but they just aren't the same without it.

Finally, James and I plopped mounded spoonfuls onto a cookie sheet, and the whole thing went into Gramma's big gas oven: temperature set to zero! The next morning, we would rush into the kitchen and out they would come: crunchy green blobs of chocolaty perfection. I learned eventually that it was the heat of the gas oven's pilot light that cooked them, but this made them no less magical to me.

**

Finally, the end of summer approached. Just one week left before our parents were due to come drag us back to the real world. James and I decided we would ask Gramma to take us to the old drive-in for a double-feature. Two awful monster movies, greasy burgers and fries, and the best chocolate shakes in the county. What better way to say farewell to summer?

Gramma was upstairs, so James and I walked up the wide wooden steps and down the long hallway to what was now only Gramma's room. We stopped in the doorway, and I was about to speak when James put his hand on my shoulder to stop me. It took me a moment to realise why, but then I saw that Gramma was crying softly as she leaned on the tall bureau. In one hand she held an old picture of Grampa, taken when he was in the Army. James and I stood there and watched, unable to move and unwilling to disturb her. There was something so very wrong about seeing her cry, something so utterly horrible about it. And then, shaking her head, she spoke:

"Nearly forty-seven years of being your wife. God forgive me, Frank, but I'm glad you're gone. *I'm glad.*"

Then, Gramma straightened, opened the top drawer, and placed the picture inside, face down. She closed the drawer firmly, wiped the last tears from her eyes, and moved to the window to raise the shades.

Finally able to move, James and I went quickly and quietly to the stairs, slipped down them, out the side door, and headed to the barn. It wasn't until we were in the loft, sitting together on a musty old bale of hay, that we spoke.

"James?"

"Yes, Elizabeth?"

"Do you—" My voice broke and I stopped for a moment, until I thought I could speak clearly. "Do you think they loved each other?"

James sat in silence. I wondered if he thought the question was stupid, but then he leaned over and rested his head on my shoulder. "I don't know," he whispered.

"Neither do I."

**

It was as if something—everything—had fallen apart that year. By the next summer, Gramma had sold the farm and moved into a small apartment near friends. Because there was only one spare bedroom, James and I never spent another summer together. And worst of all, I never learned the answers to so many of my questions. I have come to understand that most of the answers will never come.

About Meriah Crawford

Meriah Crawford is a writer, an assistant professor at Virginia Commonwealth University, and a private investigator. She has also been a horseback riding instructor, library page, programmer, prepress tech, magazine assistant editor, graphic designer, technical editor, software tester, systems analyst, program manager, and has even been paid to put M&Ms into little baggies for bingo. Meriah's published writing includes short stories, a variety of non-fiction work, and a poem about semi-colons. For more information, visit www.mlcrawford.com.

THE LYING, THE SNITCH, AND THE WARDROBE

STEVE WARD

Just after I turned nine, I asked my dad why Mum had to live in the wardrobe. I had spoken with a mouth full of Coco Puffs and for a minute I thought he hadn't understood what I'd said. But he had. He was just taking his time to answer.

He lowered the newspaper ever so slightly, so I could just make out a single staring eye beneath a raised eyebrow. His eye looked right through the middle of my forehead.

"We've talked about this before, Edmund." Edmund is not my real name, by the way. My real name is secret, and I don't tell secrets any more. "Your mother had a terrible accident and can't move around."

The newspaper was raised again, like a flag to signal that the conversation was over. It wasn't.

"Yeah, I know that, but we could lift her out and put her in different places. The garden. Or a chair in front of the telly."

This time the newspaper came all the way down on to the table. I cowered a little under the gaze of both piercing green eyes. A single vein on his elongated forehead throbbed, and his jaws clenched so tightly that I imagined I could hear the muscles working, but when he spoke it was in his usual calm tones.

"Edmund. Your mother is very fragile—"

"—Like a butterfly."

"Exactly. Fragile. Like a butterfly. She would be at great risk if she wasn't kept safe and secure the way she is. The only way we can keep her here—*the only way you can have a mother, Edmund*—is if we keep her safe and secure in that wardrobe. And, of course: what else do we need to do to make sure we can keep her, Edmund?"

I answered immediately. I had been told enough times. "To keep it secret."

"Correct, Edmund. To keep it secret. Nothing good comes to those who tell secrets."

Why, Edmund, I could tell you a thing or two about what they do to snitches in The Big House.

He didn't say that on this occasion. He had said it hundreds of times before though, and if I had waited, I bet that would have been his next line. The Big House was what he called the prison he worked at. He was a surgeon, and was in charge of the infirmary.

"I would never tell anyone. I don't want them to take Mum away," I said. I was a good boy.

"I know you wouldn't, Edmund. Now why don't you fix her up a bowl of cereal and take it on up to her?"

The Big House. Snitches. Fix her up a bowl of cereal. Take it *on up* to her.

Dad often spoke like that, the way Americans did on TV, yet he'd lived here in the United Kingdom his entire life. I don't know why he used American phrases. Or why I remember it so clearly. Some of his manner of speaking rubbed off on me. Other stuff too.

Naturally, I had done as I was told, which I was very good at doing back then. I'd fetched the key ring from the kitchen drawer, and took her breakfast *on up* to her.

**

The key ring had only two keys on it. One was the key to my mum's bedroom, the other opened the wardrobe inside. The doors were always locked. Except when we unlocked them, of course.

I'd taken meals to Mum lots of times. In fact, delivering her meals was pretty much the only time I got to see her in the years after her accident; mealtimes and when reading fairy stories to her, like she used to read to me. They'd always been uplifting stories, children outsmarting wicked witches, becoming heroes in strange far off lands, fulfilling ancient prophecies and such. Good always triumphed over evil, and the heroes lived happily ever after. If only real life were anything like that.

As usual, I set the bowl down on the bedside table to free my hands. The wardrobe lock was very stiff, and as my dad pointed out often, I was a very weak child, so I had to turn the large key using both hands.

And there, as always, strapped to the rails inside the wardrobe and wedged behind the fitted shelf we set her meals down on, was my mother, eyes as red and puffy as a pair of bee stings, and with fresh tears streaming down her paper-white face. I placed the bowl down, and her damp eyes looked at me like she was trying to tell me something. She couldn't, of course, not really. She had no tongue or larynx. She also had no arms or legs.

**

I first met Lucy two weeks after my eleventh

birthday. Her real name wasn't Lucy, by the way. Her real name is a secret, and nothing good comes to those who tell secrets.

I'd just had my schoolbag dragged in some dogshit and suffered a powerful kick to my genitals, both courtesy of the school heart-throb, Will Clements. He was repeating his final year and was the only kid in school with something approaching an actual beard. Kids at school admired Will for his manliness, his looks, and his football talent. My testicles could certainly attest to the force of his instep drive. Whilst it was true he was good at sports, looked like a model, and was the most popular kid in the school, he was also a grade A arsehole. He had bullied me for as long as I could remember.

With one hand clutching my bag and the other trying to massage life back into my balls, I turned the corner by the science labs and bumped into the most beautiful girl I'd ever set eyes upon.

The same height as me, slim, somewhat frail-looking, with long brown hair that shimmered in the sunlight and tantalising little bumps under her uniform, Lucy had eyes so wet and blue I wanted to dive into them and swim around.

I had not met her before as she was in the year above me and, as I later learned, she mostly didn't stay on school grounds during breaks and lunchtimes.

She took a step back after our collision, stared with disgust at my trouser-thrust hand, and said, "Gross! Are you *playing* with yourself?"

I was dumbstruck for a moment. She looked like how I'd imagined angels to be.

I dropped my schoolbag and stooped to pick up

the books and papers I'd scattered from her hands. It gave me a few seconds to come up with a reply, but even still, I didn't come up with anything remotely impressive.

"No. A big kid just kicked me in the bollocks."

I had turned bright red and could feel the heat radiating from me in waves. She seemed to relax a little, gave a thoughtful look, and then the look of disgust returned.

"What's that *dogshitty* smell?" she asked.

"Dogshit," I said.

Standing upright and offering her belongings, I made an effort to kick my schoolbag across the ground so that its smell would be out of range, but it left a wet brown trail behind it all the way to the wall. I'm not sure whether it was my clumsy attempts to explain, my equally clumsy footwork, the sight of my bag doing art across the floor, or my utterly mortified expression; but for whatever reason, after an awkward moment of silence, she snorted with laughter, the snort becoming a light musical giggle that instantly made everything else in the world fade into nothing. I found myself laughing with her.

When we had both caught our breath, she took her books from me, jumbled them under one arm and offered her other hand and said, "I'm Lucy".

"I'm Edmund," I had said, taking her hand and feeling like a million butterflies had just taken flight in my tummy.

**

Fragile, like a butterfly. That's what my mother was, what I was too, back then; and it seemed to me that

Lucy was the same.

**

After a few months, I guess you could say that Lucy and I were about as close to being girlfriend and boyfriend as kids our age normally got. Kids our age from *my* generation, anyway. It was a far more innocent time. Kids weren't educated much about sex or relationships. There weren't campaigns aimed at raising child awareness of teenage pregnancies, sexually transmitted infections, sexual abuse, paedophiles, domestic abuse. We didn't know how to spot inappropriate stuff. And we weren't encouraged to snitch about it if we spotted it.

Back then, victims suffered in the dark.

There were lots of secrets, and a lot of kids kept them.

Of course, we knew a little about the stuff some boys and girls got up to. A girl in the year above Lucy had dropped out of school after getting pregnant. But Lucy and I weren't going to rush into physical intimacy, we were far more sensible and content to take things slowly.

Well, that's kind of bullshit. The truth is we were both naive, clueless, and socially and romantically inept. And fragile, of course. But I guess that made us just right for each other, and we got very close very fast.

**

Lucy used to take her lunch to a dilapidated chapel in the copse just outside the school's playing fields. It was meant to be strictly out of bounds, but the school didn't seem to enforce that rule much judging by Lucy's frequent unchallenged visits. I asked her about it one time when we were sitting there on the dusty bench by the altar.

"Aren't you worried about getting caught here?"

"The teachers never come to check. They're too busy thinking up new ways to bully us."

"Aren't you afraid of the ghost?"

She looked confused. "Why would I be afraid? Clint sometimes talks to me, it's not like he's an *evil* spirit."

Clint Masters was the reason that the school had ruled that the chapel ruins were strictly out of bounds. He'd been crushed and killed under falling masonry whilst exploring the place.

"Wait," I said, sneering, "You've *seen*—and *talked to*—a *ghost*?"

Lucy gave me a look of disappointment that made me wish I could rewind the conversation. "Yes. I've talked to a ghost. The ghost of Clint Masters. He was in my registration class, we were friends. *Are* friends."

Without thinking, I quickly blurted out a derisory chuckle. "And what does Clint say?" I resisted the urge to add a suggestion that Clint might say "Woooooooooooh".

"Different things. He tells me stuff, about what happened, who comes here, things that go on at school, stuff like that. He sometimes tells me secrets."

When she mentioned secrets, I clammed up on her. I think she could tell I was uncomfortable.

"Last time I saw him, he told me this: when someone asks you not to tell for *your* own good, it's sometimes *their* own good they're really thinking of. I've been thinking about that since, I'm still not sure what he meant or why he said it. It's sort of deep. Profound."

All the talk of secrets was putting me on edge, and I was silent and fidgety. I think Lucy assumed I was uncomfortable talking about ghosts, but that wasn't it at all, since ghosts are bullshit anyway. My dad had taught me that, in the same direct and unambiguous fashion in which he'd taught me not to tell secrets.

Lucy said she had decided to tell me a secret of her own.

"My mum is always hurting herself," she said, and paused like that was it.

"You mean, like, on purpose?"

As I've said, most of us were unaware of a lot of stuff back then, there weren't documentaries and books about self-harm and such, but I'd heard from my dad about inmates deliberately hurting themselves. He'd told me that it was mainly snitches that did it, told me it was because of the guilt... nothing good comes from telling secrets.

But, Lucy was telling me this one, so I took her hand, ready to be supportive and compassionate.

Lucy shook her head dismissively, "What? No, not on purpose, silly. Accidents. She's accident-prone and clumsy, like a much older lady. She'll fall down the stairs, walk into doors, slip in the bath, that kind of thing. Often."

I was underwhelmed, "Well that's hardly what I'd call a *secret*. Not exactly a big deal, is it?"

She seemed far more angry at what I said than I might have expected.

Dad had told me that women were highly unpredictable, and often behaved irrationally; he'd told me they were at the mercy of hormones. I hadn't really understand what he was explaining at the time, and I hadn't yet noticed the phenomenon myself. But this sure looked like the kind of random mood swing he'd cautioned me about. She'd leapt to her feet and began screeching like a harpy.

"Actually, Edmund, it is. It's a fucking *enormous* big fat hairy deal, and it's the biggest secret I have. My dad told me *never* to talk to *anyone* about it, 'cause if people know what a danger to herself she is, they might move her into a special care home and I wouldn't get to see her *at all*. And I *promised* him I'd not tell. But I just told you. No big deal?! Well, clearly me and piddly little secrets are just not exciting enough for you."

She'd stomped off after that.

Our first argument, and I wasn't really sure what it had been about. Something in there for sure rang a bell though.

**

I remember when I was much younger, before her accident, my mum and dad used to argue all the time. They could argue about anything. What to watch on TV. Row. What dress to wear to a party. Row. What way round to fit the toilet rolls. Row.

Dad hated her talking back. Hated that she spent ages getting ready to go out; he'd often say she spent more time in and out of the wardrobe than she spent doing anything useful around the house. He especially hated her spending so much time getting ready to go out when she was going out without him. Which she frequently did, particularly in the months before her accident, and I don't blame her. Dad was about as much fun as cancer of the balls, and twice as nasty. Moaning about the *assholes* he had to deal with at work, moaning about what a lousy wife he came home to.

Arguing with each other was mostly what they did. Not after the accident though. After that, blinking and spitting out her food was about as argumentative as my mother could get.

**

The next few times I saw Lucy after the Big Deal Row at the chapel, she was quiet, subdued, and, I thought, quite moody with me. She hardly met me at all for a couple of weeks. At the time, I thought it was all on account of the Big Deal Row. I swear, if it had gone on like that a few days longer, I would have been ready to tell her to grow up and stop acting like a big baby. I'm glad she told me about what Will Clements had done before I made that mistake.

I'd walked her home from the bus after school, but instead of walking up her street and dropping her at her house, she'd taken my hand and walked me silently to the park nearby. Sitting at my side on an ancient bench decorated with birdshit and graffiti, she'd broken the silence by bursting into tears, loud, wailing, heart-wrenching sobs that shook her entire body and seemed endless and left me with no idea what to do or say. So I did and said the only things that I thought might do any good. I held her close to my scrawny chest, stroked her matted hair, and told her I loved her and that everything would be okay, and that I was sorry I'd upset her.

Turns out it wasn't me at all.

She told me then, in between cries and sobs and

wails, about what had happened the day after we'd rowed. About how she'd gone to the chapel without inviting me, 'cause she was pissed at me, and just needed to go and chill and clear her head some.

About how that total *cunt* Will Clements had been there, and how he'd gathered she was upset, and how he'd comforted her, and paid her all the compliments under the sun, and how he'd told her that she could do far better than that loser Edmund Hadley.

About how he'd gone to kiss her, how she'd pushed him away but he'd kissed her anyway.

About how he hadn't stopped there.

About how he'd half torn her clothes off, about how he'd pinned her down. About how she'd screamed and he'd told her that nobody could hear her out there. About how he'd told her he'd hurt her if she kept struggling, about how he forced himself inside her, about how he'd violated her, how he'd done just about the worst fucking thing to her that a person can do to another person, how he'd told her she better keep it quiet since otherwise she'd be in trouble for going to the chapel in the first place, it's against the rules, and he'd tell everyone she begged him for it and everyone would believe him too and think she's a slut so she'd best keep it a secret for her own good, about how he took a beautiful innocent warm person with feelings and thoughts and a life all of their own and took it all away from them in a poisonous ten-minute hateful act of misery and senseless fucking waste.

I carried on crying long after I'd walked her home, as did she. Sometimes, I still cry about it now.

**

I'd urged Lucy to tell her parents, the police, the school, whoever she felt most comfortable telling. She'd said she needed to think about it, and made me swear I wouldn't say anything to anyone about it until she had decided.

I did swear to that.

But she didn't ask me to swear not to *do* anything about it, and I wouldn't have sworn to that even if she had.

I told her to stay away from the chapel. But I didn't.

Over the following days, every lunchtime, every break, every moment that I wasn't sat in a class staring out of the window and being taught god only knows what, I went to the chapel. I'd go in from the wooded side so as not be too easily seen, I'd sneak around the perimetre, I'd check the entire location for any sign of him going back there. It was on the fifth day of my unholy pilgrimages that I found him there.

He may have returned for a repeat performance. I don't think he had, because he had a sheepish and worried look about him. He may have returned to make sure Lucy would keep good on remaining silent. He might even have showed up meaning to apologise, as if even the most heartfelt sorry could put her shattered soul back together.

He was sitting on the bench beside the altar, the same bench upon which I'd sat with Lucy the day she'd told me the ghost of Clint Masters appeared to her bearing a mixture of gossip and fortune cookie wisdom.

He was fiddling away on his Etch-A-Sketch, a toy he had far outgrown but only physically.

Storming him as he sat twiddling the knobs, that toy was the first but not the only thing to hit the concrete. My angry swipe knocked it flying from his hands, and its casing split as it smashed onto the ground, one of the knobs flying off from the impact. I kicked it as it landed, saw it skitter across the floor.

Will was clearly surprised that I was there, was used to me being an easy target for his bullying, and as such was clearly unprepared for what I did then. I slammed both my fists together into either side of his head. At that precise moment, I would have been happy had my hands busted through those ears, cracked his skull open, and squished his brains.

But as my dad often told me, I'm a weak boy.

Still, his ears must have been ringing good, and I caught a look of fear on his face that was immensely satisfying.

Aware that he was vulnerable seated whilst I was towering over him, Will tried to clamber to his feet. He was unsteady from the head slam, and I'm not ashamed to say I took advantage of it. I shoved as hard as I could into his chest, and he sprawled backwards over the bench.

The crack as the back of his head hit the concrete was at that moment the sweetest sound I'd ever heard. Lucy's generous giggle when we first met, my mother's voice when I was a little boy telling me how special I was, the birds singing around the chapel—*those* are things that should have been most precious to my ears. But Will had tainted every good thing in my mind, and all I had left was bitterness, darkness, and rage.

He lay blinking on the floor making the most bizarre facial expressions, seemingly unable to focus. Either hitting his head had really done him some serious harm, or he was trying to pretend that it had so I'd go easy on him. Either way, I didn't.

I leaped over the bench and drove the heel of my boot down as hard as I could on his crotch. I'm not sure if this was because of the significance of that part of him and what he'd done with it to Lucy, or because of him kicking me in the balls before, or just because I wanted him to hurt really bad and this was as good a way as I could think of. I wasn't thinking too much at the time. Whatever the reason, I repeated the move twice more before I dove at his chest with my knees, knocking the wind out of him as I landed, and then I was straddling him as he lay twitching and blinking.

I half remember shouting something about what nice fucking hair he had, grabbing it and using it to repeatedly lift his head up before slamming it down. If it were possible to punch your way through into hell with someone else's head, I think I'd be there now. Which, in a way, I suppose I am.

He tried to say something, blood gurgling from his mouth to mix with streams of it running from his head and nose. I couldn't make out what he was trying to say in his rasping.

An image flashed in the darkness at the back of my mind. My mother, lacking a tongue and larynx, staring into my eyes and wheezing impotently. Then it was Will again, trying to work his mouth to say something.

"Speak up *Mum*, I can't hear you!" I yelled, spittle

ricocheting off his face.

Sorry. He was saying sorry, over and over again.

The red mist cleared and the flashbangs stopped going off in my head. I slumped down to rest upon Will's chest, my head to the side of his. I could hear his ragged breathing.

I saw his Etch-A-Sketch by the wall and noticed what he'd drawn. An infantile rendition of a bunch of flowers and a lopsided, jagged 'sorry'.

He mumbled something semi-coherently (*'I dink yuff broken may head, I'm thelling of yooo'*), crying and blinking up at me.

I've no idea how or why, but I felt bad for him, felt pity for him. Intellectually, with what he'd done, I don't understand having any sympathy for him at all; didn't understand it then, and don't now—but I did feel bad for him. And I felt bad for feeling sorry for him, and that I *did* understand, because he'd done what he'd done to Lucy and some things a person shouldn't ever forgive on someone else's behalf, even if they can.

I climbed up from him, realised my nose was bleeding. I wiped it with my hand and walking away I said, "Tell whoever you like about your broken head, I don't give a shit. Was broken way before today. But if you tell anyone it was me that broke it, it'll be bad for you."

**

That night I sat with my mum a long while after she ate.

I guess she could tell there was something different about me, that things were weighing heavily upon me. Usually her eyes were simply sad and pleading, as if there were something I could do for her. Tonight, they showed nothing but concern for *me*. After I locked her up and called downstairs to say goodnight to my dad, I went to bed and cried.

**

I didn't sleep too well. Not surprising, I guess. I kept waking just a few minutes or seconds after falling asleep, loud flashing booms going off in the middle of my head and jolting me upright. But finally I drifted off fully.

I had a dream in which I saw Lucy in the chapel. The ghost of Clint Masters was there too. I'd never seen Clint alive, let alone dead, and had no waking idea what he looked like, but I knew in the dream that the figure at the altar was him. Dreams work that way sometimes. Clint's head hung to the side as if his neck was broken, and one side of his forehead was crumpled inward.

Clint became Will and mumbled, "*I dink yuff broken may head, I'm thelling of yooo.*"

Then he was Clint again, the snitch from beyond, pointing at Lucy and telling secrets about secrets. He said that line Lucy had told me he'd said to her: "... when someone asks you not to tell for *your* own good, it's sometimes *their* own good they're really thinking of... "

When I woke up I thought some about that. I don't know what Lucy found so poignant or mysterious about it. It seemed perfectly simple to me, banal even. Like, when Will told Lucy not to tell on him or else she'd be in trouble for going somewhere off limits and that people would think she was a slut. Will wasn't concerned about Lucy getting detention or about her reputation; with what he did he clearly didn't give two shits about

Lucy's welfare. No, Will was worried about being found out and punished, simply that.

That's all it meant. That people fed other people bullshit to stop themselves from being found out. It's not like it's new.

**

Next day, I bunked off school and met Lucy at the park near her house. I told her about my showdown with Will, the dream I'd had, and what I thought about it all. At first she could only focus on what I'd done to Will and what would happen and if I knew how he was. I told her I didn't know and that I didn't care, though that wasn't entirely true. I did care, because back then I still cared about other people, even arseholes like Will, and I was quietly worried that I really had broken his head. But even then, I was far more worried about what might happen to *me* for having broken it.

Lucy told me she thought her dad might be beating her mum, that she heard them fight and saw new bruises. She said she thought the real reason he'd been making her keep her mum's injuries and 'clumsiness' secret was not about stopping them from taking her away to a special care home for the accident-prone, but just to help him keep his habit of beating her hidden. A secret.

I think with what had happened, with what we'd seen, done, and been through, we were both forced to suddenly grow up, and were starting to see things for what they were and not the way we were *told* they were. The innocence and trust we'd had as children had been taken away from us, like a veil lifting to reveal the reality behind it. It's sad that the truth is so ugly.

I've told you my dad had often told me that nothing good ever came of snitching, that bad things happen to snitches. For years I had done as he said and kept my mum's condition secret. That day, I dared to break the rules. I told Lucy about my mum's accident, and that we have to keep her locked away.

**

We'd kept our voices hushed as we sprawled out on the back seat of the bus.

"What kind of accident does that? Arms, legs, tongue, *and* larynx?"

"It was a car accident."

"A car accident?"

"A car accident."

The more I'd talked to her about it, the less convincing it sounded to me too.

Since we'd bunked off school and dad was at The Big House, I'd decided to take her home to meet Mum, even though Dad had told me *never* to bring anyone home. I had become quite the rebel.

I'd told Lucy that she must not show any fear or repulsion, even if she felt some. I didn't want my mother getting upset.

When she saw me get the key ring from the kitchen drawer, she asked, "I don't get why you have to keep her locked away in a cupboard."

"Wardrobe."

"What?"

"We keep her locked in a wardrobe."

"Okay, wardrobe. But why, Edmund?"

"To keep her hidden in case people come round, and so she doesn't hurt herself. She's held really secure with leather straps."

"But she couldn't go anywhere even if she tried, right? What's wrong with laying her in bed or sat in a wheelchair? You could keep people out of her room. Out of the house if you wanted."

"I don't know Luce, Dad's the doctor, not me," It felt weak just saying it.

"You know something's not right about this, don't you?"

I looked sadly at my feet and nodded.

Part of me always had known something wasn't right about this. As I started off saying, I'd questioned it when I was just nine. It's a scary thing, how absolutely and unconditionally young kids trust their parents, even when they abuse that trust.

Upstairs, Lucy did her best to keep her emotions from showing.

"Pleased to meet you, Mrs. Hadley," she said in her best meeting-the-parents voice. She paused just long enough for it to be awkward, given that my mother clearly wasn't in any shape to reply.

"I've heard a lot about you," she continued. I remember thinking, somewhat uncharitably, how easily the comfortable lie came to her when it was needed.

The silence stretched out, mother looking from me to Lucy and to the straps keeping her in. As always, tears slowly ran down her face.

In a sudden abandonment of the calm and collected act, Lucy burst into tears herself and blurted, "Edmund, this is so wrong, she doesn't want to be in there, doesn't need to be in there, for god's sake we've got to get her out, this is all so wrong, we've got to tell someone."

My mother's eyes widened and she wheezed something incomprehensible. My own control slipped too, and I began wailing like I had when I was a toddler.

I'd restrained myself from crying much in front of Mum ever since she'd been this way, but I made up for it that day.

I removed the feeding shelf and started undoing some of the strap buckles. Lucy immediately joined in. We had carried Mum to the bed and laid her down on it, still both sobbing and wailing, when we heard the bedroom door bang open against the wall.

Dad was home.

**

Mum was wheezing more than she'd ever wheezed, wriggling on the bed as if she might be able to get up and do something. Lucy was screaming her head off about torture. I was standing at the foot of the bed wondering how I might protect them both if it came to that.

But Dad was just calmly leaning against the door, a forlorn and betrayed look on his face.

Amidst the din from Mum and Lucy, I heard his disappointed and disapproving voice.

"I told you *never* to bring anyone here. I told you *never* to tell anyone about your mum. I told you nothing good comes from telling. This is bad, Edmund. Very bad. I'm very upset with you."

Lucy said that no accident did that to Mum.

Dad nodded and admitted there had been complications. Complications, both during and after her stay in hospital. Complications that had come home with her. Complications that he'd had to deal with at home as a surgeon, but also as a husband who was sick of her infidelity, sick of her disobedience, and sick of her talking back.

Truth is, he was just sick.

But when he'd told me to go to my room, that he'd make sure Lucy got home okay, and that we'd talk more of it in the morning, that it was best this way—best we all stay calm and think things through and talk about them in the morning—and when I'd felt his powerful fingers grip my shoulders and guide me to my room telling me he could fix everything, I'd believed him and done as I was told. I guess I'd believed him because I'd so much *wanted* to believe him.

We did talk more of it in the morning, but he hadn't made sure Lucy got home. Not unless you count the wardrobe next to my mother's as home. And she certainly wasn't okay. Not unless you consider being strapped up tight in a wardrobe with no arms or legs okay.

"Her mouth's bleeding, Dad," I'd said.

"It will heal, son. It will all heal," he'd assured me.

But it didn't. Nothing does.

**

I guess you could say that the day Lucy bled out, I kind of flipped. I'd probably lost it long before, truth be told, but I think it was when she died that I really became the man I am today. A butterfly emerging from its chrysalis—but not so fragile after all.

There's not much left to tell. Well, there is. It's just I'm not going to tell much more of it. After all, nothing good comes to people who snitch.

Will Clements could tell you that, if he were able to speak. My dad, who taught me the best way to keep secrets, and from whom I learned so many other things— his collection of surgical texts have helped enormously— would surely tell you the same too; except I've made sure he can never speak again either.

The pair of them just wheeze nonsense to each other now.

I'm going to need to get more wardrobes or consider alternative storage solutions, I think. Especially if good-intentioned people like you are going to keep arriving to poke your noses into business that don't rightly concern you. Now all you can do is listen. You make a perfect depository for my secrets: one that can never pass them on.

I often dream of what kind of life I might have now if I'd had a normal childhood. I dream about feeling love, about being happy, about ghosts.

I imagine that the ghost of Clint Masters would disagree with my stance on keeping secrets. But Clint is as dead as a doornail; and just like dreams, ghosts are bullshit anyway.

About Steve Ward

Steve Ward is a psychologist from the United Kingdom and an author of contemporary horror and suspense. Prior to unleashing his inner darkness upon an unsuspecting world in the form of unsettling tales of dread and despair, he unleashed his inner darkness upon unsuspecting students as a senior lecturer in psychology, with interests (and non-fiction publications) encompassing fear, anxiety, pain, and crime. As well as writing, he currently donates his expertise and time in the support of people in psychological distress.

Steve Ward can be contacted at stevewardthewriter@gmail.com.

REFLECTIONS

JAMES D. FISCHER

"Bleck. Blaaahhahr. Blort..."

The sounds from Aydeen's room surprised him. He often talked to himself—aloud, sometimes. He actually experienced a sense of something like pride when he heard his daughter, apparently talking to herself—maybe imitating her dad.

"Glarp. Glllarrrppp. Glooorpitooey " It was a little louder now.

He strolled on past her closed door, then turned back. He was sure there was nothing really wrong. But he knocked, anyway.

"Yeah. What?"

"Just checking. Can I come in?"

He cracked the door open just enough to poke his head in. "Is it *safe*?" She wouldn't recognise the movie reference from, come to think of it, twenty years before she was born. "Can I come in?"

"Looks like you're already in, old man."

"Hey—little respect here."

"*You* didn't—*respect*, exactly, *me*. Poking in before you were actually invited."

"Yes—I did poke without permission. But I was really curious about the sound effects, kiddo."

"What...oh yeah. I was trying to figure out the sound of vomit. Vomiting."

"Vomit? Wait—can I come in, for real?"

"Sure."

He sat on the bed with her. "So. The vomit thing. You feeling okay? I mean, are you getting, oh, 'glarpity' or something? Something a doctor should hear about? Or a parent?"

"No. I mean, I'm not sick...I just feel terrible."

"Now, I'm really confused. What's goin' on?"

"I can't remember what Mommy looks like."

"Wow. I think she's almost asleep right now, but I can get her to come in and model for ya."

"No. Don't wake *her* up. Anyway... I mean Mommy. I can't remember what she looked like—the one who died. I can't remember, and I feel awful."

He should have seen this coming—but , then, he never did. It wasn't far from the fourth anniversary of Jenny's death. He wondered if that had triggered something. How aware is a ten-year-old of that kind of calendar? She didn't seem to need much reminding of her most recent birthday. And the pictures—he knew now that that was coming, too.

"Daddy, I should be able to remember my own Mommy! I mean, I remember her—but now I can't think of what she *looked* like. And that's the kind of thing I should know. I should be able to, you know, *picture* my own mother! And I can't, and it makes me feel bad. I mean, if I only had..."

Here it comes. And the picture thing never gets easier.

"Dad... why did you..."

"Look. I can't really explain it. It's just that... when she died... I just went kinda crazy. In some weird way, I didn't think I could stand to be reminded. And—

no, I don't mean I want to *forget*. I think of Jenny really often, and I enjoy it. These past few days, I've remembered her a lot. But I did burn all the pictures. Back then. All the pictures. I was crazy, and I'm sorry, and it was wrong, and I..."

"Daddy, don't. I'm not trying to make *you* feel bad. But it bugs *me*, a lot. I wish you hadn't..."

"I know. And *you're* not making me feel bad—I'm doing that on my own, okay?"

"Yeah. But I wish I could see her."

"Let's give it some thought for a while. Maybe there's something..."

"If you come up with something, let me know, OK?"

"Yeah, sure. But for now, let's go easy on the vomit-noises, and maybe think about actually getting ready for bed, OK?"

"Yeah, Dad. I'm sorry. You don't think I bothered... her... do you?

"Nah. She's pretty hard to shake up. But I'll talk to her—you know, make sure she's not throwing up or anything..."

"Daddy... you know I wouldn't wanna bother her... you know... *or* you."

"You can bother me, any time you wanna. 'Specially when *you're* bothered, you know? Let me know. I can't promise to be able to help... but I promise to care. And like I say—tomorrow, maybe this weekend—let's talk about, maybe, some ways to help you see your Mommy. Maybe I can, you know, dream something up."

"I sure hope so."

"Let's plan on doing some hope stuff. But

tonight's a good time for sleep stuff. No more glarping, okay?"

"You got it."

Walking back toward the bedroom—his bedroom, his wife—he thought about the mirror story. Japanese, he was pretty sure. It involved a wicked stepmother, but that would not be true now of course. But part of it might still apply. And there *is* a mirror, somewhere. Jenny actually used it, and Aydeen might remember it, and it might help. Where was it? And would it be painful to look for it, to find it?

And, if he couldn't find the mirror, could he at least find the story? How did it come into his mind in the first place? Probably, his love for many things Japanese, and the flings he'd had with Zen. That never got deep enough, but... the non-frightening way of looking at nothingness—that certainly appealed. And, over the years, he'd written a lot of what he called haiku and had taken comfort in two or three of them.

Barbara looked up from bedside reading. "Anything big goin' on?"

"Just an arrow toward the heart. Some bleeding, nothing fatal."

"The kid?"

"Pretending to be dramatic, over a memory failure."

"Okay, Jack. Should I be digging for details here? Or just let you metaphor me 'til you get us both lost?"

"Aydeen's worried 'cause she can't conjure up a visual memory of Jenny."

"Wow."

"Yeah. And the pictures of her... well, I don't have

any."

"You told me, you... did that... burned the pictures... and I never pushed you on that. Maybe it's none of my business, but it might be Aydeen's business. And she may need more information. Just 'Daddy went bonkers' may not be enough. Should I shut up?"

"That'd be convenient, god knows—but not fair. I probably need a better story."

"A true story might be a place to start."

"Malignant... melanoma. That's how Jenny died. Malignant—the right word. And ironic."

"Ironic."

"Yeah. She'd been a sun worshipper—magnificent tan—then malignant. And not really noticed until... it had really dug in, went internal. Before it killed her, it rotted away her spirit. The face, really, went last. Ugly, finally. *She* burned the pictures."

"Jenny did."

"Yeah. They were painful—brutal reminders of how... malignant things were becoming. It was summer, and Aydeen was staying with grandparents—my folks. So, Jenny had me gather all the pictures, and promise... well, actually, she didn't make me, it was my promise, not to..."

"Not to blame her Mommy."

"Yeah. Good god it was terrible to watch... that dissolving. I tried to spare Aydeen, but... I may have been wrong... And now I'm bringing you into this... secret."

"Jack, it's *your* secret. And it's safe."

"Right. How much you know about Japanese folk tales?"

"Well, you got me there, pal."

"There's a story about a mirror—and a dead mother—and I'm thinking that, somewhere, there's a little mirror around here that Jenny had. It had lights..."

"A makeup mirror."

"Really? I think it's somewhere, and... I don't know. I need to find that story, I think.

"Jack, in the attic, there's a vanity set..."

"A what?"

"Vanity set—a little table, mirror, seat, some drawers. Where a lady, you know, sits and puts on her makeup and stuff."

"That something you'd want me to bring down?""

"No. But—maybe—it'd be a place to look for the mirror. In the drawers, you know."

"That's a good idea, I bet. You'd do that—you'd store a small mirror in a drawer of the... thing?"

"I might. But, Jack—don't go up there rummaging right now, okay? I mean it is bedtime—'specially for small folk."

"Gotcha. You don't mind if I do some computer searching though, right? I could try to find the story. *Japanese, mirror, story*—might work."

"Go for it. Just don't holler if you find it."

He kissed her, then theatrically tip-toed out of the room, dodging a thrown pillow. He went, quietly, to the computer and mistakenly started the search for "japanese pillow story"—and ran in to some mildly pornographic illustrations, and to a British movie called "The Pillow Book". He was startled, but then realised he'd entered the wrong search words.

He tried "japanese mirror story", and was led to *The Mirror of Matsuyama.* He found several versions of the tale, including one with the evil stepmother, but also a lovely illustrated story with a dying mother telling her daughter to take her mirror—a gift from the girl's father—and use it to communicate with her after she died. He wept a bit as he read this story, and he resolved to find Jenny's mirror and give it to Aydeen.

When he returned to the bedroom, Barbara was sleeping. He gently wakened her and told her the story of the Matsuyama mirror. Very quietly, a bit tearfully, they made love.

Next morning, after Barbara and Aydeen got on their ways, Jack called the college and cashed in a sick-leave day. He didn't believe he ever used all those perks, and was sure the ball players in Intro to Lit classes wouldn't miss him very much.

He pulled down the attic staircase, and poked his head in. Like most humans, he spent a bit of time wondering how a human can accumulate so much stuff, and can forget the existence of almost all the stuff. She'd called it a vanity-something or other and he saw only one piece of furniture that might fit. It was a bit larger than Barb had guessed, but sure enough, in the left-side drawer was the mirror apparatus. It was about a five-inch circle or oval, held in a y-shaped swivelling cradle supported on a metal tube to a weighted stand. The outside perimetre of the mirror-circle was an ivory-tinged band, apparently the lighting element. It didn't work. He fiddled with the base switch a few times, but it didn't light. On the whole, though, he thought it was a nifty-looking device. As he studied the thing, he did a little mumbled, day-dream rehearsal of explaining it to Aydeen. He did like the mirror.

It had taken a lot less time to find the thing than he'd guessed, and the house felt lonely, so he did go to his campus office. He decided he'd tell people he had awakened with a bad headache, but it passed. He did skip his classes, but no-one complained, so he spent some time grading papers. He ended up spending a bit of an extended day in his office—the extravagant pile of essay papers was even worse than the usual embarrassing mess.

When he got home, he encountered Aydeen amid a pretty impressive pile of papers herself—wadded up piles of notebook sheets covering an impressive expanse around the dining table. She was pencil-sketching on another sheet. "Not a very productive day—unless the goal is to re-cover the floor. What's wrong with the carpet, anyways?"

"Nothing, silly." She started picking up some of the paper balls. "The carpet is fine. My drawings, though, suck."

"Can I see?"

"No, don't bother. You wouldn't like 'em either."

Barbara came in, and noticed the paper-clutter. "Wow. I was thinking about offering dinner—but would I be risking a food fight?"

Jack gave her a greeting kiss on the cheek. "I don't *think* so, hon. Kid's trying to shake off an artist's block, I think. How 'bout you? Hard day at the guidance-counsellor's office?"

"Pretty regular. Little bit of stress in the world, and... but... I'm not sure what kind of guidance I can offer, to an artist... Is everything all right, sweetie?"

Aydeen picked up a few of the paper balls. "Oh,

yeah. I'll clean up in time for dinner. I'm just a little... not happy with my sketches."

"OK. The dinner thing—I think I'll just warm up some... oh, pot luck all right with you guys?"

Jack and Aydeen mumbled and echoed each other, "Sure... okay... all right."

"Do you guys read each other's minds?"

Jack gestured sweepingly. "Indeed! We're thinking about going on the road—Mr. Mysterioso, and..."

"I'm thinking of Miss Amazing, and... this guy."

"You work out the billing. I'll warm up something amazing, and maybe a little mysterious!"

Jack made some voodoo-waves at her as she left. "Hey, kid. Speaking of amazing, I think I found something that... well... let me get it."

Aydeen took quick looks at the spaces the adults left in the room, shook her head, and went back to the paper-ball clearing project. She unrolled a couple of them, but hurriedly wadded them back up and put them in a paper bag.

Coming in from the kitchen, Barbara noticed the almost cleared floor, and picked up a loose pair of the paper balls . "Great work, kiddo! Where's the amazing Mr.... Mr.?" She pocketed the papers she'd picked up.

"Dunno. He went to get... something, I think."

"Okay. Well, while he does that something, you can do something, too. If that bag's trash, you can put it in the trash, and you can get cleaned up for dinner, which will be microwaved in a matter of moments."

"Sounds good." Aydeen deposited the paper bag in the kitchen trash, and came back through, running to the upstairs bathroom.

Barbara thought about slowing her down, but knew that would not be possible. Besides, it was good to see her in high spirits. She brought out the two wadded papers she'd salvaged, spread them on the table and frowningly studied them for a bit. She took them with her, going back to the kitchen.

Jack entered the now empty room, loudly—"OK, kiddo, I hold in my hand..." noticing being alone, he continued his speech. "Well, I guess the mystery item in my hand will remain a mystery! What a letdown." He stood the mirror on the table, and looked at his reflection. "When the hell did I get so *old*? God, I hope the kid sees something better in this thing than I do."

Barbara came in during his speech. "You know, I used to worry when I caught you talking to yourself, but I'm kinda getting used to it. Whatcha got there?"

"The mirror—for the kid. Found it right where you said I would."

"Okay. Um... Did you look at the pictures she was drawing?"

"No. She was throwing 'em away..."

"You know what they were?"

"I assume she was trying to draw pictures of... Jenny."

"Oh... that could explain... sort of."

"She showed you the drawings?"

"No. I was helping pick 'em up, and... looked at a couple. They're strange, Jack."

"Well—they're just... drawings..."

"Jack, if I saw drawings like that at school, I'd... try to find out some more about 'em."

"Look—don't go all *Guidance Counsellor* on me,

okay?"

"*School Psychologist.* It's what I do."

"Yeah, but not here, not now. Look, I'll talk with the kid, and try this mirror trick, and... let's just not get all psychological right now, all right?"

Aydeen came in, with a bouncy step. "All cleaned up, and... am I interrupting something?"

"No. Your dad and I were just... never mind. Gotta get the big feast 'o leftovers ready. Wanna help?"

"At your service, ma'am."

Barbara and Aydeen marched into the kitchen. Jack realised he was still holding the mirror, and decided to stash it beneath the couch. He put some tableware on the dining table.

The meal was pleasant. Barbara carried the leftover leftovers and tableware off to the kitchen, leaving Jack and Aydeen at the table.

"So, milady, how did you find the meal?"

"I just looked down at my plate, and there it was."

"And how did that elephant get in your pyjamas?"

"I dunno."

"So much for the hard part of the test. You know those drawings you didn't like?"

"Yeah..."

"Wanna talk about 'em?"

"You mean, about how you promised to fix 'em?"

"We'll get to that. Barb says the drawings might be... uh... well..."

"Something a *Guidance Counsellor* might wanna talk about?"

"Well, yeah."

"Look. The drawings—the scrawls—are awful—

but I already told you why. I thought I could make some pictures to... I can't remember, you know, what she looked like."

"And that's all?"

"Isn't that enough? And, anyways, what about your promise, Mr. Fix-It?"

"Aydeen, you're gonna think this is crazy..."

"Probably."

Jack retrieved the mirror from under the couch. "Okay, kid. Here's what I'm putting out as a potential problem solver. Barbara gave me some guidance on how to find it. This mirror... it was Jenny's. When I look at it, in it, maybe it just *reminds* me of her, but... I want you to have it. You know I've told you a hundred times you look like her?"

"Yeah."

"Well, here. I think, if you look in this, and hold your mouth just right, you'll see someone who looks an awful lot like your Mommy. I know you have her beauty—you always have. And there's a *chance* that this mirror can help you connect..."

"Daddy, you're right."

"Huh?"

"I *do* think you're crazy. I mean, I look in mirrors all the time. And I sometimes see what I want to see, sometimes what I fear. Some mornings, it's like 'Lookin good, girl!' Other mornings, it's total zit zone, completely awful."

"So, you've already seen some mirror magic, then. And, Aydeen, I mean this: you and Jenny have the same beauty—more and more every day. I mean, give the old 'Bibbidi-Bobbidi-Boo' a chance, eh?"

"I'll try, Daddy. Thanks."

Jack left Aydeen with the mirror, and went to the room he and Barbara shared as office-space.

The girl looked at the mirror, examined it. She stood it up on the dining table. She picked it up again, and tried the switch. "Oh well, no light. Okay... Hey, me, it's me! Gee, we're lookin' weird today—maybe the busted light? Okay, magic mirror, let's see what you really got." She looked into the mirror, then turned away and stood it on the table. She returned to it, and picked it up again, and looked. "Wow, what a bad nose. And the ears don't seem right, either. The only way this could be weirder is if someone *was* watching. Mommy... Mommy, Dad says I look like you, but I don't believe it! Maybe if the thing lit up... if, the batteries..." She opened the battery cover. "Yuck, that's ugly. If I put batteries in there, they'd never work. What *is* that white gunk?"

Barbara came in, unnoticed.

The girl replaced the battery cover. "I hope I didn't get that stuff on me." She looked again at, but not in, the mirror. "It is a cool thing. Too bad it doesn't show prettier pictures. Oh, mirror-mirror, can you be fixed?"

Barbara coughed quietly. "What'd you say, honey? Talking to the mirror?"

"A little. My dad's weird."

"I think we all know that."

"Did he tell you about this—the mirror?"

"A little, yes. He told me it belonged to Jenny, and he was going to give it to you."

"He didn't tell you... what it was for?"

"Jack's a lit teacher, and he believes in literature..."

"I'm supposed to see Mommy in it. Said I looked like her, and with the mirror, I might remember what she looked like."

"How's that working?"

"It's just me in here. And the light doesn't work."

"Well, you know..."

"You're gonna get *Guidance Counsellor* on me, aren't you?"

"You know, I'm actually a *School Psychologist*... but I'll ignore the insult for a bit. You may be trying too hard, too fast with the mirror. And about that bad light, can I take a look?" She opened the battery cover. "Whoa. See all this white stuff—you didn't get any of it on you, did you? Anyway—in the kitchen, there's some vinegar—white vinegar. And there are some batteries in the toolish-stuff drawer—triple As, it looks like." While the girl was going, Barbara did some scratching in the battery compartment. When the supplies were delivered, she wiped the battery posts with the vinegar, and installed the new cells. She handed the mirror to the girl. "Okay. Give it a try."

Aydeen engaged the switch, and looked into the lighted mirror. "This is *so* cool. Wow."

"Has the picture changed?"

"Well, no... but it does seem a little more magic now. Do you think I'll ever... see Mommy?"

"I don't know, sweetie."

"You don't think so, do you?"

"Listen. This may sound like *Guidance Counsellor* stuff... but some morning, you're gonna wake up and realise you've been talking with your Mommy—and seeing her clearly—and it's gonna feel really good."

"I used to, kinda"

"It'll happen again. And, hey—here goes the *Guidance Counsellor* again—but you can *ask* yourself to dream... and sometimes it works."

"You serious?"

"Absolutely. When you're close to sleep, try it—just ask yourself to dream... what you want."

"And it'll work?"

"Don't tell your dad I said this, but I think it could work even better than the mirror. And if you do this occasionally, you may find when you wake up, you might even know a little better, what she looked like."

"It's sort of a shame that... Dad'll be upset about the mirror."

"Oh, I doubt it. I think this... plan... has been an opportunity. I bet he's wanted to give you something... from your Mommy, and this just, you know, worked out."

"So I can tell him it doesn't work?"

"Has there ever been anything you *couldn't* tell him?"

"Not really. The lights are really neat. Can't say I *like* looking at me... but... when I hold it like this..." She turned the mirror just enough to look at Barbara.

"I see you, kid. Daughter."

"We both see... something good."

"I like it."

"Me too."

"Is that a tear?"

"Don't know why."

"Yes, you do. You know a lot of stuff."

"Thanks... Mom."

"Now I suppose I'm gonna cry".

Jack entered, overhearing just a few words. "Wow—the magic mirror is… lit up and… hey, what's…?"

Barbara started to say something, but Aydeen broke in. "The mirror was broke but… we… fixed it. And it *is* beautiful. Thanks, Dad!"

"But it looked like you guys were… sad or something."

Again, Barbara was interrupted by Aydeen. "No—we were gonna go all huggy and tear-y and everything, but… it's just a mother-daughter thing."

Jack was tempted to try to join the moment, but headed back to the office. "Glad… glad you guys like the mirror."

About James D. Fischer

James D. Fischer is retired from the faculty of Independence Community College, in Kansas. His experiences as instructor of Creative Writing and student in a series of Playwriting courses at the college have been instrumental in his continued interest in writing, and publications of (now) four pieces of short fiction.

Dodo

Sean Moreland

It had all been right here. Before tonight, there had been a room, in a house, in a suburb, on the edge of a little city, really more of a town, where Kevin had lived his whole life. It had all been right here, but now there is only the breathing dark.

Within that dark, Simon says, "She's going to college or something, and so she moves into this big old house..."

Within that dark, there are seven supine bodies. Boys, all of them, aged between eight and ten. Each is wrapped in a thick, soft, insulated bag. Their bagged bodies are strewn across the carpeted floor. The carpet was beige, before, and the sleeping bags were brightly coloured. Kevin's was red, and webbed, with Spider Man's white eyes shining up from it. Now, there are no colours; there are just indiscernibly different shades of the shifting dark. The dark has spilled in and filled Spider Man's eyes. It has taken them as its own, and Kevin supposes it watches him through them.

"The house is owned by this tall, old guy. He's a doctor or something..."

Simon tells a story, and Kevin tries to listen, tries not to think about what has happened to the room around them, for he fears that thinking about the dark too much will only bring it into and over him more quickly. But Kevin knows the carpet continues to exist, because he can feel it, itchy, against the back of his neck and his cheek when he turns his head. He knows his pillow and sleeping bag still exist because he can still feel them, too, their warmth and familiar textures haunting, here, in this obscure world in which they don't belong, any more than he does.

Kevin turns his head to better hear what Simon says, and ends up pointlessly shifting his perspective on the unshaped obscurity that coils and clenches closely on all sides.

"...and he teaches at the college where the girl is going to go, so she figures he's safe, even though he looks creepy."

The room had not been remotely creepy earlier, an hour or a lifetime ago, while it was still just a room. It was one of the least threatening rooms Kevin could imagine. Tyler's mom had called it a *rumpus room*. It was a name that Kevin had found comfortingly stupid.

There were four walls, there was fake-wood panelling, a big old TV with a pair of pellet guns crossed on the wall behind it, a big crayon-stained table with a Transformers train set, a box of tennis and baseballs, a half-deflated football, two Louisville bats, a ridiculous hat-rack that looked like the head of a goofy moose, and a legion of branded ball-caps.

Simon had even teased Tyler mercilessly about all that hokey junk, and about his mom saying *rumpus*, again and again, in that weird smiley way she had of saying it, as though it was a secret joke she didn't expect them to get.

"So she moves her books and stuff into this room, and sees this tiny door in the wall..."

Simon's teasing stopped when the dark took Tyler. Now there is nothing they wouldn't give to have Tyler's family's hokey junk back. To have Tyler's *family*, to have *Tyler*, back. But, Kevin's sure, the dark never gives back the things it has taken. He knows this without knowing how he knows. It is a knowledge of breath and bone, a certainly that is part of his flesh-circuitry, and, he's sure, part of the other breathing boys' as well.

Now even the word "rumpus" has been lent menace. It has moved from lit silliness to unsighted threat. It no longer means play, in the breathing dark, but instead that low not-quite sound, that growl felt in the chest and skull, that sensation that the dark exudes.

Of the rumpus room, now only unfamiliar, lumpish suggestions of shapes remain, and these are transformed into the stuff of the dark itself. For the darkness of the dark is not perfect, not total, not yet. It has not replaced the world—only changed it, re-made it into umber waves, obscure eddies, indistinct clumps, clusters of light's lack, voracious and active in a way lack should not be.

"The door is really small... Like, too small for anybody but a really little kid, or a dwarf..."

The difference between the boys that breathe and the dark that does is hard to define, but it is maintained by two things: their attention to the stories, and the plastic mouse in the hall beyond the door.

"The doctor tells her that the door is for a closet that belonged to his daughter, who lost the key a long time ago, so it can't be opened."

There is only one door in the dark, and it is closed, and Kevin is convinced it can no longer be opened. But the mouse shines dimly through its glass panels. The mouse is a Mickey Mouse night-light. Tyler's mother had brought it down from a drawer, in some other room. That was when this house had other rooms; when it existed in some surer, safer world, before it was winnowed down to just this not-room by the massing dark.

It was not, she'd said, that she thought they needed a night-light. They were all, she was well aware, big, brave boys. But just in case they needed to find their way to the toilet in the dark, a little light would help.

The house, she'd said, was very dark, sometimes.

Yes, thinks Kevin, *very dark*. The air is heavy, thick, with dark. It stuffs and suffocates. The dark is not cold, as you might expect, but almost *heat*, if there could be heat without hotness, heat without warmth. Perhaps the dark is nothing like heat, after all.

The mouse's light is feeble. Though the socket it sticks from had once been just a few feet from the glass-paned door, space works differently in the dark. The yellow mouse-light now has to burn across the vastness of the breathing dark to reach them. The light arrives twisted and weakened from the trip. It is a sickly glow, trickling sadly in.

Kevin wishes the mouse could offer him comfort. Instead, it only seems to mock him, its light the colour of watery pee. Just enough of an impotent gleam for him to see the moving mad mass that's been made of the rumpus room where they lay, struggling to stay awake, waiting.

"The daughter is dead or something. I don't exactly remember..."

Dead or something, thinks Kevin. There are seven bodies strewn in the fastness of the dark, but only *four* of those bodies are still the breathing boys they were before. And, Kevin thinks to himself, only *some* of the breathing in that darkness is theirs.

Kevin, Simon, Thomas, Trent. Four frightened boys, their respiration rapid, their shallow inhales and exhales audible over the inaudibly deep sound of the breathing dark.

"Anyway, she's gone, and so is the key."

Dead, or gone. This is a vital distinction. It isn't exactly that the other three, Tyler, Adam, and Dex, no longer *breathe*, as they would *not breathe* if they were merely dead. Instead, they breathe differently, now; their breathing has no rhythm, is not broken into inhale and exhale. It is just part of the ceaseless, indivisible breathing of the dark. And the dark can certainly not be said to *exhale*. It doesn't exactly inhale, either, although it does lap, suck, absorb and engulf. But what it takes in, it never breathes back out. It only swallows, swallows and spreads and grows.

"So things are going fine, she's studying hard and everything... but at night she keeps hearing these sounds, coming from behind that little door..."

Simon's story is something he saw once on TV. It could, under other circumstances, be called a scary story. But even through the lapping of terror at his edges, Kevin can see how *stupid* it is that a story about a TV show could be scary, here where the dark breathes and there are no TVs. Here in the breathing dark where their stories, and the plastic mouse, are the only things keeping them from being swallowed, as the rest of the world has been.

Through his focus on Simon's words and his scurrying thoughts about the dark, Kevin hears Trent's rhythmic breathing shift, slow. He swallows nervously, willing Trent to resist the dark, and hisses—

"Trent? Are you listening?"

Trent's breath hitches and he grunts, "yeah... yeah."

Kevin hears Simon breathe deeply before he resumes.

"So she tries prying the door open and everything, and she can't open it..."

"I don't even think *this* door is *locked*," Thomas groans, not for the first time.

"...and anyway, it's just glass and wood. Why can't we just get up and break it open and go?"

Kevin doesn't answer. None of them do. They've been over this before, a hundred times or more.

Kevin doesn't know why they can't just get up. They *just can't*. The breathing dark doesn't let them. In its world, they can't get up and move any more than they could have flown naked to the moon, in the world before. All they can do is wait, hope to hold the thread of the story, hope the mouse stays lit... or hope that the story, and the mouse, are soon swallowed up by the dark, bringing them along, concluding them.

Simon quietly resumes. "But then one night, the door just opens... and the girl looks inside, and doesn't see anything, just..."

Simon trails off. They all know he doesn't want to say *darkness.*

"Just... nothing. But she's still sure there're rats in

there..."

Tyler loved rats. He even had a sweatshirt with the Roots logo on it, but instead of Roots, it had read Rats, and had a picture of white rats below the logo. Kevin couldn't grasp what had happened to all the rats in the world when the dark began to breathe.

Kevin couldn't grasp what had happened to Tyler. Tyler isn't exactly *dead*, Kevin knows. And Tyler isn't exactly *gone*, either, because, Kevin is sure, if he draws his arm up from the hot confines of his sleeping bag, he can reach out and touch Tyler's body, just as Simon said he had reached out and touched the body that had been Dex.

But the idea repulses him. The thought of sending his vulnerable hand, its slender pallor invisible, out into the attentive thickness of the impatient dark is horrible. Worse is the thought of how the dark has changed space—what if his arm stretches out for ten metres before touching Tyler's body? Worst of all somehow is the idea of contacting Tyler's flesh. Touching Tyler's form, letting his fingers brush that fleshy void, knowing it is vacant, that Tyler is gone from it, gone to the dark.

"...because she keeps hearing those sounds at night..."

Kevin screws his eyelids shut until they ache, hoping to call up the white streaks and speckles he used to see when he did that. But nothing happens.

It no longer seems to matter whether his eyelids are open or closed. The dark is the same either way, and strangely so is the stream of dirty mouse-light. Kevin wonders whether his eyelids are gone, somehow, but he doesn't think so, because he can still feel them, sore from squeezing and blinking incessantly.

"So she tells the doctor there are rats, but he just laughs at her, says that's impossible..."

Something in the way Simon says *impossible* snaps Kevin back to attention. He's been so caught up feeling his eyelids and trying not to think about the dark, he's nearly fallen off himself and into it.

Waking from his half-trance, Kevin jerks, gasps. Simon stops his story in mid-sentence, says:

"Kevin? Are you still there?"

"Yes," Kevin hisses back. His heart's rhythm is a roar in his ears, the not-sound of gathering dark still there beneath it.

Simon says, "I can only hear three people breathing."

Kevin listens intently, listens to the sounds that skitter on the surface of the depths of the dark. Simon is right.

"It's Trent. Trent's gone," says Thomas, flatly, almost indifferently. Kevin can tell from that tone that Thomas is almost gone, too. Gone beyond caring. He's realised what Kevin himself has so far only *thought about*—that once they are *of*, rather than *in*, the dark, there will be no need for fear, or fighting to stay awake, or hanging on to hope, its weak light as dirty as that cast by the plastic mouse.

Kevin doesn't care if it *is* dirty, if it *is* stupid. Kevin still doesn't want to *be* the breathing dark.

"Simon," he says, "keep telling the story!"

"Yeah.... so... so the girl goes out and buys these big rat traps, and she puts them in that little closet..."

134

Kevin wonders if that could be where the breathing dark started, in a closet somewhere. Of course, it could just as well have come from outer space. That would make sense, somehow. He wonders, too, if when it came, it ate the rest of the world all at once, leaving only the remains of this rumpus room, or if it went through the world slowly, room by room, house by house. Person by person, as it had with Adam, Dex, Tyler. And now Trent.

Did all the lights along the city's streets go out at once, or could you have seen them going out one by one, going down like dominoes, if you were awake and watching?

And what about Kevin's family? Were they all part of the breathing dark now? Or were they waiting, trapped, in a room in their house, wondering what had happened to Kevin? Kevin, who had been so afraid, for so long, of sleeping over in a strange house? Whose mother had said she was *so proud of him* for agreeing to stay over at Tyler's?

"....and one night she hears those sounds coming from the little closet, and she hears the trap snap shut... so she sticks her hand in, into that *darkness*, trying to grab the thing..."

Kevin flinches as Simon says it. Simon says it defiantly, as if daring the dark around them to respond. He says it loudly, and then lets his sentence trail off. At that pause, they listen, all of them, as one, waiting to see what the dark will do.

The dark coils, slides, sucks at them. They listen to their heartbeats, to their breaths.

The sound of two boys, breathing.

"Thomas..." says Kevin.

"Yes," Simon says. "He's stopped breathing... by himself. It's just us, now."

They breathe together shallowly, and the dark thickens with the weight of what had been Thomas.

"Do you want to hear the rest of the story?" Simon asks, hesitant.

"Yeah... Tell me the rest."

Kevin can hear Simon's deep draw of breath. He imagines the dark flooding into Simon's lungs. He imagines the story pouring from Simon's unseeable mouth, riding on currents of the dark, and he suddenly understands the meaning of *inevitability,* a word he couldn't spell, better than any adult who ever lived.

"Well... the girl's hand gets caught in a trap, I think and she sees this thing... this monster... with big red eyes... and its skin is all wet, and waxy... it has big teeth..."

A new sound bubbles up over the breathing dark. It takes both boys some time to understand it is the sound of Kevin, laughing. He is laughing, and his face is wet, and he can feel the dark tickling in his ears, in his lungs.

"Kevin?" Simon says, uncertainly.

"Yeah... I was just thinking... how funny it is, this story... with the monster and all. I bet it looked real fake."

"Yeah," Simon says, indifferently.

In the long pause that follows, the mouse-light begins to flicker, to wane, and Kevin thinks about the light that used to fall to earth from far suns, from suns that had died before their light reached the earth. He doubts there are any stars left, in the breathing dark.

It takes Kevin a long time to realise that he is no longer thinking about stars at all, but about the dark. Maybe he's been thinking about the dark his whole life.

A gasping sound snaps him from these thoughts, brings him back to himself, his body. It is the sound of Simon's last, hitched breath, followed by the sound of Simon's not breathing, which is the sound of the dark, breathing.

"Simon?" Kevin hisses. He knows, though, that now he is speaking only to the dark. The air is now so heavy with the dark, the dark that swells like a strong smell in his flaring nostrils and dry mouth that he can barely breathe.

Are his eyelids open or closed now? It makes no difference. He thinks of the eyes in his Spider Man sleeping bag. He thinks of the dark pouring into them like oil. He wonders if the dark is really watching him, if it needs all the eyes it has swallowed to do so.

He wonders when the mouse went out, and how he hadn't noticed.

He wonders at these holes of dark, in the dark's endless whole, through which it watches itself, because there is nothing but the dark *to* see, now that the dark *can* see, in this airless breathing, in this extinction without end.

About Sean Moreland

Sean Moreland has published about two-dozen poems and a handful of short stories, mainly in independent Canadian periodicals. He is founder and a fiction editor of *Postscripts to Darkness* (find it at: www.pstdarkness.com, @pstdarkness), a serial anthology of weird fiction and art.

On the academic side of things, he co-edited the essay collection *Fear and Learning: Essays on the Pedagogy of Horror* (McFarland, 2013), is currently co-editing *Holy Terrors: Essays on Monstrous Children in Cinema* (forthcoming from McFarland, 2014) and editing *The Lovecraftian Poe: Essays on Influence, Transformation and Reception* (publisher TBA, late 2014).

DOLLS

DRAKE VAUGHN

Ella spun towards the wooden toy chest. There was a clawing sound like an animal was wiggling inside. That was silly-nilly, she wasn't allowed to have any pets, not after Captain McNugget. Mommy said she'd hugged the hamster too hard, but that hadn't been a hug. Ella had squeezed and squeezed and squeezed until the fur-ball had stopped moving. Maybe this was a mouse. She'd heard those at the old house. They went *s-s-s-scratch* all quick-like. Still, this was different. It was slow and precise as if something was climbing to the top.

Ella craned her neck and looked closer. The chest's lid was open, but she could only see the tippy-top. She was about to stand when she heard the footsteps. That noise she recognised. It was Daddy. He always walked around like his feet were pounding a drum. And now that they were living at Grandma's, the thumping was super-duper loud. The house was just like Grandma, creaky and ready to collapse. And boy, did it smell weird.

"What are you doing?"

Ella bit her lip, trying to come up with the right answer. The scratching had stopped, so she felt silly telling Daddy about the noise. And she suspected this was one of those trick questions where any answer would make Daddy mad. He asked lots and lots of those, even when Ella wasn't misbehaving.

"It's not time to play."

Ella nodded in agreement. She'd been right, Daddy was mad. He always got that way before they went over to Mommy's. Sometimes he would yell super-duper loud and once he'd even thrown a glass. It'd shattered and made a cool noise, while shooting shards across Grandma's kitchen. Ella knew she was supposed to feel sad and cry like a baby, but it'd been exhilarating. Plus, it was nothing compared to the fights Mommy and Daddy used to have.

"Why aren't you dressed?"

Ella winced. Daddy had told her to get dressed a while ago, but she'd plum forgot. Just like she'd forgot to wash her face and brush her teeth. Ella liked to forget those a lot. Once, she'd forgot for a whole four days and nobody had bugged her. A thick layer of white grime had grown on her teeth, which she'd scraped off with a long nail. She'd eaten the grime, but it didn't have much taste. Not yummy like boogers and scabs, but it wasn't bad like earwax either.

"Did you hear me?"

Ella nodded again. She'd heard everything. Ella had really good hearing; even Doctor Robertson had said so after doing all those tests with the beeps and tones. Though, her favourite was the one where he'd hit her knee and she'd kick, even if she didn't want to. Doctor Robertson was good, unlike those other doctors who asked silly questions and always made Ella feel like she was in trouble.

"Why are you still in your PJs?"

Ella didn't have an answer, but luckily, Ashley interrupted, telling Daddy he needed to take out the recycling. Ashley was always telling everyone to do one

140

thing or another. And she never ever forgot anything, not even tooth-brushing time. No wonder Daddy was always mad. But if Ashley tried to tell Ella what to do, Ella would just scream that she wasn't her real Mommy. Sometimes Ashley would cry and that made Ella super-ba-duper happy.

"You better be dressed by the time I get back."

Ella nodded, but as soon as Daddy walked away, she rushed over to the wooden chest. She stared down into the pile of toys, trying to spot whatever had made the noise. There was only the normal assortment of plastic figurines, stuffed animals, and picture-books. Ella shuffled through the contents, flinging toys across the floor. At the bottom there were a couple of rattles from when she was a baby, along with a rock hard can of *Play-Doh*. Still, she didn't see anything unusual or out of place.

After scouring through the contents a second time, she took a step back and waited for the noise to return. When it didn't, she threw up her arms and hissed. Only make-believe. She'd been a big dummy, just like her stupid neighbour Taylor. Ella hated her, since on their play-dates Taylor would always pretend to hear silly things like monsters and ghosts and the boogeyman. Once, she'd hid underneath the bed for a long, long time, crying that a tiger was outside waiting to eat her. Taylor was a real cuckoo-berry.

"Oh, hello, Marisa Clarissa. How are you?"

Ella picked up a blonde-haired doll from the floor. She brushed her hand through Marisa Clarissa's hair, trying to remember the last time they'd played together. It'd been forever long ago, like almost three days. Ella felt bad for neglecting her in the dark chest, but

141

Grandma was super strict about leaving toys on the floor.

And toys weren't Grandma's worst complaint. She was always going on about this or that. And for some reason, the weather really set her off. If it was going to rain or snow, she would launch into a barrage of naughty words that Daddy said Ella should never repeat. And when Grandma was in a yelling mood, she would slap Ella for no reason at all. One time, Ella had gotten a black eye after forgetting to turn off the bathroom sink. Daddy said they would just have to put up with her until he could get working again.

"Marisa Clarissa, would you like to come on a trip?"

Ella hardly needed to ask, she always brought Marisa Clarissa wherever she went. The only real question was who else was going to come along. Ella placed the doll next to her pink flower bag. Ashley had packed the bag, but she didn't know anything and only put in boring stuff like clothes and a toothbrush. She never packed Marisa Clarissa, even though everyone knew she was Ella's bestie.

"Five minutes. You hear, Ella? Five minutes and we're leaving," Daddy yelled from upstairs.

Ella grinned. Everything was always five minutes away and five minutes was a long, long, long time. She picked up a plastic blue brush and began to swipe it through Marisa Clarissa's blonde hair. She couldn't bring her over to Mommy's with all these tangles. Ella adored her hair, since it wasn't like her own, all curly-curly and unmanageable. She'd spend hours braiding it. Ella hoped to have hair just like Marisa Clarissa when she was all grown up. Unlike Ella, she was gorgeous and everyone loved her.

"That's right. Make her nice and pretty."

Ella jerked back, dropping the brush. The voice had been raspy and harsh, much deeper than Daddy's. And it'd come from the pile of toys next to the chest. Ella gripped Marisa Clarissa to her side and squirmed backwards. There was a booming *thud* as she slammed against the rear wall.

"Is everything all right?" Ashley asked from upstairs.

"Tell her yes," the gravelly voice continued.

Ella opened her mouth, but no words emerged. She panted deep heaving breaths, but her lungs felt empty. A layer of sticky sweat exploded across her brow, even though she was sitting completely still.

"Go on, you little bitch. Tell her everything's okay."

"It's, it's, I'm okay," Ella stuttered, shocked it'd said one of the forbidden naughty words.

She stared at the pile, trying to pinpoint the voice. At the top, there was a blue *Smurfette*, which was sprawled across a plastic red bucket. Just underneath, there was a cluster of bright orange hair that Ella recognised as belonging to *My Precious Princess*. A stuffed *Finding Nemo* jutted from the opposite side, covering half of a toy horse with a purple mane. *Lalaloopsy Silly Hair* rested just below the bucket and the doll's matching pet owl was in the lap of a nearby *Mermaid Barbie*. A wind-up green alligator was upside-down at the base of the pile.

And there were some toys she never remembered having in the first place, along with a whole bunch she couldn't see in the middle. But they all had one thing in common. Not a single one displayed any sign of life.

"Who, who's there?" Ella asked, drawing her knees to her chest. Her hands were shaking pretty bad, but she didn't dare release her clutch on Marisa Clarissa. She believed if she could keep hold of her, everything would be just fine.

When there was no answer, Ella scrambled towards an *Elmo* resting just to her left. She yanked the doll from the floor and flung it at the pile. There was a high-pitched chirp as it collided with the other toys. Dolls bowled across the floor. The red bucket shot directly towards Ella, rolling with a *tink, tink, tink*. It stopped right at her feet. She peered inside. The bucket was empty.

Ella froze, waiting for any movement. The toys just lay there, immobile and frozen. Ella jumped as the roof creaked overhead. Someone was coming downstairs. She closed her eyes and hoped they could reach her before the monster.

"Ella Claire Merriam, what in the world is going on?" Ashley yelled, rushing into the room.

"The doll said a naughty word," Ella answered the best she could.

"Dolls can't be naughty, only little girls who throw them all over the floor. This is totally inappropriate Ella."

"But I heard it. He said I was a b—" Ella paused, noticing the scowl slice across Ashley's face. "He called me that. He did, he did."

"Enough. Start cleaning up."

Ella stared at the toys sprinkled across the room. Nothing had moved since Ashley arrived and Ella hadn't heard anymore of that gravelly voice. Still, he had to be there somewhere. She remained stuck to the wall.

"Now, Ella," Ashley said, taking a step closer.

Ella knew if she didn't start cleaning soon, she'd be in for a spanking. Unlike Mommy, Ashley was always giving spankings. They weren't as awful as Daddy's, where she'd have to sit on her hands afterwards, but Ashley did hit hard enough to make her butt glow red like *Clifford*.

"You can start with that *Playtime Emily* you're holding."

"This is Marisa Clarissa," Ella said, jerking the doll out in front of her so Ashley could see. Boy, Ashley was so stupid. Everyone could see this wasn't Emily. Ella knew Emily. They sometimes played together at the swings. And Marisa Clarissa didn't look anything like her. Ashley would know this if she'd ever asked, but the only thing she cared about was dumb stuff like tooth brushing and baths.

"Put... her... in... the... box," Ashley said, placing a gap between every word. Ella knew adults talked like this when they thought she couldn't understand. But Ella had good hearing and knew what adults were saying even when they talked super fast and used naughty words.

"I'm—" Ella began.

"Don't talk back," Ashley interrupted, before Ella could explain she was going to take Marisa Clarissa to Mommy's. She really wanted to bring the doll, but it wasn't worth a spanking, so she crossed the room towards the wooden chest.

"Ashley... Ashley... Aaaaash-ley," Daddy shouted from upstairs.

"What?" Ashley finally replied.

"Where did you put the recycling bags?"

"Under the sink. Where they always are."

"I would've found them there. Where did you put them?"

"Joel, they're under the damn sink."

"Then we're out, 'cause I can't find them anywhere."

"No, I just bought some on Tuesday."

"Then show me where the hell you put them."

"You," Ashley spun back towards Ella. "Clean up this mess. And do it quick. If your father sees this, you'll be in big trouble. You hear me? Big, big trouble."

As soon as Ashley left, Ella stuffed Marisa Clarissa into her pink flower backpack. She stared at the toy chest, wanting to stay far, far away, but Ashley was right. If Daddy saw this mess, his head might just explode. Ella would surely get a spanking and not one of those good ones where he'd count the blows down to zero, but instead, one where he'd just go on hitting forever and ever.

"You little tattle-tale," the gravelly voice said. "Don't say another word if you know what's best. I'll fuck you up, I will."

Ella dropped the backpack. None of the dolls had moved, but the voice had come from right next to the chest. This time she was certain it'd been one of her dolls.

"W-who are you?"

There was no reply. Ella took a step closer. There was a stuffed octopus at her feet. She picked it up and shook it a couple of times. The octopus hung limply in her hand. She tossed it at the toy chest. It hit the edge and fell onto the floor.

That's not the one, she thought. *Be brave. Just like Princess Meredith when she confronted evil Count Krux. She didn't get her unicorn back by running away like a sissy.*

That worked and Ella took another step towards the toy chest. She picked up a pink *Barbie Glam Convertible* and tossed the car. This time, it sailed right on target, dropping inside with a *thump*. She worked her way across the floor, shaking each toy a couple of times before shooting it into the chest. The more toys she threw, the easier it became, especially as she drew closer. She'd almost forgotten about the gravelly voice as she reached for a doll with roller skates.

Whoosh. Ella bucked, dropping the doll as something whizzed past her side. She scurried back and leapt onto a blue chair in the corner. It was situated next to the dresser. She didn't hesitate climbing up its side. Only after reaching the top, did she muster the courage to peek.

There was no mistaking it. The thing had skidded past her and was now lying in the middle of the floor. Ella was certain this wasn't her imagination. Not only had she cleared that area, but she would've surely noticed this doll. Ella recognised those nappy clumps of brown hair, that tattered red dress, and more than anything, those eyes. Or at least what was left of them. The right one was missing, Ella had plucked it out with a fork. And the other she'd coloured pitch black that night when she'd stolen a *Sharpie* in order to draw tattoos on the doll's back.

"What do you want Sophia?"

The doll did not answer. Her one black eye just stared up at Ella. She hadn't thought about Sophia this entire time, but this hardly came as a surprise. If Marisa Clarissa was on one end of the pals spectrum, Sophia was on the other. She was the doll Ella always gave to her prissy neighbour Taylor anytime she came over to play. Even that cuckoo-berry would insist on a different doll, not that Ella ever gave her one.

It hadn't always been this way. In fact, previous to Marisa Clarissa, Sophia had been one of her besties. There was her and Cole, a dashing charmer who drove around in the *Barbie Glam Convertible*. He'd stolen it, but Sophia hadn't minded, since she enjoyed rogues, especially cute ones in tuxedos like Cole. They were inseparable and Ella had played with them every single day.

Then, Sophia began to sour. She became really super mean and Ella wondered if she'd had an accident, since she started using all the naughty words adults said after they hurt themselves. And instead of smiling and giggling, she'd spend all day inside the dollhouse screaming and crying and making a big, big mess.

Cole tried to cheer Sophia up and get her outside, but when he'd drive up and say "Hey babe, let's go for a ride," she would yell at him for being a bossy meanie. She'd say the only reason he wanted to go out was because he hated her cooking and liked other dolls. Cole would counter that he did enjoy her meals, especially the *Easy-Bake* ones, but he also liked to drive, play tag, and throw fetch with his pet alligator *Chomps*. Sophia would cry that nothing she did was ever good enough for him.

Eventually, Cole stopped driving to the dollhouse. Sophia still waited for him, but got super bored just sitting around by herself, so she started to huff magic markers. But not the good ones like grape and cherry. No, she liked black liquorice. She'd sniff it all the time like she had a cold. Got to the point where not a single day went by and she didn't smell like yucky black liquorice. And Ella hated that stench. It was worse than skunks, sulphur, and Daddy's farts all combined.

And when Ella tried playing with her, Sophia would throw a fit and accuse her of scaring Cole away. Ella didn't like her mouthing off, so sometimes, when Mommy wasn't watching, she'd step on Sophia and crunch her against the floor. Or she'd drag her in the mud, making her dress all dirty so Cole would really hate her. And once, Ella took one of Daddy's screwdrivers and kept digging into Sophia's back until a small hole appeared. She wanted blood and guts to ooze out, but there was only air inside. What a jip!

Nowadays, Ella didn't play with Sophia much, only when she was super-duper cranky and didn't mind being a meanie right back to her. And if Sophia was real nasty, Ella would wedge her behind the bed where there was a loose nail and jab her against it. Sophia would always cry like a little baby and this made Ella laugh. That was before she told the weird doctor with the scraggly beard and Daddy removed the nail. Still, sometimes she would put Sophia in the door and slam it shut, but that was never quite as fun.

"Sophia... what... do... you... want?" Ella repeated, doing that adult pausing for every word trick.

"She doesn't want a thing. She's too messed up to

talk right now. Let her sleep it off on the floor. That'll teach that filthy whore a lesson."

Ella glared across the room. This time she had no problem seeing the source of the gravelly voice. She should've known he would be at the heart of this. The tubby baby sat against the wooden chest, sucking on a large pink pacifier. His engorged cheeks popped with every breath and his eyes narrowed on her.

"What do you want Dean?"

"What do you think? I need a diaper change," he chuckled, in-between the *slurp, slurp, slurp* of the sucking pacifier.

Deanie Dirty Diaper, Ella thought. *Been a long time hasn't it, pal? A very wonderful long time.*

"Why are you speaking in that weird voice?" Ella asked. It was deeper and far hoarser than she'd remembered.

"You damn well know why, bitch," he said, adding a few sloppy slurps of the pacifier after the naughty word.

Ella had known Dean a long time. Back then, *Fairytale Gallant* had been her bestie. And unlike Ashley, Mommy always knew her bestie. That's why she'd grabbed *Fairytale Gallant* when Ella had refused to take off her shoes inside the house. Mommy had been super-duper mad and threatened to toss the doll into the fireplace. Ella didn't realise what was happening until the flames began to eat away at his plastic skin. Ella cried and cried and cried, but Mommy held her still, forcing her to watch, until the doll turned all brown and gooey.

Mommy said she felt bad afterwards and cried a bit herself, but Ella didn't care if she was sad. She just wanted *Fairytale Gallant* to come back and said so over and over and over. Mommy said he could never come back, never-ever, and cried a whole bunch more.

That's why Ella was so surprised when Mommy gave her Dean a few days later. Mommy pointed out that he was expensive and rare, one of those collector dolls only available on the internet. Dean was modelled on a real life baby and had a chubby frame along with an adorable cheek to cheek grin. It almost made him seem cute, that was, when she could see his smile. But when that giant pacifier was in his mouth, only a crinkled scowl remained. And Dean was always sucking on his pacifier.

Ella had introduced Dean to the others, but he was spoiled and kept calling them "mass produced trash" and "plebs." Ella stopped playing with him and Mommy thought it was because she was still mad about *Fairytale Gallant*, but really, it was because Dean was peculiar and told lies.

Dean enjoyed gossiping and spreading rumours about the other dolls, just to watch them fight. He'd always come up with nasty nicknames and pretend he'd heard a different doll say them first. And then, he'd watch from a distance and grin. It didn't surprise Ella that Dean had started to pal around with Sophia right at the same time she was having those fights with Cole.

Worst of all, sometimes Ella would wake up in the middle of the night and find him perched at the end of her bed. She would ask how he got there, but Dean wouldn't answer. He'd just sit and stare. Always sucking on that pacifier.

"Come on, don't be like that. Stop being silly and get down from that dresser."

Ella peered towards the door and heard Daddy and Ashley arguing upstairs. There was a lot of banging and clattering, so she figured they'd be occupied for a little bit longer. She kicked off and landed on the floor with a *thud*.

Dean grinned. He was still wearing the disposable diaper she'd put on him during their last encounter. It was slightly frayed at the edges, but not too bad for the wear. Certainly much better than the last one. Ella had ruined it by dumping a bottle of hand sanitizer down Dean's throat. She'd wanted to wash out his naughty mouth, but it'd run out his other end, ruining both the diaper and making a big stain on the hard wood floor. Mommy had called him Deanie Dirty Diaper after that. And for once, he was the one with a mean nickname.

"Long time, no see. You look so cute in those pyjamas."

"You got me in trouble."

"That's the last thing I wanted to happen. Will you accept my apologies, darling? I just hate to see such a pretty little girl with such a big, big frown. Can you give me a smile?"

Ella didn't feel much like smiling, but she flashed an unconvincing one anyway.

"Don't you remember all the fun we used to have? You were always laughing and smiling. Without me, you've gotten so stone-face serious. You need to lighten up, babe."

"Daddy will be really mad if he sees the mess you made."

"We'll just have to clean it up before he sees it. Out of sight, out of mind. Isn't that right, cutie?"

Dean stood on those stubby knobs he had for legs and began to hurl some toys into the chest. For being such a small tyke, he had incredible aim. Ella joined in, gathering a handful of dolls. As she dropped them inside, Dean began to whistle. She'd forgotten how well he could whistle, just like a prince.

They'd cleared half of the room, when Dean let out a groan and dropped to the floor. He heaved deep breaths as he wiped a thick layer of sweat from his brow.

"It's so stuffy. Why doesn't that old hag turn on the AC?"

"Grandma says she doesn't like the way it feels. Says it weighs down the air and makes it taste heavy."

"The only weight that cheap bitch cares about is that of her pocketbook. Can you grab me the water?" Dean asked, pointing towards a half-filled bottle next to the bed.

"We really should finish cleaning up first."

"Only thing you should do is shut that stinking trap of yours. What are you waiting for? Get me the water."

Ella stared at Dean for a second, noticing that he did look quite parched. She hissed, but grabbed the water for him anyway. As she handed it over, Dean curled his knobby fingers around her wrist and squeezed.

"It's been too long since we've played together. Why do you prefer those other dolls? They're idiots. They don't realise you're special, beautiful, perfect. We're not like those plastic cretins, we're better. Don't you understand? I'm the only one who can really love you."

"Then why are you always so mean to me?" Ella asked, hoping he would release his grasp.

"Being mean is sometimes the only way to get things done. Remember how Daddy was always playing on that fancy phone? How he would never listen to you? So we hid it under the car and he drove over it. That was mean, but he did pay attention after that. So don't take it personally. It doesn't mean I don't think you're the bestest girl in the entire world. Come on, give me a big hug."

Ella wrapped her arms around Dean and squeezed tight. He was all warm and breathing heavy, so Ella figured he was still pooped out from cleaning up.

"You always get me into trouble."

"Only if we get caught. Remember playing witch at Taylor's house? How you knocked over that glass lamp with the broom? And did you fess up? No, you did exactly what I said and went crying to Taylor's mom and said that Taylor hit you really hard with the broom. So when her mom saw the broken lamp, she believed Taylor had done it. And Taylor didn't even protest."

"Yeah, Taylor is a big dum-dum."

"And you're so smart. The smartest girl in the whole entire world. Thanks for the water," Dean said, guzzling a mouthful.

"We should finish cleaning up."

"First, I need another solid. Can you take off Sophia's dress? It's so hot in here and I don't want her overheating. People can die from that, you know."

"Really?" Ella asked, thinking that sounded strange.

"Oh yeah, it's just like cooking in an oven. Being naked is the only way to know you're safe."

"I don't know."

"Don't be like that. You have to help her out. You guys used to be besties."

"Fine," Ella said. Even if it sounded fishy, she couldn't risk wasting any more time arguing. Daddy could come down at any moment and she didn't want a spanking. There was a tearing noise as she opened the Velcro straps and removed Sophia's dress. Dean waddled over on his stumpy legs.

"She's stinky," Ella said, pinching her nose.

"Let's give her a bath," Dean said, tugging down his diaper. Before Ella could stop him, he began to pee all over Sophia.

"This is all your own fault. You put yourself in this state. Maybe next time you'll remember to keep your fat mouth shut and not flirt with the other dolls. Whore."

"That's not nice," Ella protested, staring at his little weenie as the last dribble splashed out. Ella knew the difference between girl and boy parts, but that tiny nub wasn't what those looked like. Not in real life.

"Oh shit, I got some on my diaper," Dean complained. "Can you take it off?"

"Gross," Ella whined.

"Just do it already."

Ella tugged on the diaper, sliding it down his stumpy legs. Dean was still breathing super-duper hard and Ella wondered how much more of a recess he would need before getting back to work. Just as she slipped the diaper completely off, Dean brushed his hand against her side.

"Hey, that tickles."

"Duh, I was tickling you."

"I don't like that, Dean. We need to finish

cleaning up."

"Stop being such a goody-goody. Sophia isn't going to wake up for hours and we're all alone. Let's goof around and have some fun."

"I guess, just for a little while."

"That's my girl," Dean said with a grin.

Ella giggled as he ran his knobby fingers against the sensitive part on her belly. She remembered how he would blow raspberries there and hoped he would do that again.

**

Ashley slammed the door and stormed across the kitchen. *Some start to their romantic weekend*, Joel thought as he took another sip of coffee. He couldn't wait to drop off Ella and start drinking something a little bit stronger, but if Ashley had her way, they'd spend all day tidying up. Why she had to have everything spotless before leaving was beyond him. Plus, it wasn't even their own damn house.

"Do you know what your daughter is doing?"

"No," Joel replied, but if the answer was anything other than getting ready to go, Ella was in for it.

"She's running around buck naked and refuses to get dressed."

"I thought she'd outgrown that stage. Did you threaten a spanking?"

"Yeah, and she accused me of wanting to kill her. Imagine that. Said she couldn't get dressed, since it was too hot. That clothes would make her blood boil out through her skin and she'd die. Where does she come up with this stuff?"

"It is a furnace down there."

"You know, she acts out every time before we drop her off at Maria's."

"What do you want from me?"

"To tell Maria to clean up her shit. She's always drunk and a terrible influence. Bet we could save money on all those shrinks if we just cut her out of Ella's life."

"Trust me, I know she's a mess, that's why things didn't work between us, but she's a good mother and loves Ella."

"And then there's that creepy boyfriend. Something's not right with him. I don't like the way he looks at Ella."

Joel sighed. There was something off about Gene Van Riper, but he'd lost the right to interfere in Maria's personal life a long time back. And who was he to judge? Gene was loaded, one of those financial wizards, while Joel was unemployed and living in his mother's house.

And sure, Maria wasn't the most responsible, but she'd never allow anything to hurt Ella. Plus, Ashley was the type to blow things out of proportion, like that time she'd screamed at Maria after Ella came back smelling like cigarette smoke. Gene was a chain smoker, but always did so outside. Ashley made it out as though he'd blown smoke right into Ella's lungs, which, of course, was nonsense. Joel wondered why he always fell for the overdramatic ones. A hopeless romantic, he guessed.

"Whatever, we can't change it now. I'll wrangle her up."

Joel's jaw dropped as he opened the bedroom door. How had Ella managed to make such a mess in five minutes? Un-god-damn-believable. Clothes and toys were scattered everywhere, and Ella, buck naked, was sitting right in the centre of the storm. And the little brat was grinning, almost taunting him.

Worse, she was clutching that spooky baby doll. Maria had bought it for Ella after one of her drunken tantrums. Joel loathed that thing, not only since it was damn ugly, but it also served as a reminder to that miserable part of their marriage. Why he hadn't tossed it in the dumpster was beyond him. Probably since Ella loved it and he couldn't bring himself to break her heart.

"What... did... you... do?" he snapped.

"I don't know," Ella mumbled.

"We're going to be late. Mommy hates it when we're late," he said, knowing this wasn't true. Maria was probably working off a hangover and might not even be up yet.

"Daddy, can Deanie Dirty Diaper come along?"

"Get... dressed... now," he barked.

"Can he? Can he?"

"I'm not going to repeat myself young lady. One more word and you're getting a spanking."

Finally, that jarred her into motion. As Ella dressed, Joel stared at the toys scattered across the floor. His mother was going to have a fit if she saw this. She always was so nasty about keeping the house clean. God, Joel was so tired of her nonsense, especially the way she blamed him for Ella's misbehaving. If only he'd been a better husband, harder worker, stricter father, somehow he'd still be with Maria and it'd all be roses. Whatever. It wasn't as though her and Dad had been the best role models. No, he'd leave this mess, hoping she'd find it.

"Daddy, can I bring Dean?" Ella asked after she'd

gotten dressed.

"Yeah, of course," Joel replied. He secretly hoped Ella would leave that rotten doll at Maria's.

"Oh, oh, oh," Ella panted, as though she was out of breath. "We can't forget Sophia."

Joel watched as Ella picked up a soaking wet doll. He didn't even want to know. Maybe she'd been giving it a bath, since it was quite filthy.

"That doll looks pretty beat up; do you want a new one?"

"No, Daddy. Dean likes her like that."

"Well, tell Dean he should have a better taste in friends."

"Oh, he does. Marisa Clarissa is his favourite. He hugs and kisses and loves her bestest in the whole entire world."

"That's great, honey," Joel said, rolling his eyes. "Come on, time to go."

He helped Ella put on her pink flower backpack and stuffed the dolls into the rear pocket. *Girls and their dolls*, he thought. He'd never understand it. *Girls and their goddamn dolls.*

About Drake Vaughn

Drake Vaughn is the author of *The Zombie Generation*, along with many other pieces of dark fiction. His self-proclaimed "crinkled fiction" is a blend of horror, dark fantasy, and speculative fiction with a heavy psychological bent. His tales appear deceptively simple, but transform into a wild spree of suspense, madness, and trauma.

He lives in Santa Monica, CA with his wife and a black cat named Shadow (who he is certain has come back from the dead on a number of occasions). More information can be found at his website www.drakevaughn.com. He likewise blogs on tumblr and Twitter under the handle DrakeVaughn.

THE STREET GAME

SCATHE MEIC BEORH

When I emptied my pockets that afternoon, there were things that I had not put in them that morning. Three red-painted iron jacks, a yellow cat's-eye marble, four wooden puzzle pieces, and a diminutive bottle of mignonette fragrance. I wasn't altogether surprised. A stroll down Saint George Street is never a usual one, primarily because of the children who run hither and thither, this way and that like excited puppies while they play their 'street game,' as it is called.

The week before, I pulled from my pockets a newspaper clipping of no interest to me whatsoever, a pouch of cocoa powder, a clay pipe, and a porcelain doll's head. Three days before that? A ball of purpled twine, three bent playing cards, a shrunken head, a gold Caravaca cross, and a chunk of coquina. I am aware that an expensive Caravaca cross is quite unusual, but so are the children of San Agustín de la Florida.

Edward McIntyre, a proprietor who owned the eponymous mercantile near Hypolita and Saint George Streets, explained to me the children's game. "On Treasury Street, beneath an orange tree, rests an old kitchen table some have dated back to the 17th century."

"I know the table," I said. "I pass by it all the time, but have never understood its purpose. Peculiar to say, but it seems to be waiting for something."

"It waits for something all right. Every morning,

at about seven o'clock, the children gather around that table before they begin their 'street game', as they call it."

"I am never out that early in the morning."

"But you need to be, if you want to stay in their good graces. How long do you say you have been living in town now?"

"Three months, give or take."

"Yes. Your grace period would be about over, I'd say. Believe me. You do not wish to happen to you what happened to Miss Madelia Hilloway."

"What happened to her, pray tell?"

"She left San Agustín penniless."

"The children, somehow?"

"Yes. She wouldn't play their game."

"I am not sure I understand, Mr. McIntyre. A bit more detail please."

"Good morning, Dr. Vignola," McIntyre said as he turned from me in the cordial manner of any good proprietor. "What may I get for you this fine morning, sir?"

"Good morning, Mr. McIntyre," the doctor replied as he smiled through saddened eyes and then nodded my way in the congenial attitude of a true gentleman. "Cinnamon oil. Three bottles, if you can spare them."

"I have five bottles, three with your name on them," said McIntyre as he drew a ring of keys from his belt and proceeded to unlock a glass case situated behind his till. When the transaction was complete, McIntyre pointed to the several jars of stick candy on the counter and merely said "Your daughter Susie, sir," to which Vignola replied by taking three lemon sticks and whispering "Her favourite, thank you". The good doctor then tipped his hat, nodded at the both of us, and left.

"Seems to be a fine gentleman," I said. "A local physician?"

"Yes, and the very best at what he professes, sir. Now, to your question. Many grown-ups in town play the 'street game'. If picked by the children, they *must* play. Miss Hilloway is not the only casualty we have seen."

"How does one play their game?"

"*Anything*… I say anything at *all* can be left in the morning on the table beneath the orange tree—*before* the children arrive. They are a strange lot, even for children. In a way that none of us older folk have been able to yet discern, they pick those they want to play their game and those they will always leave alone."

"I see. Well, every day after my stroll through town I find weird objects in my pockets."

"As I thought. The 'street game'. They have picked you to play. My advice to you, sir? Play, or suffer the inevitable consequence of searching for another place to live—with no money to do it with."

"But, won't they leave me alone after a while, when they see I am not interested? I really have no use for thread spools, gyroscopes, and dead beetles in tiny jars."

"My only answer to that, sir: *Miss Hilloway, destitute*. After she refused the children and their game, no matter what she did to try and appease them, she never had money. She even tried to keep most of her sizable fortune in the bank. No use. Somehow the children got to it, and spent it on candies and toys and whatever else they liked or wanted. Miss Hilloway left San Agustín in a flood of tears, and has not been heard of since."

"Oh! This is preposterous! I mean really, Mr. McIntyre. I can see being pick-pocketed by the little urchins, but having one's bank account ruined? *Foolish!*"

"Call it what you will, sir. The truth remains that the children know how to take everything you own. If you refuse to play their game, you have made yourself their enemy, and you will pay for your ignorance."

"*God in Heaven!* What about their parents? Who is raising these devils?"

"Gentlemen like Dr. Vignola, for one. His daughter Susie is one of them—an originator of the game, as I hear."

"Which, of course, explains why you gave her father candy for free."

"I give lagniappes to all the children, whether they play the game or not, sir."

"Wait a moment. Are you saying that all of the children in town are not involved in this 'street game'?"

"Oh good heavens no! Only a handful. Thirty or forty at the very most. They are a secretive group. They pick only certain children to join them. The qualifications for being asked to join are yet unknown, try as we might to decipher it."

"Their parents cannot take control?"

"Not so far, no sir. Every parent carries the same reply: it is as if their children have lost the ability to speak when the subject is raised."

"This is the strangest phenomenon I have ever heard of!"

"Believe me, sir. Live here for a while. You will hear of stranger things, be sure of it."

"Stranger than children stuffing my pockets with locks of human hair and severed monkey paws?"

"Those are odd items, I would agree, but yes. There are weirder happenings here."

"Please spare me, for the time being."

"Oh, I had no intention to broach yet another topic this morning. The 'street game' is quite enough for one day—or even a lifetime."

"You're telling me!"

"What I am telling you, friend, is to be sure that tomorrow morning at dawn, or soon thereafter, leave something on the kitchen table under the orange tree. Anything will do—but, *never* leave something that they have slipped into your pockets as they ran by. If you do, the gifts you afterward receive from them shall be far less to your liking than severed paws and dead bugs."

"That's how it's done then? They take from their table and then give back as we stroll by?"

"That is how they play the game. It seems to be a social activity with them. They *like* you, sir. Otherwise they would have never taken notice of you. Only, be careful not to cross them by not playing—now that they have picked you."

"I reckon that I have no other choice, Mr. McIntyre."

"No you do not, sir. May I interest you in my latest acquisition? Pickles barrelled in Patagonia."

"No thank you. I prefer my pickles barrelled in Jacksonville, if it's all the same to you."

"Suit yourself. They were my final acquisition for the mercantile. Sort of a last hurrah, if you will. I am selling out."

"Why is that, Mr. McIntyre?"

The man dropped his eyes.

"Mr. McIntyre?"

"Yes sir?"

"Why are you selling your store?"

"I... I ignored the children when they beckoned me to play."

About Scathe meic Beorh

Scathe meic Beorh is a writer and lexicographer of Ulster-Scot and Cherokee ancestry. His books in print include the novel *Black Fox In Thin Places* (Emby Press, 2013), the story collections *Children & Other Wicked Things* (James Ward Kirk Fiction, 2013) and *Always After Thieves Watch* (Wildside Press, 2010), the dictionary *Pirate Lingo* (Wildside, 2009), and the poetic study *Dark Sayings of Old* (Kirk Fiction, 2013). Raised in New Orleans and along the Gulf Coast of West Florida, and having undergone rites of passage in India and Ireland, he now makes a home with his joyful and imaginative wife Ember in a quaint Edwardian neighbourhood on the Atlantic Coast.

THE CYCLE OF REBIRTH

MONA ZUTSHI OPUBOR

In the South Indian village of Thiruvananthanpur there was one international telephone facility, and demand being low in the summer months, it took Ram Aggarwal three days before he found it open for business. He accomplished several tasks in the meantime. He purchased two *kurta pyjamas* for himself and two *salwar kameezes* for Agnes in the ashram gift shop. He devised a sleeping schedule to help them overcome jetlag. He left a note with the receptionist at Bhagwan Shree Bahadur's office, requesting a series of treatments. Last of all, he emptied four bottles of Agnes' pills into the Indian-style commode and yanked at the chain till they swirled away.

On his final visit to the calling centre Ram left the compound in the evening, an hour before they locked the doors. He lifted a leg to climb through the opening in the back gate and paused. The sun blazed so low in the sky, it appeared to be sinking into a sea of tropical vegetation. Ram walked down a winding dirt pathway, buffeted on either side by creeping vines. Without the attention of the ashram groundskeepers, nature had asserted herself. Ram was forced to push past the plants to follow the trail.

When Ram reached the main road, he stopped to lean forward. He rested his hands on his knees and sucked hot air into his lungs. He watched the sweat dripping off his face as it was absorbed by the cracked soil.

Ram was a man who believed in his ability to understand a higher truth. After a few glasses of Merlot at cocktail parties, he steered the conversation to himself. He liked to remark it couldn't be a coincidence that he was named for a deity.

A thin child with a pyramid of baskets tied to his bicycle pedalled by him, staring. Ram stood up to his full height, puffed out his chest, and strode toward the market, as resolute as his namesake, Rama, when a rift in the earth swallowed his beloved Sita.

Ram Aggarwal saw a group of men in loincloths squatting in the shade of a palm tree. He passed by them, his chin tilted up, studying a parrot roosting between the fronds. Ram slid his Minolta from his pocket and snapped a few pictures of the bird. The men laughed. When Ram reached the plexiglas phone booth, one of the men walked over, threw his *beedi* down and ground it into the dirt with his sandal.

"I have to call America," Ram explained to him. "Aaa-mer-icaaa," he pantomimed, pointing in the direction of the Arabian Sea. He entered the booth and hooked the door closed, staring at the naked torso of the phone operator through the streaked plastic. There was a keloid scar across the man's chest that swallowed one of his nipples. Ram looked up and saw the man's eyes resting on the price gauge of the phone. He dialled eleven digits.

He heard the gurgle of the telephone, then a tinny, echoing woman's voice. "Hello? Hello, Agnes?"

Ram turned his back towards the door. "No, Mary, it's me."

"Oh, Ram, what have you *done*? Where are you?

The hospital called the police. I've been so worried."

"I thought Agnes needed a change of scenery. We're in India."

"Are you crazy? What were you thinking? How's Agnes? How's my baby?"

Ram wiped the sweat from his face with a grimy handkerchief and stuffed it into his pocket. "She's better. I knew this would help. There's something primal about India. It's in our blood. It's only my second visit, as you know, but I never felt connected to California, even though I was born there and—"

"Ram, is she taking her medication?"

"She's fine. Yesterday she went on a children's outing to a Portuguese settlement."

"She *needs* her medicine."

"Yes, so you mentioned. I'm arranging for her to see a specialist here. A highly esteemed religious leader."

"We could have done that in San Francisco. You didn't have to kidnap my daughter."

"I have the moral authority to take *my* daughter anywhere I choose," Ram said. "The West, her mother's side, imprisoned her. The East, my side, will set her free." He glanced at the base of the phone. So far, he owed two hundred fifty rupees. Two hundred seventy-five. He looked away.

"Has she done anything unusual since you've had her? Are there any house-pets where you're staying?"

"I said she's fine, Mary. I never believed that story about the cats. No-one could prove she was involved. Did you get the divorce papers, by the way?"

"Yes, I signed them and sent them back already."

"Good. I asked my lawyer to call your—"

"Ram," she interrupted, "bring Agnes back. I'm so worried about her. She needs special care."

"I will. I promise. As soon as she's cured, I'll return her to you, as good as new. Do you know how much she enjoyed the plane ride to Bombay?"

"She was able to tolerate the flight?"

"Yes. Your daughter drank six mango juices and charmed the stewardesses. She made anagrams with their names."

"I know she's a likeable girl, Ram, but let's stay focused. I spoke with Dr. Jackson."

"That quack," he muttered.

"He's been helping with Agnes' recovery for two years. You know how close they are. He wants you to bring her back immediately. It's devastating for her to stop treatment now. He says it's imperative she keep taking her pills; she's liable to lose control."

"There's a doctor at the ashram. Agnes saw him yesterday."

"You're at an *ashram*?" Mary asked.

"Dr. Rangachari prescribed yoga classes for her circulation, massages for the release of toxicity, daily gargles with rosewater, and meditation for spiritual well being."

"Oh, Ram. Tell me where you are. I won't press charges, I promise. We'll handle this quietly. I'll come get Agnes myself."

"These are time-tested remedies, Mary. When your Jesus was still in diapers, we already had Ayurvedic medicine. I can't believe I walked through this heat to be insulted. I feel sick."

"You feel sick? Are you and Agnes drinking boiled

water?"

"We are, but I forgot to bring a bottle with me."

"Will you be okay? Are you dehydrated?"

"I'll live. I'm a survivor. There's a reason my mother—"

"Named me Ram," Mary finished. "I know. Did you tell the doctor what Agnes did to her dolls?"

"No, I didn't get into that. I'm going to talk to Bhagwan Shree Bahadur about the particulars of her behaviour."

"Who?"

Ram sighed. "He's a celebrated Indian thinker. There's a book by him in my study. *The Seventeen Laws of Spiritual Succour.* He was on Oprah last month."

Mary was silent.

"You're not seeing the bigger picture," Ram continued. "Bhagwan is the answer. And you can't believe how excited Agnes is."

"Oh, Christ. Do you know what you're doing with my daughter?"

"Speaking of Agnes, I better go. This call is overpriced, and she's by herself at the—"

"You left her *alone*?"

"I know what I'm doing, Mary. I'm showing her I trust her. Agnes is never going to recover if she's stifled. I'm allowing her to express herself without fear of rebuke. She pierced her ears this morning with a safety pin, and I bought her a pair of earrings from the gift shop. That's the kind of relationship we have."

"You let her play with a safety pin! Are you out of your mind?"

Ram turned and looked at the man outside the

phone booth. His chest was blending into the gloom of dusk. The red numbers 0-0-8 reflected off the plastic at belly button level. "Are we done, Mary? I have to get back to the ashram before I'm locked out. And this call is eight hundred rupees. That's twenty dollars, U.S. I could be spending that money on Agnes' treatment."

"I want to talk to her tomorrow. I need to speak with her."

"I told you she's fine."

"If I don't hear from her, I'll tell my lawyer. You'll lose any hope of custody and I vow to you, Ram, you'll never see Agnes again." Mary voice began to tremble. "Watch her take her pills. She doesn't always swallow them. Check under her tongue. And let me know the minute she acts up. Call me immediately."

"Mary, I can handle my own daughter."

"Will you have her call me?"

Ram reached into the back pocket of his jeans and pulled out a wad of hundred rupee notes. He peeled off eight in the dark. "You can count on it." He hung up.

**

Agnes Aggarwal trailed the Bartletts into a large, white-walled treatment room. The room was devoid of furniture save three massage tables, some cabinets, and a sink. Sitar music played through the in-ceiling speakers, slightly muffled by the hum of the AC. Mr. and Mrs. Bartlett paused to admire the Arabian Sea through the picture window.

Agnes climbed onto a table. She sat cross-legged, watching as the Indian attendant crushed clay and spices in a mortar. When the Bartletts laid down, she spread the brown paste on the couple's pale English skin.

She then prepared a quick white mask for Agnes and brushed it onto her face with a square of banana leaf. "Please stop licking," the Indian lady told her. "The herbs won't help you if you eat them." She turned to the couple lying supine beside the girl. "I'm going to leave you alone as you dry. Practice your Primordial Sound techniques in the meantime."

"All right," Mr. Bartlett said.

The woman grabbed the tail of her green sari with her right hand, adjusted a dial on the wall with her left, and swished out of the room.

"My mask is made of yogurt," Agnes announced. "If we get locked in here, I'm going to eat it, so I won't die."

Mr. Bartlett turned on his side to stare at his wife.

"That's nice, dear," Mrs. Bartlett said. "It's wise to plan ahead."

"You look like your face is on fire, mister."

The man was picking flecks of clay off his orange beard. He flipped onto his back. "I can't believe you talked me into this. I thought these rooms were private."

"They're supposed to be, but I think they mistook us for a family."

"A family!" he exclaimed.

"I'm sorry," said Agnes. She dropped her head and crossed her arms over her chest. "I was scared to go by myself."

"It's too late for that," Mr. Bartlett said.

"I can leave. I'm used to being alone."

"No, dear, don't listen to him," Mrs. Bartlett said. "We want you to stay. It will help pass the time. Tell me, do you like India?"

Agnes stuck out her tongue and licked yogurt off her chin. "Yes, very much."

"What's your favourite thing about India?"

"No rules," the girl said.

"No rules," Mr. Bartlett repeated. His face twitched. Then he grinned, sending hairline fractures through his mask. "The rupee is so weak these days that the world's ours for the taking, eh Helen?"

"We dream about moving here," the woman said.

"We discovered this country," Mr. Bartlett added. "We've been coming for five years, and now everyone in London talks about how fashionable it is and decorates with Indian furniture."

Mrs. Bartlett's face was drying to the colour of rust, and she tapped it with a fingernail. "We play the Lotto every week. If we win, we'll build a palace on the Indian Ocean, fill it with servants and jewels, and live like the Raj." She smiled. "I know it sounds ridiculous."

Agnes licked a white flake off the massage table and felt it dissolve on her tongue. "I hope I discover something. My dad does all the time. He told me that when he heard the song *Lucky Star*, he knew Madonna was going to be a lucky star. He's a genius. His name is Ram. Spelled backwards it's mar."

"Oh, are you Indian?" Mrs. Bartlett asked. She clapped her hands together.

"She doesn't look Indian," Mr. Bartlett said.

"My dad is." Agnes dug her nails into her mask. She dragged her fingers from her nose to her ears, streaking her cheeks like war paint.

"How wonderful," the woman said. "We never get

to talk to little children when we're here. We go straight from the airport to the ashram."

"That's what we did, too," Agnes said. "My dad didn't want to waste any time."

Mrs. Bartlett nodded. "What kinds of things do you like to do for fun, dear? I'm sure you have many friends."

"Yes. I love to live on the Indian Ocean with Raj, which is jar spelled backwards. I have a jar in my room with a lizard in it. I caught it yesterday. My dad doesn't know." Agnes twirled her gold hoops through the swollen holes in her ears.

"Do you have any hobbies?" Mrs. Bartlett asked. "When I was your age I loved horseback riding."

"I draw with Dr. Jackson sometimes. I like art. It's like tea. Which in India is *chai*, but they're both the same thing. If you rearrange the letters of *chai*, you get *achi*, which means good in Hindi. Art is good, too.

"You put leaves in a strainer and pour hot water over them and it becomes tea. But tea is not leaves or a strainer or hot water. It's eat, if you spell it wrong. When you take crayons and a piece of paper and you draw whatever you feel, your picture turns into something different than your feelings, the crayons, and the paper. It's a surprise. The inside of a cat looks nothing like the outside, but if you draw that, it's not art. I love surprises."

"My mask is hard," said the man. "When is that woman coming back?"

Mrs. Bartlett pressed her palm against her belly and exhaled. "Do you ever regret not having children, Henry?"

He snorted.

Agnes sat up. "I want to ask the Bhagwan about it. How come it's okay to lick something but not kill it? It's practically the same word. And who *says* the outside of a lizard is better than the inside? What if you do something people say is ugly, but you think it'll be lovely? Then how can it be wrong?"

"You can do anything for love, dear. When my father courted my mother, he stole apples from his neighbour's tree because he knew she loved them."

"Dr. Rangachari says the *Bhagwan* is love. And he does miracles on people who believe in him."

"He is very enlightened," Mrs. Bartlett said.

"When the Bhagwan cures me tomorrow, I won't have to go back to the hospital. I can live with my mom again."

Mrs. Bartlett smiled at her husband. "Bhagwan Shree Bahadur is in Los Angeles. He summers there and winters here. *Everyone* knows that. He's the spiritual leader to Michael Jackson, Geena Davis, Shirley Maclaine, and lots of other stars. He's a very busy man. We know him personally. We've attended two of his seminars."

"He's—not—here?" Agnes asked.

"No," the woman said. "If you don't need a private audience, it's best to come now. You get all the ashram amenities for half the cost."

"I thought he was named Bhagwan for a reason," Agnes said.

"There are a billion Bhagwans in this country," Mr. Bartlett said.

"My father told me he was named Bhagwan for—" Agnes began yanking at her new gold hoops. Her biceps contracted. She tugged until they tore slightly, and her hands were warm and sticky.

"Stop that!" the woman cried. "You're bleeding. Henry, make her stop. There's something wrong with her."

Mr. Bartlett's eyes widened.

Agnes pulled harder. The hoops ripped out of her lobes. She placed them in a neat pile in her lap and then fingered the flaps in her ears. She wiped her bloody hands along the front of her *salwar kameez*. "I caught a lizard in my room yesterday. My dad doesn't know. But I didn't hurt it. I was going to give it to the Bhagwan. I *really* don't want to hurt it."

"Are you all right?" the woman whispered.

Agnes licked the blood from her thumb and then raised her arms toward Mrs. Bartlett like a baby in a cradle.

"I think you should leave," the man said. He jumped off his massage table, stood between his wife and the girl, and pointed to the door. "Stay away from us. You're sick. You don't belong here."

**

Agnes unscrewed the lid of the Pond's Cold Cream jar and stared at the dead lizard. She plucked it out, then raised it to her lips and kissed it. She buried the creature's emerald body in the trashcan, underneath her *salwar kameez*. She replaced the empty bottle on the shelf.

Agnes crossed the bedroom and stood in front of the mirror. Her feet sank into the soft Indian rug. She pulled at the neck of her pyjamas until her armpit was exposed. There were two new black hairs erupting from her smooth flesh. Agnes adjusted her sun hat so it hid her earlobes. She frowned at her reflection.

A key turned in the lock and Ram entered, dripping with sweat. He emptied his pockets onto the night table, stripped to his underwear, lifted the mosquito net, and sat down on the bed.

"Come here, Agni baby," he said, patting the batik bedspread. "Let's go to sleep. I'm exhausted."

The girl lit a match and held it against the green mosquito coil. When it began burning, she blew on it and extinguished the flame. A small stream of smoke rose in the air. Agnes watched the ember glow at the tip. The orange spot would circle around and around through the night, leaving nothing in the morning but a circular pile of ash.

She climbed under the gauze netting and lay beside her father. He flicked off the light with a switch dangling from the wall.

"I took a picture of a pretty green bird for you," he said, rolling onto his side to drape his arm over her. "Is green still your favourite?"

"No. Now it's red plus yellow equals the Englishman's face. Guess what colour that is."

"Is that a riddle, Agnes?" He ran his hand up her back and stopped at the base of her neck. "Hey! Don't you want to take your hat off?"

"No."

"All right. Do whatever you want."

"Did you talk to my mom?"

Ram pulled the sheet up and smoothed it over their chests. "I did. She misses you. I told her you were feeling much better, and she was glad."

"Do you think mom still has my dictionaries?"

"Everything in your room is just how you left it. After we see Bhagwan Shree Bahadur and you're cured, you can play with your books as much as you want. I'll take you straight to Mary's house."

"What if he's not here?"

He encircled Agnes with his arms and pulled her against him. "That's impossible. Who's the one person in this world you can count on?"

"You."

"And who's the one person who's always right?"

"You," the girl repeated.

He kissed the tip of her nose. "You're my cuddly little baby, and daddy's going to make it all better."

Agnes squirmed away from him. "How was your lecture?"

"Very interesting. It was about the second chapter of *The Bhagavad Gita*." Ram yawned. "I'll tell you about it in the morning, and then you can tell me how your day was. Right now I'm sleepy."

"I'm not." The girl wiggled under the covers until she was an inch away from her father's chest. She pressed her mouth against him.

"Eeew! What did you do that for?"

"I wanted to wake you up. Talk to me."

Ram rubbed the saliva from his nipple. "Fine. For one minute, that's it. Okay, I went to the lecture in the afternoon. This man—I think he's famous, but I forget his name—talked about two guys in the book, and one of them tells the other that it's okay to fight his cousins because he can't really kill them."

"Because they're already dead?"

"No. Because the soul is immortal, and when someone dies they're reborn into a new body. It's like changing your clothes."

"And then they go to heaven?"

"No. There is no heaven. Don't listen to your mother; she doesn't know what she's saying. The truth is that when you die, you get to start all over again. You're a new person. Or if you weren't that nice, you might be a cow or a donkey or a flea."

"What if I die?" the girl asked. "Will I still be sick?"

"No, you'll be all better, Aggie, as good as new. Now will you let me sleep? I'm tired."

"Yes," she said. She found her father's cheek in the dark and kissed it.

"G'night. I love you," he mumbled.

When Ram began snoring, Agnes slipped out of the netting and tiptoed to the bureau. She blew on the mosquito coil and the ember burned brighter for a moment. Agnes felt along the dresser for a small cardboard box. Her fingers closed around it and she slipped it into her pocket. She stretched her arms toward the shelf and located a bottle of sandalwood oil. She unscrewed the cap and splashed half the liquid on the bedspread. Agnes took off her hat and poured the remainder on her head, as if she were showering. When her hair was soaked, she crept back to Ram and rubbed his chest with her oily hands. He groaned in his sleep.

Agnes lay against her father. She fished the box from her pocket and shook out one slender match.

About Mona Zutshi Opubor

Mona Zutshi Opubor is an Indian-American writer living with her husband and children in Lagos, Nigeria. Mona received her BA in English Literature and her MA in Fiction Writing. She was a 2012 Farafina Trust Creative Writing Workshop participant. Mona's work has been published in *The Kalahari Review, Descant Magazine,* and *The Foreign Encounters Anthology.* She blogs for intent.com.

Court Out

Shaun Avery

Oh my God.

She just saw, didn't she?

She just saw what my little Henry was doing.

It's my own fault. I shouldn't have pushed him, shouldn't have shouted at him. He didn't want to get up when the alarm went off this morning, and he's been cranky ever since then. Still, I didn't think it would happen... that as we drove to school he would forget himself and—

Now she knows.

She lives on my street and she saw, and I just know that she's going to tell everyone.

**

Starting with the other mums at the school gate.

I watch them as I drop Henry off.

Certain that they're watching me, too.

Watching.

And judging.

Because of what has just happened, I don't talk to them this morning. This doesn't require much effort—I very rarely talk to them *any* morning. It's hard to relax around them, you see. I can't let myself go too much, get too loose with them. In case my mouth runs off with me.

On the other side of the school gates, Henry runs off and joins his friends, their ranks opening up to let him in. Before he vanishes around the corner and into his class, though, he looks back, calling, 'bye, Mom!'

I wave. Thinking, as I do so, that he now looks so cute. So normal. Not like before, in the car, when that nosy bitch from my street Mrs Cuthbert passed us by, and she saw him snarling, wearing his special face.

The memory makes me frown.

Makes me worry.

I have so much to lose, now that I'm married, now that I'm happy.

But maybe I'll get lucky, I think as I turn back from the school.

Maybe she'll think it was just her imagination.

**

That's what I keep telling myself, as the day goes on.

But I still find myself walking past the house where she lives, trying to catch a glimpse of her.

Marcus finds me brooding over it later, staring out of the window at the distant shape of the Cuthbert residence.

'She's away,' he says, bending down to kiss the top of my head. 'On business, for a few days.'

The thought should bring me comfort.

She must have been heading out of town when she saw me—saw Henry, I should say. So my secret should be safe, at least for now.

But is it really?

She can still call people.

Still text.

Still e-mail.

I'm thinking about this as I walk up the stairs and into Henry's room.

Where he leaps at me as I open the door, wearing the face that Mrs Cuthbert saw this morning.

The first few times he did this, it scared me. Now, though, I've got used to it, and I just say, 'Darling, didn't we talk about this?'

He nods his head, switching back to his usual face, a suddenly very grown-up expression upon it. 'Yes, Mom,' he says. 'But this time I'm practising.'

'Oh really?' I say. 'For what?'

He just looks at me.

Seemingly knowing something that I don't.

**

The next few days are rather strange. I keep expecting Mrs Cuthbert to appear at the door, accusations in hand.

But she never does.

That should make me feel better. Feel more secure. But it doesn't. It makes me more certain that the noose around my neck is tightening. That she's taking her time, letting me think I've got away with it before turning up with a kangaroo court made up of the rest of our neighbours.

Marcus notices.

He doesn't know what is wrong—I can't quite bring myself to tell him—but he knows that something is bothering me. So he tries to cheer me up. Tries to lift my spirits with an extra dose of hugs and kisses when he returns home to me from work.

It usually works.

I've always loved his kisses.

Except for that one night when...

It's my hen night and I've had a bit to drink before I've even left my house and he doesn't like some of the people I'm going out with, he's never approved of Bessie and Joan, he says they've always been a bad influence on me, but they're my oldest friends and I love them, and he says but don't you love me too *and I hate the emotional blackmail that I see in his words, and I shout at him, I call him names, I use words I've never said before, words that always made me blush when I heard people say them in films...*

And then later on I'm in this bar and there's this guy who's looking at me, and he's making my stomach and some body parts lower than that feel funny, and Bessie says look at him *and for the briefest of seconds I think to myself that Marcus was right, she* is *a bad influence on me, but the thought is fleeting, and before I know what's going on, I'm talking to this guy, and then suddenly we're doing* more *than talking, much* more, *and then we're back at his place and my legs are up in the air and I'm thinking and saying rude things as he slides up into me and—*

But I swear I didn't know.

I didn't.

I thought that he was human.

Until three months after Henry was born.

Marcus knew what had happened by then, of course.

But he stood by me.

Even after that night, when Henry started crying, and got so upset and angry that his face, his sweet baby-face, became something else.

Something black and twisted, with horns and a tongue so long that it flopped out of his crib and touched the floor far below.

We kept it a secret.

When he was old enough we told Henry that he must never let his other face show in public.

A request that he'd followed faithfully until the tantrum in the car the other day—the one that Mrs Cuthbert had witnessed.

**

Late on Friday night I find it hard to get to sleep, and when I finally do I dream that I'm in court, that all of my neighbours are judging me, and Marcus, too, he's with them, and he's kissing Mrs Cuthbert, even though she's so much older than us, and his tongue is a huge, living thing, and he's whipping it up her face to lick her devious prying eyes.

I wake with a gasp.

And realise what I have to do.

**

Henry is lying awake, too.

Waiting for me.

Wearing his special face.

'I knew that this would happen,' he says. 'That's why I was practising being scary the other night.'

I bend down and plant a kiss on the ridges that have appeared in his forehead.

'Good boy,' I say.

A few minutes later, we're standing outside of Mrs Cuthbert's house.

The lights are still out.

But this time, I can tell she's home.

I reach out and ring the doorbell.

Then I look to Henry as we wait.

'What else have you been practising?' I ask him. 'What else can you do when you're wearing that face?'

He smiles.

The door swings open.

And he answers my question.

About Shaun Avery

Shaun Avery is a crime and horror fiction fan who has appeared in many anthologies and magazines. He has won competitions with prose and comic scripting, and was shortlisted in a screenwriting contest. He thinks the child he has created for this anthology is really quite scary. He hopes you agree.

PULP ADVENTURE

LAIRD LONG

Max Dower walked into the school cafeteria clutching his environmentally-friendly nylon lunch bag in one hand, his mathematics and science textbooks in the other hand. His classmates spotted the tall, lean, studious teenager and quickly piled books and coats up on the empty chairs at their tables, or spilled food and drink on them, as Max looked around for a place to sit.

He finally located a clean, uncluttered chair at the back of the cafeteria. Sitting across from each other at the table were Ben and Belinda Thomas, redheaded twins who were both in Max's social studies class. Max carefully placed his books down on the left hand corner of the table, his lunch directly in front of the empty chair, and then sat down.

"Hello," he greeted the twins.

They glanced at the brown-haired thirteen year-old, their mouths moving like rabbits, chewing up identical peanut butter sandwiches. Kids snickered all around the trio. On the cafeteria society social scale, the painfully shy Thomas twins were just about at the bottom, just above Max.

"You know," Max began, to show what he knew, "whole grain bread is much better for you than white bread." He carefully removed a cheese and tomato sandwich, on whole grain bread, from his lunch bag, as the Thomas twins silently munched away on their white bread. "It contains far more nutrients."

The twins simultaneously swallowed the remainder of their sandwiches, unwrapped and nibbled on a pair of snack-sized chocolate bars.

Max methodically opened up his container of skim milk, then took a measured bite out of his own sandwich. He noticed among the stacks of textbooks on the table, copies of the latest boy vampire and girl wizard volumes. His blue eyes lit up with the zeal of the scientific debunker of fairy tales. "You actually read that supernatural and magic junk?" he said.

The Thomas' jaws moved even faster. "We enjoy them," Belinda said, her nose twitching.

"They're interesting," Ben said, his eyes darting left and right.

"They're full of more bologna than Mrs. Leonard's lunch menu," Max stated.

Lunch Lady Leonard had a penchant for bologna in all of its forms—in sandwiches, salads, and casseroles, on crackers and toast, fried and deep-fried on sticks.

"Take that girl wizard," Max went on, oblivious to Johnny Detweiller behind him curving out an egg shape with his hands behind Max's head. "All those spells and curses and magical powers are just totally made-up. There's no scientific basis for them, no attempt made to even explain or justify their existence or properties. A broomstick that can fly? What's the propulsion mechanism supposed to be that—"

"Gotta go!" the Thomas twins gasped as one.

They swept up their books and lunch boxes and bolted from the table. They might not be part of the middle school in-crowd, but they still wanted nothing to do with myth-busting fun-killer Max Dower.

Students at nearby tables choked on their laughter, and Mrs. Leonard's bologna soufflé. Johnny Detweiller poked his blonde head over Max's shoulder and breathed egg salad into the teen's face, pointing at the empty chairs and chirping, "Hey, Max, sitting with all your friends again, huh?"

That brought on more laughter, more bologna spittle. Max simply shrugged his bony shoulders and opened up the science textbook he'd read through twice already. He started taking notes, chewing evenly and precisely on his sandwich.

**

"Do I have to go to Grandma's house?" Max asked his mother the following Saturday morning. It was a bright, sunny spring day. Max had been looking forward to staying in his room and conducting some admittedly rudimentary experiments using his chemistry kit.

"Yes, you do," his mother answered. She was standing at the kitchen counter, packing a cooler with the picnic lunch they were going to eat in the backyard of her mother's home. "You know how much she enjoys telling you her stories—about Grandpa, the way life was back in the old days."

Max almost rolled his eyes. But as a sober, budding young adult, he eschewed such juvenile antics. "Stories! That's all they are. Made-up tall tales. I know Grandma's not senile or anything, but—"

"She just has a vivid imagination. Like your grandfather did. It's too bad he died when you were just little, so you didn't have a chance to get to know him. He was a very interesting man."

"He was a small town bank clerk," Max pointed out. Then added, "Imagination is simply a childish escape from reality. The psychologist Dr. Herbert Kleiner said that—"

"No note from a doctor is going to get you out of *this* trip," Max's father said, slapping the teenager on the back as he entered the kitchen. "All ready to go, honey?"

"Yup!"

Max's grandmother lived in an old house located in a quiet residential area near the centre of the city. It was a turn-of-the-last-century two-storey wooden structure, painted yellow, with a wide, screened-in veranda at the front and a tiny patch of grass yard at the back. The house moaned and groaned at the slightest gust of wind, chattered with the least little bit of rainfall, and the interior creaked more even than its 90 year-old occupant.

Max reluctantly accepted his grandmother's customary peck on the cheek. Knowing how germs were spread, the bacteria incubator that was the human mouth.

"And what sort of mischief are you getting into these days, young man?" she asked him, when they were all seated in the parlour of the ancient home.

"Well," Max responded, glancing around at the faded wallpaper and age-darkened door and window frames, "I was reading an interesting article on termite colonies the other—"

"My, but your grandfather used to get into all sorts of exciting adventures. Why, one time I remember, he—"

"I have to go to the bathroom," Max interrupted,

before his grandmother could get up a head of steam.

"Ah, young boys—so full of vinegar and—"

"Mother!" Max's mother cut in. "Go ahead, Max. But hurry back down."

The teenager hurried out of the parlour, with no intention of hurrying back in. He snagged a meatloaf sandwich out of the cooler his mother had placed in the kitchen, stuffed the wrapped edible into one of his jacket pockets, and then ran up the rickety stairs that led to the second floor of the house, the ancient bathroom at the end of the tiled hallway.

Max didn't go into the bathroom, however, having just gone before he left his own house. Instead, he opened up the doors and looked into the two dusty, cluttered bedrooms on the second floor.

He entered the bedroom nearest the bathroom and peered around at the heaped boxes and stacked chairs and other assorted sticks of furniture. He tried to pull the closet door open. It stuck, the wood warped. Tugging hard, he at last managed to yank the door open. More boxes, some old clothes on wooden hangers. He jerked down on the frayed cord hanging from the overhead light fixture, and nothing happened.

"Bulb probably burnt out back in the '50s," Max muttered, pulling his pocket flashlight out of a jacket pocket. Max always came prepared.

He shone the pencil of light around the closet, saw nothing of interest, just dancing dust motes. He shone the flashlight upwards, and noticed for the first time a second cord hanging from the closet ceiling, to the left of the light cord.

Max stepped into the closet and pulled down on

the second cord. The ceiling opened up and a flight of stairs cascaded down, almost bashing the startled teenager right in the face. He let go of the cord and jumped out of the way just in time. Then he pointed his flashlight beam up into the attic of the old house, and carefully ascended the swaying, creaking steps.

Max was hoping to find some interesting spiders or bats or even rodent carcasses to study up in the attic. But he was disappointed, as he stepped out into the low-ceilinged room and swept his light around. There were only more boxes and broken pieces of junk, more dust. Not a spiderweb in sight, no flapping of little wings or scurrying of little feet within earshot.

Stooping down slightly, Max walked amongst the cardboard, wooden and metal relics. In one corner of the attic he found an old wardrobe. He opened its doors, rusty hinges squeaking. Inside hung coats of an ancient vintage. He pushed them aside, but found only a solid pine wall in back. "How unsurprising," the teenager muttered.

There was a pile of clothing in another corner of the attic, old dress shirts and pants. Max touched the pile, and the clothes tumbled to the floor in an avalanche of dust and must, revealing a large black and blue steamer trunk.

Max knelt down in front of the trunk. "Perhaps some artefacts for anthropological study," he mused.

He flipped the hasps up on either side of the trunk, then tugged at the latch in the middle. It was locked, but the lock was as mouldered and mauled as the rest of the trunk. The lid flew open.

Max stared down at the contents of the trunk.

And his expression drooped from one of mild interest to one of resigned disappointment. (Max wasn't given to wild mood swings.) Inside the trunk were stacks and stacks of old magazines, their acrid, decaying odour assailing Max's sensitive nostrils.

He picked a magazine up off the top of one of the stacks. The semi-glossy cover bore the title *Strange Adventures* in blood-red letters, and an eccentric painted picture of a giant spider descending from an enormous web just above a terrified, trussed-up man in a dungeon cellar. The illustration was liberally splashed with red, yellow, black and green, making the outlandish scene appear even more garish. Dripping down the right hand side of the cover in crimson was a partial list of stories and authors.

Max yawned, opening up the magazine. The paper inside was rough and thick and browned, crumbling to the touch. The table of contents listed ten short stories by various writers and the latest chapter in a serial story, 'Men Without Limbs', by Max Mann. The interior pages were crammed with typewritten words and black and white illustrations as outrageous as the one on the cover of the magazine.

There were hundreds of such magazines. Most were titled *Strange Adventures*, or *Weird Wonder Stories*, or *Astonishing Tales*. And as Max flipped through the pulpy pages, he noticed that each fiction-packed issue contained at least one story by Max Mann.

The teenager began skimming through some of the Mann stories by the light of his flashlight. They were wild, rip-roaring tales set in exotic lands inhabited by even more exotic creatures and foliage. Usually, the fate of a woman or the world hung in the balance, compelling some man to perform superhuman tasks of daring in order to rescue one or the other or both. The wildly improbable, but well-paced and plotted stories, were peopled with more evil doctors, mad scientists, lurching henchmen, rugged heroes and beautiful heroines than a comic book convention.

Max scoffed at the astounding happenings, yet he read on, consuming the purple prose like a kid consumes candy at Halloween.

He tossed down the July 1937 issue of *Astonishing Tales* and snatched up the September 1938 issue of *Weird Wonder Stories*, with the cover story 'Emperor of an Invisible World', by Max Mann. But as he did so, he accidentally knocked over a stack of the magazines, exposing a pen lying in one corner of the old trunk.

Max picked it up. It looked to be of the same vintage as the magazines. It was about five inches long and one-and-a-half inches around, the barrel gleaming black lacquer, the cap black, as well, with a shiny gold clip. The pen felt light, but solid in Max's hand.

He tried to pull off the cap. It wouldn't budge. He twisted the cap, and it easily unthreaded from the barrel.

It was a fountain pen, the kind you refill with ink when they run dry. The long, curved nib appeared to be made of solid gold. Max fitted the cap smoothly onto the end of the pen and held it by its barrel. It fit his writing hand perfectly, well-balanced and at home like a sixth finger. The pen seemed to pulse right along with the teenager's suddenly accelerated heartbeat.

Max pulled his trusty observational notepad out

of his jacket pocket, flipped it open. And the pen and his hand leapt at the blank ruled paper, anxious to write something down. Max swallowed hard, pressed the straining nib into the paper.

Expecting nothing more than a dull, dry scratch, he was amazed to see black ink flow out of the golden nib of the pen, flow smooth and thick and wet onto the paper, the pen almost writing by itself. Because not only did the ink flow, but so did the words, pouring out onto the paper, the pen moving swiftly in Max's damp hand. Before he knew it, he had a whole page filled with his attic observations, his script neat and clear like never before.

Max jerked the pen up. The night-black, gold-embossed writing instrument seemed to vibrate in his hand, its ink coursing through his fingers and up his arm and into his brain, filling his head with sudden wild ideas, pushing aside his normal doubt and natural scepticism. The fountain pen yearned to write, to take up where it had left off, capped for too long, compelling Max to let loose, as well.

He gazed down at the piles of thrill-inspiring fiction magazines, and grinned, his eyes glittering like the pulsating pen in his hand. He'd uncovered more than some dusty old magazines; he'd uncovered a world of excitement and adventure and imagination, beyond the realm of rationalisation. It lay right before his very finger and pen tips, ready to be written, and enjoyed.

Max applied pen back to the paper, and he instantly began writing again. Only this time, it wasn't dry scientific observations that he documented; it was the exciting opening of a pulp action story that he began furiously scribbling, similar to the ones he'd been recently reading. Inspired by the magazines, inflamed by the racing pen that seemed to write anything possible. He was...

Surrounded by an oozing army of giant slugs.

The bloated, banana-yellow gastropods humpback slithered towards him in their slime, the sickening sluicing sound of their mucous-aided march filling the air, along with their primordial swamp stench. They were all at least four-feet in length, two feet in engorged girth.

Max anxiously backed away, but was stopped cold by a rocky, ten-foot-high ridge behind him. He plastered his sweating hands and body against the shale barrier and stared at the undulating mass of slickened, larval-like bodies that blanketed the level ground in front of him as far as a green sea of slime in the distance, from which more disgusting giant slugs were emerging.

He shot a glance right: more ridge; a glance left: the same, except for one notable exception—a man. A man had his back flattened to the ridge not twenty feet away from Max. He wore a battered felt hat and a black leather jacket, whipcord tan pants, a white shirt and a grey bowtie. A lariat and sheathed knife hung from his belt.

Max gulped with relief. "Help!" he cried.

The man twisted his head away from the ever-advancing legion of slugs and looked at Max. "I was going to ask the same thing of you!" he yelled back.

Max's hopes plummeted lower than a slug's belly. For all his attire and equipment, the man had a plain, homely face, grey eyes enlarged by ultra-thick glasses.

His chin was receded and his shoulders stooped, his chest shallow and skin sallow.

"Great!" Max hissed.

Yet the man's knife gave him an idea—to pull his own Swiss Army all-in-one knife out of his jacket pocket. For what purpose he didn't immediately know, because neither the small blade nor bottle opener nor nail file was going to be nearly enough to repel the horde of insidiously swollen, shunting slugs, now closing within feeler distance of the trapped teenager and man.

The pair pancaked themselves against the ridge, desperately trying to melt into the rock. A giant slug raised its blinded head right in front of Max, its bulbed antennae bending grotesquely forward, honing in on the terrified teen's presence.

"What can we do?!" Max yelled at the man.

"Sprout wings?!" the equally horrified man responded.

Unfortunately, there was no such convenient magic to be conjured to get them out of the mess they were in.

Max looked up, down. His frantic eyes fell upon a small dome-like uprising in the otherwise flat terrain a couple of yards away to his right. He stared at the formation, desperately thinking. With his mind at fever-pitch, he rapidly riffled through his mental catalogue of topographical oddities, the Periodic Table of Chemical Elements.

"Halite!" he rasped. It was a small halite dome, thrust to the surface at some geological point by the pressure of the earth's plates beneath.

"What?!" the man shouted. "Did you just swear?!"

A slug's ooze-covered bright yellow head pushed against Max's chest. He screamed, smacking the hideous creature away with the flat of his hand. Mucous slimed his hand and chest. The slugs were upon them.

Sliding along the ridge like the wind, Max moved quickly over to the halite dome. He kicked an encroaching slug in the snout, his sneaker sinking into the spongy body. Then he dropped down and scraped the blade of his Swiss Army knife against the small rock formation, chipping off some pieces. He scooped these up in his hand and flung them into the rounded, unseeing faces of the slugs right in front of him.

They recoiled. Max chipped, flung. The slugs in front humped backwards, squishing into the mass still advancing. The man rushed over and got in on the act. He and Max hurled chunks of halite out into the writhing body of slugs, sowing confusion and panic.

The slimy surfaces of the slugs so struck by the rock shrivelled and hissed. Pandemonium broke out in the ranks of the unhelmetted snails. Max and his companion rained halite down on the slugs, and they wheeled and slithered in retreat, oozing back on their trails for the safety of the green sea of slime at top slug speed.

The man mopped his brow with relief. "I'm Arthur, by the way."

"Max," the teenager replied.

"What is that stuff, anyway?" Arthur asked, gesturing at the whittled-down dome.

"Rock salt," Max answered proudly. "The mineral form of sodium chloride, NaCl. The natural enemy of leeches, snails, and slugs. See, the salt draws moisture up out of the slug's body, causing them to dehydrate. Osmosis is—"

"We haven't time," Arthur interrupted. "We have to save the golden-haired girl, Felicity Chapell, from the evil clutches of Lord Talordor, ruler of the Nether Regions!"

The man rapidly explained that Lord Talordor had seized Felicity from her parents' home, was holding the golden-haired teenager captive at his castle in the Nether Regions.

"To be used as a human sacrifice?" Max gaped.

"No," Arthur replied.

"To become his bride?"

"No."

"Then why did he kidnap Felicity?!"

Arthur gulped. "Because he means to subjugate her as his personal servant, with no life outside the castle."

Max grimaced. It sounded a little too 21st century for a 1930s pulp scenario. But there was no time to argue. Because Arthur was already racing along the ridge towards the emerald-green forest that lay off in the distance. The teenager ran after him in hot pursuit.

Had story-boy Max looked up into the brilliant blue sky, beyond the glowing yellow sun, he would have seen story-writer Max looking down from the heavens, furiously spilling ink into words and sentences from his flying pen, the paragraphs forming up at a penny-a-word pulp writer's frenetic pace.

Max and Arthur soon skidded to a halt at the edge of the forest, panting for breath. The deep foliage was thick with trees, the thick trunks of the trees swarming with vines.

But with not a moment to lose, the two intrepid adventurers plunged into the forest. And were instantly ensnared by the coiling green vines that suddenly sprang to life, wrapping themselves around Max and Arthur's limbs. The pair stumbled backwards, barely squirming free from the crushing grasps of the snake-like vines.

"The Tendril Forest," Arthur breathed.

"So I noticed," Max commented, rubbing his arms.

"We have to get through it, if we're going to reach Lord Talordor's castle."

Max scratched his head. The forest stretched away for miles on either side of them. "Any ideas?"

Arthur skinned off his hat, ran a small, soft hand through his slick black hair. "None."

Max admired the decisiveness of the man's mind, if not its agility. He fingered his pocketknife, staring at the sheath hanging from Arthur's belt. They'd need buzzsaw machetes to cut their way through this vegetation. The bright sun glinted off Arthur's 'do, and Max suddenly had another idea.

"Do you put something in your hair to make it so ... slick?" he asked his companion. "Or just not wash it?"

"Both," Arthur replied. He pulled a red tin out of the back pocket of his pants. "I use this." He handed the tin to Max. "Like a lot of men of my generation."

The tin was labelled Hair-Glo Pomade. Max grinned. "You know, the main ingredients in these hair gels are petroleum jelly and mineral oils."

"You don't say? So?"

"So watch me," Max said, stripping off his jacket

and 'Science Fare' t-shirt, his jeans. He slathered his bare legs and arms with the hair goop, then handed the tin back to Arthur.

The man smiled, catching on, baring and slathering his own limbs, as well.

And now when the pair dove into the Tendril Forest, the lashing vines found no grip on their slippery limbs. Max and Arthur dashed through the foliage like greased pigs, sliding their arms and legs easily out of the futilely entwining vines.

"You gotta love it when a plan gels!" Max quipped.

But the teenager's grin turned to chagrin, when he and Arthur leapt out of the forest on the other side, and faced the vista that now that lay between them and the golden-haired girl Felicity Chapell: an endless ocean of sand, shifting and sliding and sharding with the blowing of the wind, piled high in drifted dunes here and there and everywhere, as far as the eye could see.

"The Sinking Desert," Arthur breathed.

The pair used handfuls of sand scooped from the desert's edge to scrub the hair tonic off their limbs. They reclothed themselves. Then Max ventured out into the sand. And instantly sank down to the beltline. Arthur scrambled to pull him back out again.

"Maybe if we ran really fast, we could sort of skim over the surface," Max gasped.

Arthur picked up a flat stone, tried skimming it across the sand. It skipped once, then was swallowed up by the sand.

They looked out at the interminable expanse of desert.

"Felicity Chapell is being domesticated as we speak," Arthur noted.

"Of course!" Max yelped, his scientifically-trained mind springing open like a steel trap, freshly unhinged to its full potential by the recent exponential rise in his imagination. "Snowshoes!"

"Snowshoes?!" Arthur rasped, squinting at the blazing sand. "Is that a joke?"

"Nope. It's a method of human transportation across any soft particulate surface—like snow... or sand."

Employing their knives again, the pair quickly cut out the necessary wood and vines from the Tendril Forest. They then fashioned the wood into square frames which they lashed together and across with the vines, constructing crude snowshoes of the type Max had worn on a winter outdoor education exercise at school.

Fitting them to their feet, they stepped out onto the sand. They sunk down several inches in the fine grains, but didn't bog down to their waists. They began loping over the sand, hot on the trail of the tall grey castle that shimmered like a mirage far up ahead.

Later, they lifted their leadened legs out of the desert and onto the rocky ground at the foot of Lord Talordor's castle. They unfastened the sandshoes and stepped off of them. Then stared up at the sheer stone walls towering a hundred feet over their heads.

"There's no way we can climb these walls," Max said, frustrated at having come so far horizontally, only to be stopped vertically.

"And the gate is solid oak!" Arthur called over from the massive closed and barred front entrance of the castle. "Not a hinge showing anywhere!"

Max pointed up at the parapets crowning the mammoth castle walls. "Look at those ugly gargoyles!"

Gigantic ash-grey, bald-headed, hook-beaked birds perched on the edge of the parapets, glaring down stone-faced from their long, grotesquely bent necks.

"You don't have to yell," Arthur said, at Max's side once again. "And those aren't gargoyles. They're vultures."

"What? They're so big, and grey."

"Yes. They're big, grey vultures. They feed on the defeated bodies of Lord Talordor's would-be conquerors, no doubt."

"Carrion."

"Carrying us? How?"

"No," Max said. "Vultures feed on carrion—the rotting carcasses of dead—" He stopped talking, started digging around in his jacket pockets.

"What are you looking for?" Arthur asked.

"This!" Max responded triumphantly, pulling out the meatloaf sandwich he'd pocketed earlier in the day. He unwrapped the sandwich and discarded the bread, held the thick, square slice of ground hamburger high up above his head.

The pair of vultures stirred on the parapets. Beady eyes gleamed downward, necks stretching, claws grating on stone. Max threw the chunk of meatloaf into the air, and the huge birds swooped, spreading their wings and plummeting off the parapets, greedily trying to be the first to reach the dead meat.

The meatloaf had only time to bounce off the ground once, before the raptors were on top of it. They each grabbed a side, their sharp beaks meeting in the middle, their sharp claws clattering on the rocky ground.

They fought over the sandwich meat with a fury that would've made Lunch Lady Leonard proud. Their mighty wings beat at one another, feathers flying. They hopped around, each trying to tear the densely-formed hamburger from the other.

"All aboard!" Max shouted, leaping onto the back of one of the vultures.

The bird squawked. But refused to let go of the meatloaf.

Arthur gritted his teeth and leapt onto the back of the other bird.

Wings flapped furiously and claws scratched frenetically. Until, at last, the square of processed meat rended in two. The birds gobbled down their portions and then took flight, with the pair of adventurers hanging on for the ride. Max's ornithological studies had taught him that just as surely as a rooster crows at the crack of dawn, an enraged or frightened bird will instinctually fly back to their roost.

And the vultures did exactly that, sailing up to their parapets and alighting on the edges. Max and Arthur scrambled off the feathered backs of the birds and jumped through the wooden trapdoors set in the stone floors of the parapets, just ahead of two ferociously snapping beaks.

Man and young man half-tumbled, half-clambered down the winding stone staircases and shoved through the wooden doors at the base of the parapets—inside Lord Talordor's castle. They regrouped. Just in time to see a small, black-cloaked, staff-wielding figure pull a frightened golden-haired girl through the entranceway of a crypt, and vanish within.

Max got only a brief glimpse of Felicity Chapell's anguished face before she disappeared. But he noted, with only mild surprise, that she bore a striking resemblance to Inga Hansen, the popular thirteen year-old who occupied the desk right in front of his in language class.

Max and Arthur gave chase, bounding down gloom-laden stairs deep into the bowels of the castle. They shouldered their way through a heavy oaken door and burst out into a subterranean vault.

"Gosh!" Arthur marvelled.

Lord Talordor stood on a raised stone platform in the middle of a molten ring of fire. He clutched Felicity around the waist with one arm, brandishing his silver staff with the other. "The girl is mine!" he roared over the burbling brimstone in the encircling moat.

The pair of adventurers desperately looked around for some way across the hissing, steaming lava, and found none. The walls of the immense chamber were bare, as was the stone floor and overarching ceiling.

"We're stymied!" Arthur yelled.

"Stuck!" Max shouted.

They stared up at the opaque image of Max hovering just above the fiery chamber. His brow was furrowed, the magical fountain pen stuck in a corner of his mouth, as he pondered a way of resolving the situation, without resorting to the cop-out deus ex machina of many such similar yarns; when a guardian wizard suddenly appears from nowhere in the story, for example, and blows the lava cold with his winter mouth, allowing the heroes to cross the moat; or one of the leading characters suddenly remembers the previously unmentioned enchanted toad they've been carrying around all this time, and said toad, with the appropriate incantation and rear rub, uncoils its sticky pink tongue to form a bridge for the rescuers to cross over.

Max and Arthur looked at one another, up at the puzzled face of their creator. Lord Talordor smirked complacently, grasping poor Felicity with a chattel impudence.

Then, suddenly, Max snapped his fingers, concluding that there surely must be some sort of bridge to straddle the superheated contents of the moat, else how did Talordor and Felicity get over onto the stone platform? And the person who would best know about that bridge and its operation would be: the evil Lord himself.

Max hastily explained his plan to Arthur. The man nodded, unhooking the lariat from his belt. He began swinging the rope over his head in ever-widening circles.

"You will cross on a bridge of flammable strand?!" Lord Talordor exclaimed derisively.

Arthur answered pulp Western style, throwing the lasso. It sailed across the moat and looped down over Lord Talordor's shoulders.

"Bulls-eye!" Max yipped.

Arthur jerked on the rope, tightening it around Talordor, pulling him forward. The ruler of the Nether Regions let go of the golden-haired girl and struggled to rid himself of the encircling twine, still clutching his staff. Max joined Arthur at the other end of the noose, dragging Lord Talordor closer to the edge of the stone platform and certain flaming oblivion.

207

Talordor squirmed, writhed, tried to dig in his heightened heels, his round face going red as the brimstone drew ever closer. He was pulled to the very edge of the platform, the glowing lava snapping and spitting up at him.

His bully strength and courage shattered at the same time, in the teeth of the steely resolve of the pair of adventurers across the way. He frantically lifted his staff and gave it a furious shake. The metal instrument snapped out to moat-spanning length. Talordor fumbled the tip of the fully-extended rod into a slight indentation high up on the stone wall opposite, above Max and Arthur's heads.

A stone bridge instantly rose up out of the magma. It locked into position on either side of the moat, spanning the lava expanse just above the jumping flames.

"I'll get Felicity!" Max yelled at Arthur. "You hold onto Lord Talordor!"

"But it's still too hot!" Arthur grunted, grimly clinging to the rope.

"No! You see that white carpet across the top of the bridge?! Asbestos—inflammable!"

Max ran across the bridge, the heat-retardant carpet and the stone arch protecting him from meltdown. He grabbed Felicity Chapell by the hand and pulled her towards the bridge.

"Wait!" she cried. Running over to the hog-tied Lord Talordor, she seized his staff and pressed the tip of it back into the wall indentation. The bridge began to sink into the molten moat.

"Hurry!" Max wailed.

But Felicity wasn't finished with her evil captor

just yet. She tore the silver staff right out of his hand and threw it into the moat. The lava swallowed it up, liquefying the metal on impact.

The teenage boy and girl raced back across the lowering bridge, flames licking at their high-stepping feet. They leapt the final yard, just as the bridge sunk into the boiling brimstone. Arthur caught them in his arms, flinging his rope aside.

Leaving Lord Talordor exiled on his barren stone island, surrounded on all sides by the hellish fires of his own creation.

Arthur watched with a sheepish grin, as Max and Felicity embraced, then...

The world of adventure faded. Max's grandfather's pen had run out of ink.

Max capped the pen and carefully placed it in his jacket pocket. He heaved a sigh and wiped sweat from his forehead, his face flushed and pulse racing. He'd never been so alive, so excited. He gazed down at the pages and pages of rip-roaring story that filled his notebook, hardly believing he'd authored it all.

Then he scooped up an armload of pulp magazines and climbed down out of the attic. His parents and grandmother were in the backyard, finishing up their lunch.

"Good heavens, where have you been all this time, Max?!" his grandmother asked. "We thought you'd disappeared."

Max plopped the magazines down on the picnic table. "Tell me about Max Mann, Grandma."

"Oh, dear," the old woman clucked, staring at the glossy-covered, rough-edged magazines. "You've discovered our secret."

She looked up at Max. "You see, Max Mann was your grandfather—or, at least, his penname. You've heard me tell you stories over the years about what an exciting, adventurous man he was. Well, that's what they were—stories; stories he made up and sold to the pulp magazines. He had such a vivid imagination, you know."

Max's grandmother looked down at her hands. "But, well, the pulps were considered trashy at the time—back in the '30s and '40'—beneath the dignity of a respectable bank clerk. So, we kept his writing a secret, turned his flights of fancy into real-life adventure tales."

She fumbled a small leather billfold out of the enormous purse she always kept at her side. "I don't think you've ever seen a picture of your grandfather, Max." She opened the billfold and handed it to the teenager. "It's the only photograph I have of him, after the funeral parlour lost all of the pictures we'd set up for his service."

Max looked down at the small black and white photo in its protective cellophane jacket. It was a posed studio picture of a man dressed in a battered felt hat, a leather jacket and whipcord pants, a sheathed knife and coiled rope hanging from his belt. The man had a weak chin, was stoop-shouldered, and wore thick eyeglasses. He was holding up a copy of *Strange Adventures*, and grinning at the camera.

Max grinned, realising that while most things in the world can be explained scientifically, all people—bank clerks and middle school students alike—need a little magic in their lives, to add joy and excitement and adventure.

He handed the photograph back to his grandmother, clutching his grandfather's black-barrelled, gold-embossed fountain pen in his pocket. The pen pulsed in his hand to his heartbeat, thirsty for more ink, bottles of which were still stored in the old steamer trunk up in the attic. Enough ink for many, many more exciting adventures, the only limit: Max's imagination.

About Laird Long

Long pounds out fiction in all genres. Big guy, sense of humour. Writing credits include the magazines *Blue Murder Magazine, Orchard Press Mysteries, Futures Mysterious Anthology Magazine, Plots With Guns, Hardboiled, Thriller UK, Shred of Evidence, Bullet, Albedo One, Baen's Universe, Sniplits, 5 Minute Mystery, Woman's World, Tales of Old, that's life!, knowonder!*; the anthologies *Amazing Heroes, The Mammoth Book of New Comic Fantasy, The Mammoth Book of Jacobean Whodunits,* and *The Mammoth Book of Perfect Crimes and Impossible Mysteries*; and the book *No Accounting for Danger.*

Run Like A Girl

M. Kate Allen

Jesse looks around slowly with wide, sparkling brown eyes, his mouth agape. His slim arms hang at his sides. All he can do is stare.

Moments ago he had lead his kickball team on the playground to victory; two of his strongest guys were carrying him across the field as the rest of the team cheered. Now?

The normally blue sky is now fuchsia. The blades of grass, the clover, the stems of the dandelions—all darker, lighter, brighter, and paler shades of pink. Jesse blinks, then blinks again. He checks his black digital watch. 12:00PM.

"Hey, Sissy, time to come in!" Jesse looks over and sees Jill Howarth staring at him. Giggles erupt behind her. Jill smirks as Jesse jogs toward her. "You run like a boy," Jill says, letting the door shut just as Jesse reaches it. He opens the door and has a sharp retort ready, but Jill is already gone.

He scurries back to his classroom and slides into his seat just as Mr. Francis begins the math lesson. His eyes widen as he pulls his math book out of his desk. The hunter green textbook is now the colour of cooked crab, and the front picture of the boy with brown hair and khaki pants raising his hand from his desk is replaced with a girl with red hair and pale skin, wearing a bubble-gum coloured polka dot jumper.

Jesse opens his book, his hand trembling. Whispers from his left draw his attention. His gaze shifts to Maddie Jennings who glances in Jesse's direction before holding her hand up to Jill's ear and whispering again. They giggle. "Hey!" he says, angry.

"Ah, Mr. Wilson, how nice of you to volunteer." Jesse looks up at Mr. Francis, whose eyes are fixed on him. Jesse blushes, silent. He didn't hear the question, or he'd be able to answer easily. Math is his best subject.

Jill raises her hand. "I know the answer, Mr. Francis. One hundred and twenty-six divided by seven is eighteen." Jill flashes a triumphant grin at Jesse. Jesse seethes.

Girls suck at math, especially *Jill Howarth*, he thinks to himself. *And what's with all this puketastic pink?*

Math is over when final bell rings, and Jesse flings his backpack over his right shoulder, rushing out of his classroom and down the hall.

"Look, there he goes! Sissy's running home to Daddy! Crying like a boy because he got outsmarted again." Jesse slows and turns toward Jill's voice. Jill's eyes sparkle behind her thick, boxy glasses as she places her hands on her narrow hips, inviting a challenge. A crowd gathers around her. Jesse rises to his full height and approaches her.

"Listen, nerd," Jesse says, his voice rising to a screech, "you may be a girl, but I have no problem punching you from here to the next block." He balls up his right fist as he says this and prepares to swing.

A moment later, he's laying flat across the floor, unable to breathe. Jill's high-pitched voice sounds in his ear. "You should know better than to pick on someone who's smarter and faster than you," she says in a low, slow drawl. "But a dumb boy wouldn't get that, would you? Try acting like a girl next time. Maybe you'll grow some girly parts."

Jesse's breath comes back to him just in time for a flood of white-hot pain to shoot through his body, starting from between his legs. Jill's freckled face hovers over his, and then all goes black.

**

Jesse's eyes open slowly, weighted with sleep. He's in bed. Slivers of pale light stream through his brown curtains. He sits up with a yawn. The clock says 7:30AM. His alarm will go off in fifteen minutes. He moves the switch from "alarm" to "off", tips his legs over the side of the bed, and stands up.

Downstairs, pouring himself a glass of orange juice, he sees his dad sitting at the breakfast table in a white shirt, red and blue striped tie, and a glossy pair of black slacks. He's reading *USA Today*.

"I had the worst nightmare," Jesse says, skipping the cereal cupboard and moving directly to his breakfast chair.

"Mmm?" Jesse's dad murmurs, his fingers curled around the handle of a cup of black coffee.

"It was a kickball game during recess. I had just won when suddenly everything turned pink."

Jesse's dad looked up from his paper, raising an eyebrow.

"Seriously. It was like walking into an antacid bottle, except it made me sick. This gimpy girl in my class did better than me during math and then kicked my a—."

214

Jesse's dad raises his eyebrow further. "I mean, she messed me up. Can you imagine a world where the whole world is pink and girls are better than boys?"

"No, son. I don't have the sort of imagination you do," his dad answers before turning back to his newspaper.

Jesse looks at his dad to see if he's joking. He can't tell. Shrugging, he grabs a piece of cold toast from the toaster on his way out to the bus stop.

**

It's 11:40AM and Jesse's classmates gather around in a loose circle, hoping to be among the first selected for his or Antonio's team—or, if not among the first chosen, at least chosen for Jesse's team, since his is the one that always wins.

Four-eyed Jill is among those gathered for the game. Jesse glances at her. She's wearing a pink polka-dot dress and her hair is pulled back on top of her head in a mauve denim scrunchie. She meets his eye. He looks away. "Hey, Jesse," Antonio barks, "get a move on!"

Jill is the last person standing when all other teammates have been chosen. She's also the seventeenth person in line, which means her presence on either team will make the numbers uneven. "I want to play!" she calls out in her high-pitched voice.

Laughter ripples through the two teams. Jesse quips, "Hey, Antonio, wanna flip for it? Heads, you win, and I end up with Four-Eyes. Tails, I win, and you're stuck with her." Antonio grins and pulls out a quarter to flip. He tosses it and it lands on the ground, rolling across the pavement and falling flat near Jill's stocking-covered feet. Tails.

Antonio groans while Jesse high-fives his classmates, giving Jill a wide berth as he assumes his place on the field.

Ten minutes later, Jesse's team has twice the number of runs as Antonio's team with a score of six to three. Antonio's team has loaded the bases. Jill is next in line to kick, and as she approaches the plate, Antonio's brow furrows. Jesse is in the pitcher's position and chuckles, turning to his teammates and calling out in a stage whisper, "Oooh, I think we're in trouble." He turns back to see Jill's face turn as pink as her dress. Antonio crosses his arms, frowning at Jill.

"Make sure you run like a girl!" Jesse calls out, just before rolling the ball down the line. Jill kicks and delivers the ball across the foul line. Catcalls erupt from Jesse's teammates. One of Antonio's players grabs the ball and tosses it back to Jesse. He holds it up like a bowling ball, then delivers it down the line again. Jill swings her leg, but her foot catches on an invisible barrier and she nearly falls. The other members of Antonio's team groan aloud. Antonio shakes his head and walks over to her, standing between her and Jesse, speaking in a low voice.

It's down to the third and final roll before the bell sounds. Jesse smiles broadly as he delivers the ball expertly down the line. Jesse swings her leg and makes contact just as the ball reaches her. The ball soars just above Jesse's head. He reacts too slowly and misses catching it by inches for the out. The ball lands well beyond the base guards. Antonio's base runners fly into motion. Billy, one of Jesse's outfielders, reaches the ball and throws it hard to Jesse. At that moment, the last of Antonio's runners reaches homeplate and Jill touches third. "Run!" her teammates scream.

Jesse whirls around and runs full speed toward homeplate to beat Jill to it. His distance to home is shorter than hers—he's got this in the bag. When each one is just steps away from homeplate, Jesse trips, losing the ball and sailing headfirst into the plate.

Jill jumps to avoid colliding with him and touches homeplate with her right heel. Her grand slam is met with wild cheers and the ringing of the recess bell. Antonio pulls over another of his teammates and they lift Jill on their shoulders. "Go, Jill! Go, Jill!" their teammates chant.

Jesse's teammates help Jesse off the ground, but he shrugs them off. As his classmates head inside, he slinks along behind them.

The excited twittering dies down as he enters Mr. Francis' room. Mr. Francis asks Jesse to take his seat. As Jesse walks down his row to his desk, Antonio says to him in an exaggerated whisper, "Maybe you should have run like a girl."

About M. Kate Allen

Kate is a writer, an editor, and a thealogian (and no, the "a" isn't an accident— thanks for asking!). She's also the mother of two delightfully precocious children and the wife of a once-upon-a-time precocious boy. In her free time, Kate enjoys tending her garden, riling up the patriarchy, and wooing people with her Russian tea cookies.
Website: www.lifeloveliturgy.com
Twitter: @lifeloveliturgy

CUPID'S STRIKE

MARTIN DAVID EDWARDS

"I'm going on strike," Cupid declares to Venus inside her boudoir. Crossing his arms, he waits for her to respond.

"Don't be so ridiculous. You can't stop working on a whim. It's Valentine's Day," she replies, pursing her lips in front of the mirror.

"But I'm a god. I can do what I want. And there's no better day for making a statement."

"Your father has been filling your head with nonsense again. You're not a proper god and can't do whatever you like. Think of the unhappiness you would cause for your mother in particular."

As Venus leans over to ruffle his hair, Cupid catches a glimpse of the purple-laced corset underneath her dressing gown and blushes.

"You exist to make mortals fall in love. Speaking of which, where are my roses and champagne? My admirers always want something for nothing," she murmurs, before returning her attention to the mirror.

"Making mortals fall in love is boring. As a job, I would call it superficial. It's time that I discovered myself. I'm capable of being so much more. I'm nowhere near my full potential."

"Be a good mother's boy and fetch me my stockings from the closet. Mars is coming for his regular appointment. I'm surprised he could even manage to become your father. He can barely last five minutes," Venus replies, spraying herself in a cloud of myrtle.

"I'm not a child anymore," Venus replies, tugging at his diapers to keep them from falling down from his waist. "I'm going to discover my true self."

"Who is that precisely, my baby?"

"I have no idea. That's the point of looking."

Cupid loosens the straps holding his wings to his shoulders and hangs them on the corner of Venus' mirror. Twisting his back, he then pulls off his bow and the quiver containing two sets of arrows with sharp, gleaming golden and blunt, grey lead tips respectively.

"While I'm on my journey, please don't prick yourself with the lead arrows. I wouldn't want you to start hating whoever you first see," he warns Venus.

"No men can ever hate me when they see me. I'm all they dream about," Venus says, applying slender, black lines of mascara to her eyelashes.

"No-one's going to dream about love while I'm not working. Try gardening instead. Your sleep could be more productive."

"Go and have a swim in the lake to cool yourself, my baby. You know how glad Apollo will be of the company."

"I'm not going to hang about Olympus trying to make friends. London is where I'll find myself. Cool Britannia, here we come."

Cupid sweeps aside a curtain and opens a window, flooding sunshine into Venus' boudoir. She shields her eyes with her mascara brush and squints at him as he climbs through the window frame.

"If it's entertainment you want, I'll unfreeze a

Vestal Virgin. I never liked those stone statues anyway. They stare at the most inopportune moments."

"I don't want entertainment. I want wisdom," Cupid replies.

Licking his finger, he checks the wind direction and jumps through the window frame into the sky below. As the air whistles through his hair, he passes through a cloud and wraps his arms around his head to protect himself from the ground. With a bump, he lands on top of Big Ben. Reaching out, he grabs hold of the minute hand on its clock face to steady himself. But its grip is slippery from pigeon droppings and he slithers downwards to the grey slate roof of Parliament. When a policeman looks up startled at the noise, Cupid shrugs his shoulders. But his diaper bounces on a gargoyle to catapult him out of sight of the policeman and over the Thames. Landing on a concrete walkway by the Southbank, he shivers as a rain drop splatters on its nose.

"Dude, you are one spaced out party animal," a boy resting on a skateboard calls out to him. Scratching a baseball cap turned backwards on his head, he stares at the diapers.

"Let's go skateboarding. In my heart, I'm a teenager," Cupid says.

"I want whatever you're taking," the boy replies.

Cupid follows him to a graffiti-covered underground walkway. Then he picks up a skateboard parked next to a boy busy texting on his phone.

"Hands off," the boy says, placing a hand on the skateboard's wheels.

"Don't mess with me. My dad could turn you into a firework display," Cupid snarls.

"Respect. My dad's an accountant," the boy replies, letting the skateboard go.

"Watch me. I've had eternity to practise," Cupid says.

Mounting the skateboard, he runs up to a concrete ramp. As he nears the top, his feet lose their hold and he collapses onto the concrete in a heap. "Just a warm up," he adds, righting the skateboard for another turn.

But his path is blocked by a group of girls standing facing the boys with their hands on their hips.

"You promised me a date at lunchtime and I'm not thinking of a Happy Meal," a girl says to the boy holding the mobile phone.

"Dating is so like yesterday's news. If you want kissing and cuddling, go and get yourself a puppy," he replies to sniggers from the other boys.

"You're texting another girl. I knew you were cheating on me," the girl says. Snatching the phone from him, she looks at its screen and hands it back. "Skateboarding championships. You could have come back to my place for dessert afterwards, but I'm pre-ditching you instead. Come on girls. Let's go shopping. February 14th, and all guys are so stupid and immature."

With a collective tut, the girls click on their heels to leave the walkway in unison.

"Girls. Who needs the aggravation?" the boy asks Cupid.

"I've decided I'm too old to be a teenager. You've become too bitter and jaded about life, and you're not even properly grown up," Cupid replies, handing the skateboard back.

"I'm not the one wearing the diapers," the boy says.

Leaving the South Bank, Cupid crosses the river and follows the overcoats of the girls as they head through the crowds towards Oxford Circus. When they stop at a set of traffic lights to cross the street, he carries on walking past them with his pace quickening. At the end of Regent Street, he slows to a stop in front of a shop with large clear glass windows. A flashing neon sign proclaims he has arrived at Hamleys, the world's favourite toy store. Inside the empty shop, a man is scurrying around the ground floor pushing teddy bears into a cardboard box.

"I want a Valentine special, just for me. Fluffy and squeaky," Cupid says.

"We're closing," the man says, picking up a stray teddy bear from a shelf.

"You can't shut. I'm discovering my childhood."

"Haven't you heard? Nobody's falling in love anymore. There won't be enough babies being produced to sustain the store. I've had to fire a hundred part-time students already today and it was Valentine's Day."

"Don't think about blaming me. I'm on strike. Ever heard of workers' solidarity?" Cupid asks, picking a teddy bear from the box.

Outside the toy store, his eye is caught by a male mannequin standing in the window of the adjacent shop and wearing a white suit. Dropping the teddy bear into a bin, he hurries inside.

"I'm fed up with being treated like a child. Give me something sophisticated to wear," he says to a woman with a tape measure draped around her neck.

"Sir will certainly be chilling in the February cold. Could I suggest a coat?" the woman replies in an Italian accent, looking down at his diapers.

"The white suit in the window is just the ticket for a sophisticated adult like myself. Find me your smallest size, but I'll want letting out in the waist," Cupid says.

"Sir is surely flattering himself," the woman mutters before she disappears.

Left alone in the shop, Cupid's eye wanders to a stand advertising racks of unsold red socks and silk underpants embossed with horns. When the woman returns carrying the suit, he shakes his head and waves her away.

"You'd be amazed how a spell of industrial action can open your eyes. All these years I thought I was being original," Cupid replies, eyeing the rows of identical gifts. "Instead, I've just been a factory. Mass production stinks," he says, strolling out to the street in his diapers.

Outside in the cold February air, he passes Piccadilly Circus and sees the statue of Eros balanced on its plinth and accompanied only by a solitary pigeon.

"Here's looking at us, sweet eyes. We've been wrong all along. Instead of trying to find ourselves, we should be worrying about what's going on inside. My stomach is definitely rumbling. We're supposed to be *bon viveurs*," he says to the statue, patting his belly.

The pigeon drops a stream of white goo onto his shoulder in response.

"Don't be looking to me for favours when you want to hatch another egg. My strike applies to the animal kingdom as well," he says to the pigeon.

Picking up a discarded flyer from the foot of the statue to wipe away the mess, he reads an advert for a restaurant offering candlelit dinners for two. "The gods can't avoid bestowing their favours on me. Lonely ladies, here we come," he says to the statue.

As he approaches Covent Garden, Cupid recognises the restaurant from the flyer. Banging the doors open, he stamps his feet to warm himself up.

"*Bon soir,*" a waiter says to him. With a bow, he hands Cupid a menu. "You are coming for a Valentine's Day rendezvous perhaps, monsieur?"

"A table for one, but for the starter only. By my main course, I expect to be having company. It's only a question of applying the tricks of the trade."

The waiter leads Cupid to a table, pulls out a chair and removes a napkin with a flourish. Looking around him, Cupid sees a single woman sobbing into a large glass of red wine, while a solitary man is sucking spaghetti into his mouth with his shoulders slumping.

"I thought you were having a Valentine's Day for couples," Cupid says.

"Monsieur is incorrect," the waiter replies, sweeping the napkin at the other tables. "Meals for one are highly popular this evening. You are lucky to have a table free. A cancellation due to the flu. Everyone in London is ill with the horrible weather. Bring me the sunshine of Cannes any day," he sniffs.

"I'll have anything that doesn't feature honey or ambrosia. *Foie gras* and a fillet steak with mushrooms. Rare, with plenty of blood. And give me a bottle of Mum's Gordon Rouge, but send a glass to the table over there. A single girl needs a man with experience to console her," he continues, gesturing to the woman crying into her wine.

When the waiter returns with a bottle, he opens the cork with a loud pop.

"Remember who's the customer," Cupid says under his breath as he sends the waiter over to the table.

The woman looks at the offered glass and bursts into another fit of tears before she runs to the washroom.

"I never liked cry babies. They have a habit of making my arrows sodden," Cupid says to the waiter when he returns from the kitchen carrying a plate of *foie gras*. Tying the napkin around his neck, he licks his lips in anticipation.

"How will monsieur be paying?" the waiter asks, hovering behind the table. "Monsieur will surely appreciate that the bill will be over a hundred pounds, and I am concerned that monsieur might have left his wallet with his jacket at home."

"I don't have to bother with the trivialities of mortals. Send the bill to Olympus, marked for the attention of Venus."

"We have a more practical solution. If monsieur would not mind following me to the kitchen, he will find the chef will be most appreciative of his dish-washing techniques," the waiter replies, removing the plate of *foie gras* from the table.

In the pale dawn light of the following morning, Cupid limps out of the restaurant with his diapers covered with kitchen grease. Hugging himself in the freezing cold, he bumps into a stand outside a doorway advertising a 24-hour gym. Stepping inside, he rings the bell on a reception desk. A man steps out in a sleeveless t-shirt and holding a towel, his muscles bulging.

"G'day sport. You been before?" the man asks in an Australian accent.

"I'd like a six pack by lunchtime," Cupid declares, gawping at the muscles.

"We have an eight-week programme guaranteed to produce results for only five hundred pounds. If you sign today with a disclaimer that is, sport," the man adds.

"If you're trying to say I'm big boned, I'll take my business elsewhere. After the exercise of washing up last night, my inner karma tells me I'm secretly a champion body builder."

"Sure thing sport," the man says, handing Cupid the towel. "Men's changing rooms are down the corridor to the left, but children are usually companied by their *au-pairs*," he confides with an accompanying ripple of muscles.

"You should be more appreciative of my age. I remember introducing your parents to each other. Your mother complained that your father had sheep manure underneath his fingernails until I struck her with an arrow."

"My parents got divorced ten years ago. You need to keep more up to date, sport," the man replies, handing him the towel.

Removing his diaper in the changing room, Cupid wraps the towel around his waist and heads towards the sound of whirring and an occasional grunt from behind a closed door. Opening its handle, he enters a spot-lit room and steps onto a vacant running machine.

As he begins to run, a man lifting weights points at Cupid's waist with his dumb bell. Looking downwards,

Cupid sees his towel has dropped on the floor. Turning crimson, he stoops to pick it up and leaves the room, the door swinging in his wake.

"My poor darling needs comforting. He has such pretty curls," a female voice purrs from behind him in the corridor.

Cupid looks over his shoulder. A woman with platinum blonde hair and strawberry lips totters towards him on high heels.

"I wanted a work out, but I on second thoughts have a much better idea for exercise. Gyms are so inconvenient when you're wearing make-up," she says, flashing her teeth.

"Mars always remembers to look after his son. I don't even mind the specks of lipstick on your molars. Finding yourself is an exhausting business," Cupid replies. Outside the gym as the woman raises her hand to hail a cab, he gives a celebratory skip.

With a click of a key turning in a lock, the woman invites him inside her flat.

"Baby won't mind watching where he steps," she says, pointing at his feet.

"As long as you don't mind staying up all night," Cupid replies, pressing his toes into the thick pile of a carpet.

A meow followed by a sharp jab to his leg makes him suddenly yelp in pain. From the carpet, a white-haired cat hisses at him, before it wraps itself around the woman's legs.

"If I had a lead tip and an arrow free, I'd aim right between your eyes. Then the feeling would be mutual," Cupid whispers at the cat.

"My baby is being so cheeky," the woman replies, giving him a peck.

Kicking off her heels, she leads him to her bedroom and turns off the lights.

"Skipping the preliminaries was going to be my suggestion," Cupid says, his heart racing.

The woman pulls back the duvet on her bed and smoothes down the sheet. Jumping onto the bed, Cupid leans back on the pillow.

"Throughout my journey, I knew my ultimate destination was to become a pleasure machine. Just start with a massage before we move onto extras. After my work-out, my shoulders are bunched up into knots," he says.

"I've got an extra-lovely treat for my cutey curls."

As he closes his eyes, Cupid feels a cold, round tube being placed in his hands. Opening his eyes, he sees a glass of milk, condensation dripping from its side.

"Baby needs his goodnight drink and his sleep," the woman says, pulling the duvet up to his neck.

"I was going to make you the immortal you deserve to be. If the massage is the issue, we can make it mutual at first."

"I'm only offering you what all men deserve," the woman replies. "When they tell you they love you, it's a lie. They only want to use you and then expect to be treated like babies. Revenge is best served straight from the fridge," the woman declares, pouring the milk over his head.

**

An hour later, Venus glances up from the mirror

in her boudoir as Cupid climbs through the window, his hair covered in dripping white streaks.

"You're back," she says, reaching for a powder pad.

"Pleased to see you too, mother," Cupid replies, shaking his hair dry.

"Have you found yourself yet? You better be brief in case you have. I've got another appointment in ten minutes. Your father's discovered blue endurance pills, so he's staying for an extra hour. It's about time mortals invented something useful."

Cupid picks up his wings from the corner of her mirror and straps them to his back. Lifting the quiver, he counts the arrows and tests the bow. "I know exactly who I am, mother. My journey's come full circle," he says.

"My baby has come to his senses. You are exactly who I made you to be," Venus replies, padding her cheeks.

"Look in the mirror, mother. I want us to appreciate your beauty together."

"You should take a break more often. Then I'd consider you for promotion to become a proper god. You might eventually get to exchange the diaper for a toga if you treat your mother nicely."

Looking into the mirror, Venus blows a kiss at her reflection. At its side outside her view, Cupid selects a grey, lead-tipped arrow from his quiver, fits it to his bow and aims for her heart, his hand never wavering.

About Martin David Edwards

Martin David Edwards is a writer living and working in London. He has published short stories previously with *Psychopomp, Bento Box, The Metric* and *Street Cake* magazines. Martin is currently working on a novel, *Death's Last Complaint*. He studied History at Oxford University and at the European University Institute in Florence. Martin is also a photographer and has exhibited in collections in London, New York and Bradford (England). His website is www.storiesbymartin.com.

HEX MCGOWAN AND THE CAT'S MEOW
PATRICK SCALISI

Hex McGowan was a very unlucky individual. Born on Friday the 13th at 1:13 p.m. (that's 13:13 for those of you who prefer the 24-hour clock), Hex was delivered after his mother had spilled a shaker of salt at breakfast that same morning and by a doctor who had dropped his shaving mirror just before coming to the hospital.

If you think it's not possible for someone to have been born under so many bad signs, then join the club— Hex had felt this way for most of his life.

Hex first learned that he was unlucky on his fourth birthday when a tornado—a rare occurrence in Connecticut—totally disrupted his birthday party. Though no party guests were injured, the magician who was hired for the event was never seen again.

At the age of seven, Hex caught one of only 63 reported cases of the measles in the United States that year—despite being immunised. At the age of ten, he was bitten by a black dog named Grim. And at the age of eleven, another tornado touched down on his birthday, a coincidence that was so statistically high that any gambler could have won the lottery three times by comparison.

As a sophomore in high school, Hex was dumped by his girlfriend one week before the big homecoming dance, only to see her show up with a different date. As a junior, he received a car for his 16th birthday. Unfortunately, the engine was stolen the following day as part of a bizarre crime spree that began with Hex's Dodge Neon.

Forced to walk home for the rest of the school year, Hex was not altogether surprised to find that he was being followed by a black cat on an unseasonably warm day in late April. Hex turned to the cat, said hello and continued walking, enjoying the warm spring air. After all, Hex's daily walks were not usually this pleasant. Often, it began raining or snowing just as school ended. Once, toads began falling from the sky like something out of the Old Testament.

"But not today," Hex said to himself. "Today is warm and breezy and the trees are finally starting to bloom."

"You wouldn't know it by how dead they still look," said a voice in response.

"Give 'em a few more weeks," Hex said with a smile. "Then spring'll really be here."

He stopped walking as the words left his mouth.

Who said that? Hex thought.

He turned his head in both directions and found that he was utterly alone, except for the black cat, who was still two paces behind.

"What *are* you looking for?" the voice asked.

"Who's there?" Hex replied aloud, worried that he had finally had the bad luck to go insane.

"I did, clearly, since there's no-one else around."

Hex whirled and caught sight of the cat, who was doing a handstand on his front paws while his tail stood rigid in the air like an exclamation point.

"That got your attention, didn't it?" the cat said as it dropped again to all four paws. "So undignified..."

"You can talk," Hex stated.

The cat sat upright and began washing its front paws. "Wouldn't have gotten very far in life if I couldn't talk," it said.

Hex considered this for a moment. "I guess you're right," he conceded.

"I'm glad you agree," the cat replied. "Now that we've debated my linguistic abilities, perhaps we can get down to business. First thing's first—my name is Rupnik von Whiskers the Third. For simplicity's sake, you can call me Rupnik. Let's walk."

The cat began trotting ahead of Hex, agilely avoiding the pebbles on the side of the road. Hex took a few steps to catch up, then walked alongside his new travelling companion.

"You seem to have gotten over the shock of a talking cat rather quickly," Rupnik said conversationally.

Hex shrugged. "I've had so much bad luck in my life that a talking *black* cat doesn't really faze me, I guess."

"And that's exactly what I need to talk to you about," said Rupnik, who stopped dead in his tracks. "Your bad luck is what we need to save the Cat Guild."

Now Hex really did stare. Brows furrowed, he dropped down to his haunches and looked directly into Rupnik's green eyes. "My bad luck has never helped *anyone*."

Rupnik lifted his front paws onto Hex's knee and replied, "That's about to change."

Dropping to the ground again, the cat resumed

walking without a backward glance.

"What'd you mean?" Hex asked as he hurried to keep up.

By way of an answer, Rupnik replied, "Let me ask you something: Who is a cat's natural enemy?"

"Dogs," Hex said immediately.

Rupnik shook his head. "Incorrect. Modern social teaching would have you think otherwise, but the feline-canine dynamic is much more complex than you realise." The cat stopped, seemed to realise that he had gone off topic, and swished his tail to clear the air. "No, the cat's age-old enemy is the rat. We've been fighting a battle with the armies of the rat king since the dawn of civilisation. In ancient China, the battle was fought over a race to become part of the zodiac. In Europe, in the Middle Ages, campaigns were waged for control of whole castles. While rats sowed the Black Plague among humans, cats fought back against the disease. And in America, rats came to the New World aboard Columbus' ships, seeking a whole new continent in which to wreck havoc."

Rupnik continued, "While the war between rat and cat has lasted for thousands of years, the scales have always been evenly balanced. Victories and losses for both sides, but neither one holding a distinct advantage over the other. Until now. And that's because the rat king has stolen the Cat Guild's most sacred, most powerful weapon—the   Cat's   Meow!"

"I've seen that on TV!" Hex replied. Then, in an imitation spokesman voice, he added, "'Treat your cats special at meal time—Kitten Mix is the cat's meow!'"

Rupnik's whiskers drooped. "You're not taking

this very seriously," he said.

Hex put his hands on his hips and said, "I just don't see what any of this has to do with me."

"You're the only one who can retrieve the Cat's Meow!" the cat answered. "No cat can safely step foot in the court of the rat king, and no human has ever been there."

"Then what makes me any different?" Hex asked.

Rupnik replied, "Your luck. Or rather, your lack thereof. You see, no human would ever be so unlucky as to be kidnapped by the rat king and carried off to his court; no human would have the misfortune to be thrown in the rat king's dungeon; and no human would be so ill-fated as to be forced to escape from such captivity. Except you. You are the only person who can help us."

Hex did not reply. With the cat beside him, he resumed walking the rest of the way home and remained silent until he reached the end of his driveway. Then he looked down at Rupnik once more.

"Suppose I believe you," Hex said. "What's in it for me if I can rescue the Cat's Meow?"

Rupnik nodded knowingly. "We expected that you might ask for some kind of compensation and are prepared to pay it. The head of the Cat Guild is a powerful feline. Lady Nile can provide many things—she may even be able to turn your luck around."

"I'll think about it," Hex replied. He turned and began stalking toward his house.

Rupnik did not give chase. Instead, he shouted out, "You won't have time to think about it. Be prepared. And remember that the rats hate freckles!"

Hex waved over his shoulder, then crossed the

last hundred feet to his front door. His conversation with Rupnik was mostly forgotten by the time he burned his dinner in the microwave and realised that he had taken the wrong textbooks home to do his schoolwork.

**

By the time Hex went to bed, he had convinced himself once more that there was no such thing as talking cats, rat monarchs, or a war between felines and rodents. Still, it took him a long time to fall asleep. When he did, he dreamed that he was floating on his back through a dark void, unable to move or speak. Yet there was also something comforting about the darkness, like the swaying of the sea, and Hex gave himself over to the motion. Cares and worries and even his bad luck seemed to drop away as he floated through the nothingness like a piece of stray newspaper on the wind.

Like most dreams, Hex lost all sense of time and place; he may have been asleep for hours or minutes. All he knew was that it was pitch black when he awoke— and that the swaying motion of his body did not disappear with the dream. He tried to move and could not. He tried to speak and could not. Somehow his dream had bled over into reality.

"Hey, I think he's waking up!" whispered a voice urgently next to Hex's right ear.

"Don't worry about it. We're almost there," replied another gruff voice.

Hex began to struggle now, desperate to break free or wake from what he thought might be a dream within a dream.

"I told you he was awake!" exclaimed the first

voice.

"Can't be having that," answered the second. "Milt, give him a poke!"

Hex felt something sharp poke into the small of his back. He jumped as the point pressed into his skin, then stopped struggling.

"That did it," said the second voice, and the swaying continued.

Hex shut his eyes tightly and willed himself to wake up. That didn't work, and he realised with stark terror that he was no longer dreaming. Somehow, he had been carried off from his bed, just as Rupnik has predicted. Hex could also guess the identity of his kidnappers without looking down at the multiple small bodies that carried him.

In moments, the darkness began to pull back like a set of stage curtains. Craning his neck, Hex saw that the light came from torches that were set along the battlements of a large castle. The gray walls of the keep were so worn that they were almost black, having seen countless ages of wind and weather. Window slits broke the wall at intervals, where defenders could shoot arrows, spears or stones at an attacking force.

The swaying continued without pause, and Hex was carried under the castle's main portcullis. As he and his captors passed into the main courtyard, Hex could hear the sound of footfalls underneath him as many clawed feet *click-clacked* on the cobblestones. Then he was through another doorway and into the castle proper.

Through his peripheral vision, Hex could make out tapestries lining the walls as he was carried through countless hallways. Finally, the company stopped before a massive wood-and-iron-bound door.

After what seemed like hours, during which Hex's body became more and more cramped, the doors swung open with a great groan, their weight taxing the hinges. Hex was carried to the centre of a large room with a high, buttressed ceiling, where he was finally allowed to sit up.

If the room appeared large to Hex, it must have seemed enormous to the rats. The chamber, which appeared to serve as the throne room, was lined with rats in mismatched pieces of armour, bearing swords or wicked-looking pikes. At the centre of the room was a stone dais decorated in mosaic and topped by a golden throne. And on the throne perched a rat that was easily the size of Rupnik von Whiskers the Third, if not larger.

The large rat swung his feet onto the dais and lurched forward. He, too, wore a suit of armour, as well as a cape made from the hide of a calico cat. When the rodent was still a few feet away, he stopped to examine his captive, twitching his bent gray whiskers and sniffing loudly with a nose that resembled scarred brown leather. Hex recoiled from the rat's carrion stench.

"Report, Lord Mange," said the large rat to a member of the kidnapping party.

Another rat, this one wearing a helmet made from the skull of a kitten, stepped forward and dropped to one knee. When he spoke, Hex recognised his voice as the second of his two speaking captors.

"My liege," began Lord Mange, "we captured the human as you ordered. He definitely had a meeting with the cats, sire—he outright reeks of them."

The large rat nodded in agreement and said,

"Human, I am King Longtail Plaguespreader the Twenty-eighth, ruler of the rat kingdom. Why did the cats reveal their presence to you?"

Hex, exhausted and suddenly angry at having been dragged from his bed in the middle of the night, screwed up his face and said, "I'm not telling you anything." The words sounded very brave as they left his mouth, but their pitch changed as they echoed off the buttressed ceiling. As the word "anything" repeated itself, it became shriller and shriller with each reverberation.

The king shrugged and said to Lord Mange, "Throw him in the dungeon, then. He can rot there for all I care."

At a gesture from Lord Mange, the rats began to circle their captive. Hex shrank back from their weapons when he suddenly remembered what Rupnik had said about freckles. Knowing that he had a number of the marks on his arms and shoulders, Hex lifted his pyjama shirt over his head and yelled in triumph.

The rats stared back at him, confused.

"He's mad," muttered Lord Mange.

Hex thrust his left shoulder forward, holding the freckled skin inches from the advancing rats. But the rodents only stared at one another in perplexity, then shrugged and continued their advance.

In seconds, Hex was on his back again, being carried through another endless series of corridors with his shirt crumpled atop his bare chest. The light dimmed more and more as the party descended into the lower depths of the castle until Hex was finally placed in front of an empty cell and prodded inside.

Lord Mange stepped into the cell's doorway.

"We'll be down to check on you in a week or two. Maybe then you'll feel like talking."

The rat kicked the cell door shut, which echoed terribly throughout the dungeon. Then the party of kidnappers marched away, leaving Hex utterly alone and naked from the waist up.

**

Hex replaced his pyjama shirt and examined his surroundings. His cell was about the size of a small bathroom with bars for walls. The bars themselves were sunk several inches into both the floor and ceiling, and despite being worn and rusty with age, they were no less immobile. The rear wall was made out of stone blocks, windowless, and featured intricate tapestries of cobwebs and moth cocoons.

Hex sunk to the cobblestone floor as terror and despair began to attack him from all sides. The cell seemed to contract, the walls and shadows getting closer and closer. Hex closed his eyes and tried to breathe, all the while muttering, "Freckles, they were supposed to be afraid of freckles."

Something stirred in one of the other cells as claws scraped first on the cobblestone floor, then rang out as they gripped the metal bars.

"Did someone call my name?" a voice asked.

Hex opened his eyes and looked for the speaker. Two cells away stood a large tomcat, his fur mostly orange except for his face, which was white. Hex noticed that one of the cat's eyes was missing and that his left ear was ragged with old cuts and scars.

"Leave me alone," Hex said miserably.

The cat cocked his head to one side, his good eye glowing in the dim light.

"Who are you?" the tomcat asked. "How did you come to be here? The rats have never taken a human before."

By way of an answer, Hex said, "Rupnik lied."

"Rupnik!" the cat replied. "You know Rupnik von Whiskers the Third?"

But Hex plowed on without hearing: "They were supposed to be afraid of freckles. I showed them my freckles, and they didn't even flinch."

Then the cat started to laugh, a frail sound that was swallowed by the dungeon almost as soon as it began.

"*I'm* Freckles!" the cat exclaimed. "And of course they're afraid of me. Why else would I be down here?"

It took some time for this statement to sink in. When it had, Hex's surprise quickly gave way to embarrassment as he recalled his actions in the throne room.

"Tell me how you know Rupnik," the cat insisted.

Hex looked up at his fellow prisoner. "Tell me why they call you Freckles," he retorted.

Freckles nodded. "I guess you deserve that much." The cat began pacing back and forth in his cell, "My name's not really Freckles, of course. It's Tigerpaw."

A pause followed this statement in which the cat waited expectantly.

"And?" Hex prompted.

"You've never heard of me?" Tigerpaw (or Freckles) exclaimed. "Never heard of the legendary cat warrior Tigerpaw? Never heard of the famous Rout at

Red Barn? I led that battle!"

"That doesn't explain why a warrior cat named Tigerpaw is called Freckles."

The cat sighed. "It's because of the orange spots on my face."

Hex peered through the dim light and could just make out a series of small orange spots on the cat's otherwise white face.

"So," Tigerpaw continued, "I answered your question. Now it's time to answer mine. How do you know Rupnik?"

"Rupnik—I wish I had never met him!" Hex said. "He's brought me nothing but bad luck—even more than usual!"

"Yes, but how were you captured?" Tigerpaw pressed.

"That's just it!" Hex said. "It wouldn't have happened if Rupnik hadn't asked me to get back something called the 'Cat's Meow.'"

Tigerpaw's jaw dropped. "The rats have the Cat's Meow?!" the tomcat exclaimed. "We have to get it back!"

Before Hex could argue further, Tigerpaw began throwing himself against the walls and door of his cell. The echoes of his body crashing against the metal bars reverberated throughout the dungeon. To this ruckus, Tigerpaw added a series of sorrowful meows, and the noise created such a cacophony that Hex pressed his palms against his ears to keep sane.

"What are you doing?!" Hex cried, but Tigerpaw didn't seem to hear him above the ruckus.

Presently, a pair of rat sentries descended through the gloom to stand before Tigerpaw's cell.

"He's finally lost it," said the first rat in a calm, sensible voice.

"He's giving me a headache!" said the second rat irritably.

"Just leave him be," continued Sensible Rat.

"I'm going to knock his head off," finished Agitated Rat.

Agitated Rat unsheathed his sword and removed a set of keys from his belt. As he entered the cell, Sensible Rat smartly moved to block the doorway.

The rats, though, would have had better luck trying to stop a thunderstorm. As soon as the rodents were inside his cell, Tigerpaw leapt into action. His movements stopped being frantic and instead became fluid bursts of militant energy. Using all four paws and his tail, the cat bounded from the floor to the wall, launching himself upon the first of his jailers. Agitated Rat fell in a heap, his sword hitting the floor with a clatter as his head slapped against the cobblestones. Instantly, he was unconscious. Sensible Rat turned and tried to escape, but not before Tigerpaw slipped his tail between the cell door. With a yowl of pain, the cat forced the door open, even as Sensible Rat tried to slam the portal closed again. In seconds, Tigerpaw had shoved his way into the dungeon corridor and was raining blows down upon the second rat sentry.

Hex watched all of this with a mixture of horror and amazement. The skirmish was over in seconds, and Tigerpaw made his way to Hex's cell with the set of keys held in his mouth.

"Why didn't you escape sooner?" Hex asked as the cat tried one key after another.

"Couldn't do it alone," Tigerpaw replied. Then, finding the right key, he swung open the door to Hex's cell. He continued, "With you around, I'd give us even odds of finding the Cat's Meow and getting out of here alive."

Hex shook his head. "I'm getting out of here *now*. Forget the Cat's Meow."

Tigerpaw sank his teeth into Hex's pyjama-clad leg. Hex cried out and jumped back against the cell door.

"What was that for?!"

"To wake you up!" the cat replied. "The rats know who you are now. They won't leave you alone without the protection of the Cat Guild. And without the Cat's Meow, the Cat Guild can't protect anyone. So you see, boy, you're stuck with me retrieving the Cat's Meow whether you like it or not."

Hex bent down to rub his leg. "You didn't have to bite me," he said sullenly. "And don't call me 'boy'. My name is Hex."

"Well, I hope our luck is better than your name," Tigerpaw said.

Hex scoffed. "Don't count on it."

Tigerpaw returned to the unconscious rats and retrieved their weapons. He took one of the swords for himself and handed the other to Hex. And while the sword looked positively threatening in the paws of the cat, the weapon seemed no larger than a steak knife to Hex.

The rats thus disarmed, Tigerpaw began shaking Sensible Rat awake. The rodent slowly came back to consciousness, only to find a sword at his throat.

"I'm only going to ask this once," Tigerpaw said

while pressing the confiscated weapon into the rat's flesh. "Where is the Cat's Meow?"

Sensible Rat looked down at the sword with crossed eyes and stammered, "It's ... it's in the king's private chambers. Off the throne room."

"Directions, my dear rat," Tigerpaw continued. "How do we get there?"

In a quavering voice, Sensible Rat outlined the route from the dungeon to the throne room. When this was done, Tigerpaw brought the handle of his sword down on the rat's head, then tossed both sentries into one of the empty cells.

"We're going to have to fight all the way there," Tigerpaw said to Hex. "Are you with me?"

Hex looked sceptically at his steak-knife sword. "Do I have much of a choice?"

"Not if you want to get out of here and stay alive."

Hex rolled his eyes and followed Tigerpaw up the stairs to exit the dungeon. Expecting opposition from the rats at any moment, they were shocked to find that no guards were there to stop their escape.

The two companions continued unchallenged out of the dungeon and into the castle proper. They navigated down corridors and through assorted castle chambers without encountering anyone, and the entire fortress was quiet except for a muted noise that seemed to come from somewhere just out of earshot.

"What's that sound?" Hex asked, stopping in the middle of another empty passageway.

"I don't know," Tigerpaw replied, his ears twitching. "More importantly, where are all the rats?"

The answer came moments later as Hex and

Tigerpaw arrived at a terrace overlooking the courtyard. The thick stone walls of the castle had muffled the sound they had heard for what it really was: a battle! Rats lined the castle walls and ramparts, trying desperately to defend against an invading force. A breach had been made in the castle's main gates, and through the splintered timbers, Hex and Tigerpaw could see the armies of the Cat Guild engaged in furious combat with the rat legions.

"C'mon!" Tigerpaw exclaimed. "The Guild is giving us the chance we need to get the Cat's Meow!"

Hex and the cat warrior raced from the terrace and toward their destination. Here they encountered their first resistance: sentries left to guard the entrance to the throne room. Before Hex could even bring his "sword" to bear, Tigerpaw was moving like an orange blur, toppling the sentries and cutting into them with his weapon. In seconds, the way was clear, and the two companions barrelled their way inside.

More rat warriors waited within. Tigerpaw charged forward with a hiss, followed less enthusiastically by Hex. When one of the sentries broke from the main group to raise the alarm, Tigerpaw cried out, "Stop him!"

Acting purely on instinct, Hex kicked out and caught the fleeing rat with the tip of his foot. Though not a particularly powerful kick, the blow sent the rat flying across the throne room. Tigerpaw and the sentries stopped their fighting to stare at Hex.

For the first time since his kidnapping, Hex realised how much *larger* he was than most of his foes, and with that realisation, his fear began to drop away.

Brandishing his sword, Hex charged into the remaining sentries with what he hoped was a fearsome war cry. For their part, the rats seemed finally to realise how foolish they had been to kidnap a human. They scattered to all corners of the room before fleeing altogether.

"Well done," said Tigerpaw, rubbing up momentarily against Hex's leg.

"Uh ... thanks," replied Hex, with a lopsided grin.

With the throne room empty, cat and human began to scan the area for the rat king's chamber. Hex spotted it first—a door behind the throne dais. The two companions charged forward, expecting to find more sentries within.

The room, though, was unoccupied, which was quite a shock considering that it held the rat king's personal horde.

The chamber was perfectly round and piled high with chests full of missing rings, assorted charms and broken bits of golden bracelets. There were other oddities, too, like a golden shrimp fork, a dozen gold paperclips and one very large gold needle with a pearl head.

"How are we going to find it in all this junk?" Hex asked.

"It's right here," Tigerpaw replied as he pointed with his sword to a pedestal in the centre of the room.

Hex was nearly beside himself. "*That's* the Cat's Meow?!"

Tigerpaw shrugged. "What did you expect?"

Hex wanted to reply that he had expected a sword inlaid with precious metals and stones, a weapon to strike fear into the hearts of the rats. Or a sceptre topped with the biggest ruby he had ever seen that would be used to lead the feline armies into battle. Or even a silver collar studded with spikes and a large bell—a symbol for the cats to rally around in times of trouble.

What Hex did not expect was a mason jar filled only with a small green glow, like a single emerald firefly.

Hex cocked his head. "Huh?"

"This is the treasure of the Cat Guild, handed down from the time of Bast, our greatest hero," said Tigerpaw reverently. "It is passed from one leader to the next, endowing him or her with the Commanding Roar that is feared by rats everywhere." Tigerpaw paused and looked from the mason jar to Hex. "Small cats like us can't roar, just as big cats like lions and tigers can't purr. That changes with the Cat's Meow. One of our number can use the Commanding Roar to send the rats fleeing and to rally the armies of the cat nation to a shared cause."

"Then let's take it and get out of here," said Hex.

"You're not going anywhere."

Hex and Tigerpaw turned toward the door of the chamber—only to find it blocked by the impressive bulk of King Longtail Plaguespreader. Taking another step into the room, the rat king removed his cloak of calico cat fur and unsheathed the two swords that hung on his belt, holding one in his hand and one with his tail.

"Your plan was exceptional," King Longtail continued. "An outside diversion while the 'prisoners' steal back the Cat's Meow. But you and this human will now die like the rest of the cat army."

King Longtail launched himself at the intruders, the points of both swords lunging forward. Hex and

Tigerpaw leaped to either side of the room to avoid the attack, crashing into the treasure that was piled high along the circular walls. Tigerpaw recovered his balance quickly and brought his sword to bear. Hex, however, slipped on the bracelet fragments and went barrelling into a treasure chest full of mismatched earrings. In the process, he lost his sword among the collapsing debris and could only watch as Tigerpaw danced around the room in single combat with King Longtail, dodging and parrying blows from the rat monarch's two swords.

"I have longed to fight the one they call Freckles," the rat king said. "When I kill you, I will wear your tail as my new scarf."

By way of reply, Tigerpaw swung furiously at King Longtail, overbalancing and nearly falling forward into his adversary. The rat king thrust forward agilely with both swords, and while Tigerpaw managed to avoid the blow from one, the second glanced his head and took off the top of his good right ear.

It was Tigerpaw's scream of pain that prodded Hex into action. Lifting himself from among the scattered treasure, Hex saw that the cat warrior was backed against the wall by King Longtail, blood streaming from atop his head. The rat king lifted both his swords for a killing blow.

Hex grabbed the closest weapon at his disposal: the large needle with the pearl head. In his hand, the needle was nearly the size of a small machete and deadly sharp. Charging forward with a grimace and eyes closed, Hex swung blindly at the rat king. The needle met some resistance about halfway through its arc, which was followed by the clatter of metal and a cry of agony. Hex opened his eyes to find that he had severed the rat king's tail.

Tigerpaw rolled away from the wall and out of range of King Longtail's remaining sword. But the rat monarch was no longer interested in fighting. Pushing Hex down with his free claw, King Longtail fled the room with large drops of blood pulsing from his hindquarters. In moments, Hex and Tigerpaw could hear the rats calling a retreat.

Tigerpaw stood over Hex and offered to help him up.

"Thank you," Hex said. He looked down and saw that he was still holding the golden needle. When he returned his gaze to Tigerpaw, he saw that the cat warrior was sitting back on his haunches with head bowed.

"Don't—" Hex began to stammer.

"You saved my life," Tigerpaw cut in.

"C'mon," Hex replied. "I just want to get out of here."

**

The scene in the castle courtyard was one of utter destruction. Abandoned weapons and armour were strewn everywhere, while cat soldiers piled up rat carcasses in one corner and prisoners in another. Voices and meows filled the square, and in the centre of it all stood Rupnik von Whiskers the Third and a regal Siamese with beige fur and brown points on her tail and ears.

A few of the cats saw Tigerpaw and Hex emerge from the castle proper. Cries of "Freckles!" went up from those nearest, attracting the attention of the Siamese.

"Lady Nile," Tigerpaw breathed as he bowed his head respectfully.

"Freckles!" the Siamese purred affectionately. "We thought you were dead."

"Much to the rat's dismay, I have survived," Tigerpaw replied. "Though I fear my grooming is not appropriate for an audience." The cat warrior flicked the remains of his right ear, which was crusted now in dried blood.

"See to it that a physician examines you," Lady Nile commanded.

Tigerpaw nodded, then stood upright and left Hex alone with Rupnik and the head of the Cat Guild.

"And this is our saviour," Lady Nile continued, looking at Hex and his golden needle.

"I knew he could do it," Rupnik added.

"Tigerpaw—er, Freckles—did most of the work," Hex insisted, pointing to the cat warrior, who was being examined by another cat in a snowy white coat.

"Please," Lady Nile insisted. "Tell us all that has happened to you."

Sitting cross-legged on the ground with the Cat's Meow in his lap, Hex related the tale of his kidnapping (but excluded the part about removing his pyjama shirt) while Rupnik and Lady Nile sat on their haunches and listened. He told about being brought to the rat castle, his meeting with Tigerpaw, their escape from the dungeon and their battle with King Longtail Plaguespreader.

When he finished, Lady Nile nodded solemnly and said, "I have one final task for you, Hex McGowan, if you would be so kind as to accept it."

"I'm listening," Hex replied cautiously.

The head of the Cat Guild batted gently at the mason jar. "Would you kindly open this? I'm afraid without thumbs it's a task we cats have never been able to master."

Hex smiled and unscrewed the jar. As he lifted the top, the green light floated gracefully into the air. Lady Nile inhaled deeply, drawing the light into her mouth and swallowing. Then she flicked her whiskers and licked her jowls.

"Thank you," she said.

Rupnik turned to the Siamese and said, "I promised Hex some kind of compensation, and I think it's only fitting seeing as what we put him through."

Lady Nile nodded. "I'm afraid I have a confession to make, Hex. It was not your bad luck that resulted in your kidnapping. We desperately needed the help of a human, and I'm afraid our intelligence agents alerted the rats to your presence. If not for their intervention, the rats would have never taken you."

Hex couldn't form a reply. And yet, it was difficult to remain angry at the regal Lady Nile, whose blue eyes held more than a hint of intelligence. Indeed, Hex saw that the Siamese was deeply troubled by the Cat Guild's deception.

"There are times when we must be no better than the rats," Lady Nile said quietly to Hex.

Hex sighed and nodded. "I understand," he said. Then he paused, as if considering, and added, "If anything, I'd like to find a way to break my unlucky streak."

"That started with the warm weather when we

walked home together yesterday," Rupnik said. "And it ended when you cut off the tail of the rat king. Among the Cat Guild, Hex, the tail of a rat is a sign of valour and good fortune."

Lady Nile stood, stretched and nuzzled against Hex's knee.

"I believe your bad luck may finally have ended," she said.

**

Hex returned home that same day with Rupnik and Tigerpaw as his escorts. The rats' castle, he discovered, was part of a derelict amusement park in the next town over. Knowing this, Hex was amazed that the rats had been able to carry him so far.

Hex was allowed to keep the golden needle as a souvenir of his adventures. He promised Lady Nile that he would keep it safe and hidden, but with his luck, he knew it was only a matter of time before his parents would find it.

And luck was something that dominated most of Hex's thoughts on the way home. While Tigerpaw related to Rupnik a blow-by-blow account of their battle with King Longtail, Hex considered Lady Nile's claim that his bad luck had finally come to an end. He was encouraged by the fact that it was not snowing or sleeting or raining toads, but it was only when Hex walking inside that he noticed something had changed.

His parents, both sitting in the kitchen, greeted him warmly and asked about his morning walk. Then they commended him on his commitment to exercise. Neither seemed to notice that he had been missing all night.

"Oh, and before I forget," added Hex's mother, "the police called this morning."

Hex's growing happiness sputtered.

"Don't make that face," she chided in a cheerful voice. "They finally caught those car engine thieves. All the parts have been recovered, and the insurance is going to pay to fix your car."

Hex was at a loss for words. Finally, he said, "I think I'm gonna get a little more fresh air."

Walking outside again, Hex saw Rupnik sitting on the front stoop licking his flanks while Tigerpaw stalked a pair of squirrels.

"Anything different?" Rupnik asked between licks.

"Yes, as a matter of fact," Hex replied. "I... don't believe it."

Rupnik stopped his grooming and turned to Hex. "That Lady Nile is really something," he said. "I think she'll go down as one of the greatest leaders in cat history."

Rupnik rose, stretched and called to Tigerpaw, who had managed to chase the squirrels across the street. "Time to get back," Rupnik said. "Don't worry, Hex. The Cat Guild will keep an eye out to make sure the rats don't bother you."

Tigerpaw bounded forward and bowed his head once more. "It was an honour fighting with you," he said. "Do you think we'll see each other again?"

"I think so," Hex replied. "Knowing us, it would be just our luck."

About Patrick Scalisi

Patrick Scalisi is a journalist, magazine editor and author from Connecticut. He has published fiction in several magazines and anthologies, and served as editor of *The Ghost Is the Machine*, an anthology of steampunk-horror stories from Post Mortem Press. His first book, *The Horse Thieves and Other Tales of the New West,* will be released in early 2014. When he's not writing, Pat enjoys watching way too many movies than are good for him, reading more books than he has shelves for and listening to music (his tastes range from classical to classic and modern rock). Visit Pat online at patrickscalisi.com

MONSTER

TERENCE TOH

Lily had been eight years old when she first saw the Creature under her bed.

It had been a quiet night. She had been reading a book of fairy stories, when there was the sound of snarling.

Curious, she had peeked under her bed, and regretted it instantly.

There was a creature lurking in the shadows. He had dark crimson eyes, which glittered like rubies, and five curved horns that formed a crown on his brow. Long talons, jagged little razorblades, extended from his hands and feet.

"Hello, little girl. I want to eat you up!" the creature licked his lips. His voice was heavy and guttural.

Lily screamed and ran to her parent's room. The creature's mad laughter echoed from behind her.

Her father, a tall man with a bushy moustache, held her hand and led her back to her room with a flashlight.

"See Lily? There's nothing here," he said, waving the flashlight under the bed. "It's all in your imagination, honey."

Her father hugged her, and planted a kiss on her forehead.

"Don't you worry about monsters," he said. "As long as I'm around, you have nothing to fear."

**

Her Daddy stayed with her for two more years.

Lily would forever remember the day he left.

She and Mommy had been baking muffins in the kitchen. They had been talking about a trip to the zoo: Lily had been especially excited to see the elephants and the bears. And then the phone had rang, and Mommy went to pick it up.

When she walked back into the kitchen, Lily noticed Mommy's eyes were wet.

There had been an accident at Daddy's workplace.

Mommy sat Lily on her lap. Daddy had gone to a better place, and they would never see him again, she told her. And Lily didn't understand all this, but Mommy was crying, and that made her sad, and so Lily started crying too, and for the whole night, they held each other, mother and daughter, weeping.

The next few days were very confusing. They made Lily dress in black, and they went to the church, which they normally only went to on Sundays. Many aunties and uncles she had not seen for ages were there, and most of them were weeping around Daddy, who they had put into a long wooden box.

They told her that Daddy was having a long sleep, and would never wake up. A man in a black robe and funny collar corrected them: no, that was not true. He would wake up, someday, in a time far, far in the future, and all of them would be reunited, forever in happiness, for the rest of eternity.

But Lily didn't want that. She wanted her Daddy

now, with his smile and laugh and hugs. She wanted him to pick her up again, and pat her on the head, and take her to the garden to show her things like beetles and millipedes, although she found them scary.

Lily wanted her Daddy, who would protect her from the bad things, like the Creature.

She still saw him under the bed from time to time.

Most of the time, she only heard him. The *clink-clink* of his talons as he tapped them against the bed's steel frame. His low, heavy breathing and his bestial snarls. Sometimes, he would mutter to himself, saying strange things like "The blood rain pours on the innocent and the guilty alike. Yes it does, yes it does."

Many nights, he was not there at all, and Lily was glad for it.

Other nights, however, he was restless, and that was terrifying. The Creature would shake the bed, curse and scream, and threaten to kill her in her sleep.

On one occasion, the Creature had ripped his own head off and left it by her pillow, where it had grinned at her. She had nightmares for a week.

Lily usually dealt with these things by hiding under her blankets, and crying for it to go away. When things got too much, she would call her Daddy, who would appear with his torchlight and trusty attack pillow. He'd shine his light under the bed, which always scared the monster away, and then make her laugh with a joke. Sometimes, he'd even make her a mug of hot chocolate, with marshmallows in it.

Without her Daddy, however, Lily had no defence against the Creature.

"Go away!" she'd scream as he laughed and gibbered and cursed.

"Where is your knight now?" He would respond mockingly. "Gone, all gone, leaving you cold and alone!" He would gnash its teeth, and Lily would tremble and cry.

The Creature never actually touched her: he had no need of that. His voice alone was enough to terrify this lost little girl.

The year Daddy left was an extremely difficult one for Lily.

The little girl found herself doing poorly in school. Lily had few friends, as most of her classmates didn't understand why she was so gloomy all the time. Some of them made fun of her for not having a father. They were difficult days.

And one day, things got worse.

Mommy brought a man to the house. He was tall, with spiky brown hair, and had ear-rings, which Lily found strange because she thought only girls wore those.

They had met at a company picnic, Mommy explained, and she was very much in love with him. They had been seeing each other for quite some time now, and soon, they would get married.

Lily did not understand.

In short, Mommy explained, he was going to be her new Daddy.

Lily found this even harder to understand. She only had one Daddy, who was now resting in a coffin beneath the earth. She still loved him, and had no desire to have a new Daddy.

Besides, she did not like this new Daddy. There was something off-putting about him. His smile did not seem real: New Daddy did not smile with his eyes.

She couldn't even bear to call him Daddy. No, he would never take her old Daddy's place. She took to calling him 'Uncle', the term she used when calling other men, and when her Mommy made her call him 'Daddy', she combined the two, referring to him as 'Uncle Daddy'.

Her new father was not amused, but she would not call him anything else.

Uncle Daddy was a very strange man. Sometimes he was nice, giving her sweets and making jokes while watching TV with Mommy and her.

Most of the time, however, he was unpleasant.

He liked going out late at night. While Daddy always came home by nine, just in time to read bedtime stories, Uncle Daddy usually returned at midnight or later. He would smell terrible, and be awfully rude, shouting bad words that kids at school would get punished for saying.

Mommy asked him to stop, but Uncle Daddy refused. He would get angry, and there would be an argument that would last long into the night. Sometimes he would hit her, which would make Mommy cry.

Uncle Daddy was mean to Lily too, finding fault with her over the smallest things. He often asked her to bring him snacks from the fridge while watching television, and if Lily brought the wrong thing, he would fly into a rage. Once, he caned her so hard she could not walk properly for a day. She had cried and cried.

Uncle Daddy would be sorry after that. He would come to her contrite, tears in his eyes, begging for forgiveness.

But it was when he was remorseful that Lily was

most afraid of him.

Uncle Daddy's apologies were very *touchy*. When he hugged her, his hands would wander all over her body, touching her in places that made her uncomfortable. Once, he tried to kiss her on her mouth: if not for Lily's squirming, he would have succeeded.

But it was when he used his tongue that Lily really felt terrified. Lily remembered a morning when she had woken up to see Uncle Daddy bent over her, shirtless. He had unbuttoned her pyjamas, and had apparently been kissing and licking her chest.

His trousers were half-open.

Lily asked what he was doing, and Uncle Daddy told her it was a special way for fathers to show love for their daughters.

"So you can't tell anyone about this, okay?" he said. "Pinky promise? No-one would understand it."

Lily however, could never believe him.

Her old Daddy never did anything like this. His touch was kind and loving. Uncle Daddy's touch however, felt *wrong*, felt grown up and disgusting and hollow, and made her feel dirty all over.

The strange thing was even he seemed not to like it. Once, Uncle Daddy had broken away from her during a hug, and rushed to the kitchen, where he downed a bottle of beer. There was a look of repulsion on his face, and tears in his eyes.

"What am I doing?" he kept muttering. "Bloody hell, what am I doing?"

And for the next few days, Uncle Daddy would not even dare come near her.

But then something would happen, and the cycle

would repeat itself. Lily would somehow make Daddy upset, and he would try to make things up by touching her, tickling her, caressing her everywhere. Occasionally, he would still look disgusted with himself, but those times grew fewer as time went by.

Lily started locking her door when Uncle Daddy was at home. Her Mommy scolded her for doing so, but it was all right.

She'd take her Mommy's anger over her Daddy's love any day of the week.

**

One day, Lily got into serious trouble with Uncle Daddy.

She had forgotten to put her shoes on the rack upon coming home from school. You couldn't blame her: she had had a stomach-ache at the time, and had raced to the toilet as fast as her little legs could carry her.

Uncle Daddy, however, had not been happy.

He had stormed into Lily's room, screaming her name. Lily had just came out of the bathroom: he grabbed her by the ear and forced her on her bed, before pulling off his belt.

He beat Lily seven times on her legs, ignoring her screams.

When she started crying, however, Uncle Daddy softened. He sat by her, and kissed her gently on her forehead.

"I'm so sorry, Lily," he cooed. "I've got a bad temper, and I can't control it. But always know that Daddy loves you. And he'd never do anything to hurt you."

Uncle Daddy started to caress her. He stroked her chest, and was about to move down to her legs, when there was suddenly the sound of the front door opening.

He stopped.

Mommy was back.

"Goodnight, child," Uncle Daddy said. He ignored her squirming, as he kissed her lips, and left.

That night, when the lights were off, the Creature emerged from under the bed.

"I want to eat your flesh," he had said menacingly, clinking his talons on the bed-frame. "I want to rip your skin and feast on your bones!"

Lily's eyes were red with tears.

"Do it," she said.

There was a brief silence.

"What?" the creature was perplexed.

"Come on," Lily cried. "What are you waiting for?"

She stretched out her hand to the Creature defiantly.

"You are no longer afraid of me!" the Creature said, and there was frustration in its rough voice. "Why, child?"

"You are a very scary monster," Lily said. "But my new Daddy... he scares me more."

"What? Why?"

And Lily broke down into tears, and told the Creature everything her Uncle Daddy had done.

The Creature listened in silence.

Her stories filled him with rage. It was no wonder she was not afraid of him anymore, he realised. What her stepfather was doing violated the natural order. Fathers, whether through blood or not, were supposed to protect their children.

He really should pack up and go, he thought. He would find no nourishing fear here. He should find another kid to terrify. A nice juicy screamer, maybe, whose nightmares would make him fat.

After all, Shadow-Beasts were solitary and reclusive by nature. Empathy was a foreign concept for them.

Yet the Creature found himself staying, and listening.

It was the first time one of his victims had actually spoken to him. And the Creature had to admit, he found that fascinating.

**

As the nights went on, Lily and the Creature had many conversations.

Lily told him of the terrible things Uncle Daddy did to her and Mommy, and how she hated him so much it made her stomach hurt. Uncle Daddy made Mommy sad, she said, and they fought a lot. Uncle Daddy spent too much of their money on beer, while Mommy wanted to save money for Lily to go to college.

Whenever Mommy tried to talk to Uncle Daddy, he hit her. Once he had hit Mommy so hard she had fainted. Lily had never felt so scared.

"You have to tell someone," the Creature had said. "You can't keep letting him do this."

"I can't," Lily said. "Uncle Daddy would hit me."

"You have to be brave, little girl."

"But I'm not," she said sadly.

Lily told him about how embarrassed she was

about going to school with red cane marks all over her legs, and how her classmates always teased her and called her names. One girl had called her 'Stupid Face', and Lily had chased her and slapped her across the face: she had gotten into serious trouble. The headmaster had scolded Lily and made her apologise.

"I felt crummy after that. But I'd do it all over again," Lily said defiantly.

The Creature laughed.

Lily told him of funny episodes of Spongebob she had seen. Of bunny-shaped clouds in the sky, of her teacher's jokes, of the delicious peanut butter and cheese sandwiches her mother made for her to take to school. She told the Creature of the little dog that had followed her home one day, only to be chased away by Uncle Daddy. She told him of the time she and Indran, a handsome curly-haired boy she hoped she would marry one day, spent recess blowing bubbles outside the canteen. She told him of the man with the funny hat she had seen on the bus, and the time she, Mommy and Daddy had gone to Japan, and eaten ice creams after a fireworks display.

Yes, Uncle Daddy was still doing things to her, and Lily was still doing badly at school. But despite all that, there was happiness in Lily's heart, a hope that kept her strong. For now, for the first time in her life, she had someone to talk to.

Lily had always wanted a friend. She would never have expected, however, to find it in the shape of a shadowy monster with fangs and talons.

The Creature told her about his life, as well.

He told her his true name, Volstrak, and his clan,

and of the day he was spawned. He told her of all the children he had scared over the centuries. Francois, the bed-wetter, Benjamin, who prayed every time he came close, Xiao Li, whose aged grandmother would rush in to comfort her every time she screamed, Motabi, the sleepwalker, and dozens and dozens more.

The Creature confessed to her that despite the nature of all their threats, his kind rarely ate children. It was the fear they thrived on, fear that was delicious and live-giving and gave their bodies strength. Child-flesh was stringy and bitter. Not for him at all.

Lily asked why he and his kind scared children, and the Creature said it was how things were. For ever since the first day of creation, when the Great Spirit had willed light into existence, there had been shadows, and there had been beings that lurked in them to feed on fear.

He apologised for all the nightmares he had given her, saying he could not help his nature.

But you should count your nightmares as blessings, the Creature reminded Lily. For often, a Shadow Creature forces a child to be brave, and find inner strength that otherwise would have been hidden. Little boys and little girls who found it in themselves to face the monsters under their bed would find the courage to face other monsters in their lives. They would never be shaken, no matter what life threw at them, and greatness would be their only destiny.

Lily asked about others like him, and the Creature was glad to oblige. He told her of the spider-bellied Xephir, who lurked in closets. He spoke of the Idtiliss, the long-fingered man with the scarred face that tapped at windows, begging to be let into houses. He told of the Lady Suffocate, a bloated corpse that hung upside down from bedroom ceilings in the dark, and of the Clown King, and the Inside-Out Man, of the Skeleton Witch and the Faceless Beast, the Seven Disgraces, and the Scream-By-Night.

And he told of Jerrifux, the prettiest Shadow-Creature he had ever laid eyes on, with her seven venomous tentacles and her hair that was a mass of writhing serpents. She had laid him a dozen eggs, which they had taken care of for about a month before each going their separate ways. Such was the way of their kind: never remaining together for longer than was necessary.

And the Creature said times were difficult for his kind now. The world was a terrifying place these days, and children were harder to scare. Movies and television, with their special effects, creating legions of monsters just as scary as a real Shadow-Creature. To say nothing of real life: why would anyone be scared of his night-time threats, with war, crime and injustice to worry about?

Many were the times when the Creature had visited old friends, only to discover their shrivelled bodies lying beneath beds and armchairs, in empty closets and under staircases. Members of his kind could not go too long without being nourished by fear, after all.

And he hoped he would never suffer such a fate.

**

One day in December, Uncle Daddy had a bad day at work.

His boss had caught him sleeping at his desk. There had been yelling, and cursing, and Uncle Daddy had been forced out, with barely an hour to pack his things. It had been very humiliating.

Cursing under his breath, Uncle Daddy had gone to a nearby bar, where he drank until midnight.

He drove home in a haze. It was a miracle he did not hit anything on the way.

When Uncle Daddy reached his house, the first thing he saw was Lily's shoes on the ground outside the door.

HOW MANY TIMES HAD HE TOLD THAT GIRL TO PUT HER SHOES ON THE RACK WHY WAS SHE SO DAMN STUBBORN...

"Lily! Lily!" he bellowed her name loudly. Furious, Uncle Daddy grabbed the feather duster from the table.

Stupid girl, he'd teach her to answer when she was called...

Lily was reading a magazine when Uncle Daddy burst into her room. She cried with fear as Uncle Daddy grabbed her and tossed her to the floor. With every ounce of strength, she apologised for what she had done, but her pleas fell on deaf ears as Uncle Daddy struck her again and again.

Whack. That was for his stupid boss. *Whack.* That was for his stupid mortgage. *Whack.* That was for his stupid wife, always nagging him, never supporting him...

Love. That was all he wanted. Why was it so difficult to find...?

His head was spinning. The effects of twelve shots of vodka were still affecting his mind.

He looked at his daughter, who was sobbing, her legs covered in red marks.

It was just then that a strange urge took over him. He picked his crying daughter off the floor, placing her gently on the bed.

"I'm sorry, Uncle Daddy," Lily wept. "I won't do it again, I'll be a good girl, I promise..."

"Shhh, Lily. It's all right. I'm not angry anymore. You can stop crying."

"Okay, Uncle Daddy. I promise I won't—"

He put his arm around her.

"Take off your dress, Lily."

"No Daddy! Please, no!"

"Take it off, Lily. You want to be a good girl, don't you?"

"But I don't want to, please—"

Enraged, Uncle Daddy sprung on Lily, his hands trembling as he fumbled with the buttons on her dress. Lily screamed and tried to fight him off, but he was too strong.

Just then, her room door opened, and there was a scream.

Mommy stood in the doorway, white-faced.

"What the hell are you doing?" she screamed. "Get your hands off my daughter, you pervert!"

Uncle Daddy gave a strangled cry. Furious, he picked up the feather duster and started hitting Mommy, who shrieked and did her best to try and protect herself.

Lily curled up in a corner, sobbing, only able to watch as her stepfather rained blow after blow on her mother. One punch caught her right in the mouth, knocking out a bloodstained tooth.

She wanted to scream.

It was just then that Lily heard a voice.

"You can't let him do this, Lily. You have to be brave."

"But I'm not," Lily wept. "I... I'm scared."

There was a laugh.

"You've faced down a Shadow Beast, and lived to tell the tale. Do you know how few people can say that? How can you still say you're not brave?"

Lily closed her eyes, and prayed.

She stood up, and turned to her father.

"Leave Mommy alone."

Uncle Daddy's hand stopped in mid-air: he had been about to land another blow on Mommy, who was sobbing, her hands over her face.

He turned towards his stepdaughter. "What the hell did you say?" he demanded.

"Leave Mommy alone," Lily said, louder. Her hands were trembling, but her voice was clear and firm. "Stop it! It's making her cry!"

"Little bitch," Uncle Daddy spat. "How dare you!"

Uncle Daddy marched towards her, feather duster in his hand raised. Lily wanted to scream, but forced herself to be brave.

Her stepfather did not manage to reach her.

For a pair of powerful claws lunged at him from beneath Lily's bed, ripping his flesh and causing him to fall to the ground.

'What the fu—"

To his horror, a hideous beast emerged from the shadows under Lily's bed. It was huge, with sharp claws like razor-blades, and piercing red eyes that blazed like the fires of hell.

"Monster!!!" it shouted at him, the shriek of a

demon.

Uncle Daddy was too terrified to speak as the thing lunged toward him, its claws outstretched, its teeth bared. Whimpering, he tried to crawl away, but fear had rooted him to the spot.

Mommy screamed: Lily, however, looked on in awe. This was the first time she had seen the Creature's full form.

"You have assumed the role of this child's daddy," the Creature said, "and that role comes with responsibilities. You are supposed to love her, and cherish her, and make her happy. Teach her right from wrong and educate her in the ways of the world. You are supposed to protect her from the monsters of the dark. That is the way it has always been. Yet you have perverted these sacred roles!"

Uncle Daddy was too terrified to respond. The Creature had never felt so powerful: the wretch's fear was overwhelming. He had never supped on the fear of a grown-up before: it was surprisingly nourishing.

Why had he been only scaring children till now? Adult fear was delectable. Adult fear was rich and flavourful, with a texture that was rough yet pleasant...

"Get out of this place, Lily," the Creature said. "Your mother needs help. Call an ambulance. Then call the police."

"And please, don't look back. I do not wish for you to see what I am about to do."

Lily nodded. "Thank you, my friend," she said. Supporting her Mommy, she headed downstairs.

Behind her came the clink of talons being unsheathed, a mighty roar...

...and the shrill screams of Uncle Daddy.

About Terence Toh

Terence Toh writes newspaper and magazine articles by day, and fiction by night. He is a merry wanderer of the night, constantly searching the world for fulfilment, inspiration and affordable plates of pasta. His short plays have been performed at the Short and Sweet Theatre and Musical festivals in Kuala Lumpur and Penang. Most recently, his short stories have been featured in the *KL Noir White* anthology published by Fixi Novo, and read on BFM Radio.

THE CHRISTMAS DRAGON

TOM TRUMPINSKI

Will Prentice itched everywhere. With winter here, his skin touched nothing but wool and wool had always made him itch. He and the other servants of the village of St. Eligius were restricted to the gallery at the rear of the church. They rose, sat, and knelt as one. Latin was beyond his understanding, but years of attending Mass gave him the general idea of what was going on. He didn't mind attending at all. The Saint's Day service—today, December first, the town's namesake's day—gave him a half-day off of work. And St. Eligius was the patron of blacksmiths, so the homily was going to be interesting.

Will always enjoyed the homilies. They were in English, after all. Sometimes, the instruction and correctives were directed at important parishioners. There were also tales of bloody martyrdoms and famous miracles, which showed him that the past was indeed much more interesting than today. He'd wager that the Romans didn't spend all of their time scratching beneath their togas.

The biggest problem was that as Father Albert aged, his voice grew weaker and weaker. Each week, Will found it harder and harder to hear the sermon. It didn't help that the gallery, presently free from responses, were whispering to each other about this morsel or that of gossip. If he was going to hear, he was going to have to get closer to the front.

The main floor of the church was filled with better-dressed townspeople—merchants, landowners, and trades-people. The wealthiest families—of the Mayor and those who ran the town—sat on the front benches and the least important near the back. The chill leaking in around the closed doors kept those folks shivering. The Lord in the manor atop the crag had his own priest and chapel, so his household only came down for Easter and Christmas.

Will carefully made his way down the stone stairs, keeping to the shadows. Boys like him were not allowed on the main floor and if he was caught, he'd get a thrashing at the very least. He hid behind an arch in the wall halfway back and listened as the Priest told tales of the life of the Saint.

Eligius had been a blacksmith like Henry Smith, the man he worked for, and as Fr. Albert continued, Will pictured the Saint with the strong shoulders and bulging muscles of his trade. The last story concerned a horse possessed by demons that had been brought in to be shod. The horse would not hold still for the smith to work, so St. Eligius, his patience gone, removed the horse's leg and nailed on a shoe while the horse waited patiently on three legs. Afterwards, the Saint miraculously reattached the leg and the horse, now demon-free, left the smithy tame and gentle.

Towards the end of the sermon, Dick, the miller's spoiled son, noticed Will lurking in the shadows. The fat boy made a fig with his fist, shook it toward the apprentice, and then reached for his father's shoulder, probably to tap it and point him out. At the last moment, Dick paused to gloat about his victory and Will saw his chance.

The apprentice, hiding behind the edge of the arch, threw his voice—imitating the sound of the bully breaking wind (and smiled while he did it, giving it all he had). The miller and his wife both turned and frowned at their son, and Dick flamed scarlet and sputtered, his enemy forgotten for the moment. The homily ended, the congregation rose to come forward for the Host, and Will slipped up the stairs and back into the milling crowd in the gallery.

**

Communion for the gallery-folk went quickly and then it was back onto the road from the church to the smithy. Will took his time, even though his stomach was rumbling, since when he got back, there'd be plenty of hard work after he ate his midday bread and cheese. Snow crunched beneath his shoes and his breath came out in great clouds. As he passed the waist-high wall at the edge of the village proper, an icy ball smacked the back of his head. Turning, he saw the miller boy and two villiens on the other side of the wall. Grasping snow in their hands, they leapt over the wall and came running at Will, the look in their eyes clearly indicating that maiming him was foremost in their thoughts.

The apprentice was tall and lean and capable of sudden bursts of energy. The boys chasing him were less used to hard work. Will had a lead, and it was long enough that they would not catch him before he reached safety. The trio stopped in place and readied their missiles. Hunching his shoulders, Will anticipated the next snowball striking him—last month, after the first big snowfall, they had filled them with rocks.

Two narrowly missed him and he was looking back over his shoulder to dodge the last of the volley when the Dragon-horn sounded. One note meant the Duke of Lancaster was on his way south; two meant that Yorkists were counter-marching. It was fortunate for their community that both armies, whether they belonged to the White or the Red faction, depended on the services of blacksmiths and the townsfolk who supported those smithies. Non-essential towns were often burned by one army to keep them out of the hands of the other. In any case, the armies would be on the lookout for young conscripts and all the boys would have to hide until the soldiers passed by. Therefore, the four of them stopped dead still, eyeing each other and looking for possible advantages while there was still time to take them. If they clubbed him, they could leave him dazed in the road for the press gangs to find.

The horn sounded a third time, which meant one or more dragons. Will jumped and dashed for the armoury next to the smithy, moving so quickly that his feet slid out from under him. Lying on the ground, he saw a flying beast high overhead—its dull red wings tipped into the shape dragons used to dive and skim the ground, looking for untended sheep.

St. George had led his knights on their extermination mission around Europe a thousand years before, killing the huge beasts wherever they found them. But whole flocks still lurked in the hills and crags of Scotland and now those were moving south, growing fat on the bodies of men and horses left behind on the battlefields. Will's grandfather had chilled him with fireside tales of dragons walking on their wingtips across the killing fields of France, their feathers brilliant in the sunlight, as they fed on casualties not yet dead. Only English longbowmen stood a chance of driving them off.

That meant that he had to reach the smithy and pack arrows, as many as he could, and make sure that Henry Smith had a constant supply. The village's men were coming out of their houses now, stopping to bend their bows and string them. Will made it to the armoury just as Henry was strapping on his bracer. "Boy, take those bundles and be quick. Follow me—the Lords' troops haven't left enough stock that we can afford to feed these monsters."

The archers lined up, rank and file. The yeoman on the far side of Will had no-one to provide him with arrows. Henry nodded towards him so the boy stuck six arrows, point down, within the yeoman's reach. Twenty men pulled back as one and when their Captain shouted, "Loose," the arrows flew toward a spot in the sky ahead of the dragon. The volley pierced its wings and a few arrows stuck in its side. In the past, visiting dragons had taken that as a warning—flying off to areas where no-one was shooting at them.

This time was different. It gave a great, shrill cry, which made Will want to cower with his hands over his ears. Rising into the sky and turning, it launched itself straight at the square of men, narrowly missing the first two rows with its talons. The boy struggled to keep his balance when the wind of its passage buffeted him. Over the church, it arced back up for another pass. This time, the archers were ready and it flew directly into a dozen direct hits. The scream was even louder now and definitely one of pain. *Why isn't it running away? They'll kill it next pass for sure.* It stopped for a moment, landing on the byre where Smith kept the milk cow and sheep during the winter. The scene was silent except for the sound of men panting as they held their bows taut. With one final scream, the monster launched toward the bowmen and landed in front of them, mortally wounded. It lifted itself on its legs and wingtips and its long neck whipped back and forth, looking for something to reach with its sword-sharp bill, easily the length of a man's arm.

Henry and Will were directly below its head now and its golden-eyed gaze fell upon them. It opened its mouth to strike and then collapsed, dying in the middle of the road.

The townspeople seemed stunned—they were certainly silent. *No-one expected to kill it. There aren't any stories about people nowadays taking down dragons—at least none that I've heard.*

John Farmer, who owned a house a league past the smithy on the London Road, was first to speak. "Is it dead? How can you tell?" He poked it with his bow—nothing happened.

Several men answered at once. "Looks dead."

Another added, "We need to be careful, though, could be a feint."

Henry reached out with calloused hands and brushed the ruddy feathers on its head with the back of a finger. "It's dead all right. Send a runner to the Manor—the Lord needs to know about this."

The crowd swelled, now that it was deemed safe. Oldsters, women, and girls came from the houses of the village to see the wonder. The younger girls tittered, fingers over their lips, and stared at the fallen beast. The younger boys ran around its body and two brave ones tried to climb atop it, but fell off when its rib bones broke beneath their feet.

The Seneschal and two men rode up on black horses. It was the closest that Will had ever seen the old soldier. He surveyed the crowd and dismounted, handing his reins to one of the village boys. He cupped his hands and shouted, "Is the Reverend Father here?"

Father Albert came forward, parting the sea of folk. "Yes, Sir James."

"Is this a beast of the air or a devil from hell?"

"There has not been a Papal decision on this subject, to the best of my knowledge."

The Lord's man stepped closer to the Church's man, now less than six feet from Will, and lowering his voice so that it would not carry said, "It has to be forty or fifty stone. Can we eat it? Can we salt it away, perhaps? So far the warring Lords have left us alone, but winter campaigns make for hungry men. What say you?"

"You could not eat it on Saint's Days or for a Friday meal, but on another day, it might not hurt to try to cook some of it and test the virtue of its humours."

"Good enough. Butcher?"

"Here," the town's slaughter-man answered.

"Skin it. Bring its feathers, skin, and meat to the Manor. Save all of the rest of it for Father Albert to send to whichever Archbishop is currently in London or to the Oxford dons." With that, he remounted and led his men up the crag-road toward the keep.

**

Henry and Will walked back to the smithy together, the older man limping slightly from the sprain he had taken during the dragon's first rush. "You comported yourself well, William," he said, "at least as well as any Lordling's page in his first battle. Did you see those other boys run away?"

Will nodded.

"If you run in battle, you're already dead, though the breath in your body may fool you for a time. Mounted knights will race through a mob of cravens—slicing, stabbing, and killing them from behind. The only way to stand a chance against a strong enemy is to meet it face-on, preferably with a weapon from our forge." They reached the front door of Smith's house. "Wait here. I will have Anne bring you out a basket with a slice or two of mutton added to your loaf and cheese. A young soldier deserves a decent ration." He prodded Will on the shoulder with his fist. "No work this afternoon. We will begin anew tomorrow at sunrise. There is barstock ready to make horseshoes—outriders said this morning that there's a big battle brewing north of us in Yorkshire."

Will crouched outside the door, waiting. Sitting upon his haunches, he looked at the low sunlight glinting from the snowdrifts, like jewels before his eyes. He felt alive—the Miller boy and his gang of thugs were nothing compared to the ferocious jaws of a dragon, after all. He wiggled his fingers. Everything still worked—all over his body. Glancing around first, he dipped his fingers beneath his corded belt and scratched, stopping immediately when the cottage door opened and Anne

Smith, the eldest daughter, brought him his basket of food. She kept her eyes averted, but her cheeks were flushed—perhaps with excitement or concern.

"What was it like?" she asked. "Was Father brave? Were there more than one? Was it hard to kill it? Mother kept us inside, baking bread and cutting up turnips and carrots for stew. I so wanted to see the battle."

"It was frightening, but your father never wavered, even when it flew at us. When that happened, some of the other archers froze in place and a few of the boys helping them ran or lay in the snow, crying."

"You didn't, though, did you?"

"No, I handed him arrows when he needed them and he fired, again and again, until the beast fell before us. It was red as dried blood, large as the spring-house, and had feathers like the biggest goose God ever made."

She lifted her eyes and smiled at him. "Thank you, Will, for helping keep him safe. It is good that you're here."

**

Will did not have idle time often enough to know what to do with it. He took the basket to the forge and sat next to the furnace, the heat making him comfortable and removing the stiffness from his fingers and toes. Fatty chunks of mutton floated in the stew and he tore off pieces of bread and dunked them in, savouring the juices. There was even a whole carrot in the bowl—Anne must have dropped that in when she was getting it ready. When he was nearly finished, Will could still see sunlight coming through cracks in the wall.

Brindle-cat has kittens in the byre's loft. There's a crust or two left, maybe I could get them close enough to pet. Some of the other boys tormented cats and kittens, but Will admired their self-reliance and speed. He wished that he could hide like them, wait for prey to come close, and then leap out and seize it, faster even than a ferret. When John Farmer brought his plow horse in for shoes, he claimed that cats were good luck and villages that tolerated them were less likely to have plague. *Sounds like a Wives' Tale to me*, Will thought. *Doesn't matter anyway, they were made by God and named by Adam in the Garden—if they did no harm, they deserved to be left alone.*

The byre was built into a hillside and had two levels. The top level had a cart-path to it and was used to store sheaves of wheat and sacks of grain. The lower level was where they kept all the livestock—Brownie the milch cow, Spots the piglet, and five pregnant ewes and a ram—that the passing armies had left them from the past summer. At sundown, he would throw down enough grain into their pens for them to eat. In the morning, as soon as his breakfast loaf was finished, he'd shovel the muck from the pens and pile it next to the byre. There it would sit until spring, when Smith would sell it to the neighbouring farms to be spread upon the fields.

Will pulled open the door to the top level and stepped inside. *It isn't usually this bright inside. What's going on?* He spotted a hole in the thatch, up near the top—and a big hole it was, too. Brindle and her two kittens were lying on a grain sack, the mother cat holding them down with one paw and washing them thoroughly with her tongue. They had been born in late September—

fall kittens were not usual, and often didn't last until spring.

He moved to a clear spot an arm's length from the cats and dropped the soggy bread-crusts onto a bare spot on the floor. Backing away, he reached a corner and sat, folding his legs beneath him.

"BLAAAAAAT!" Around the corner of the stacks of grain came what Will at first thought was the largest goose he had ever seen—a scarlet one at that. *No, it's not running on two legs, it's also pulling itself forward on its... wing claws. Oh, the Saints save me—a dragon.*

The mother cat hissed, reared up on its hind legs, and swatted the baby dragon twice across the face with its claws. The creature tried to stop, but instead slid forward, as if it had not yet fully learned to use its limbs. It gave another loud honk as it moved its long neck back and forth, looking at the bread, the cats, and Will. After a moment or two, the mother cat relented and the dragon tossed the bread crust into the air and caught it on the way down. The kittens jumped at its scaly legs, which looked just like a chicken's. It prodded them away with the side of its head.

"What is *that*?" Anne asked.

Will jumped two feet into the air. He recovered, red-faced. "The big dragon left a baby behind. No wonder it didn't fly away."

"What should we do about it—the baby, I mean?"

"We'll have to tell your father. They're dangerous and destructive."

"Look," she said, "it's sitting on the floor right next to the kittens. It doesn't look all that troublesome."

Will moved closer. The dragon hissed at him, so

he retreated a step. "Why isn't it eating them? They're burrowing into its feathers, as a matter of fact."

"Remember the baby duck that hatched while its mother was missing? It saw the old sow and followed it around for months. It thinks Brindle is its mother."

Will rummaged in the loft. "That's so curious." When he set a small pile of grain near the dragon, its head whipped around, jerking forward several times as it pecked up the grains of wheat.

"Let's keep it," Anne said.

"You'd not tell your father? When he catches us, we'll both be tanned—and for good reason. They eat people... and horses... and cattle... and sheep."

"It eats grain, too. Brindle will probably teach it to catch rats and we can give it some of the grain each night. There's enough additional for even a hard winter."

He shook his head, trying to think. "All right, but promise me this, Anne. If your father finds out, tell him that you had nothing to do with this. Protecting the dragon was my idea—you should pretend that you didn't even know about it. Swear!"

"By Holy Mary's cousin Elizabeth, I pledge to tell my father that the dragon is yours. Does that do it? I need to get the milk to the springhouse. When I'm in the byre tomorrow morning, I will feed it and we can look at it together at evening milking time—they won't notice if I'm a little bit late coming back, but now I have to hurry." She climbed down the ladder to the lower level and carried the pail out of the door.

Will sat on his haunches and watched the animals. The purples and reds of winter sunset shone through the hole in the roof. A cold breeze kept him from dozing off for a while, but when his chin hit his chest for the third time, he left the loft by the side door, went to his mat in the forge, and curled up, falling into a sleep inhabited by clawed, feathered wings.

For the next few weeks, the two children worked hard with their animals, adding extra work to their schedules so that Henry and Dame Smith would stay away from the byre. It worked, not least because Henry had received commissions to shoe the horses of York's knights as they moved to follow their Duke toward Wakefield. Dame Smith prodded all three daughters in the preparations for Christmas—new outfits to be sewn for Midnight Mass and a special dinner for the family on Christmas Day.

The baby dragon chased rats and mice around both floors of the byre. By the week before Christmas, it could leap down from the loft for a hunt and then fly back up to reach its nest on the upper floor. To keep the dragon from escaping, Will piled sacks of grain until they were close to the hole in the roof and then covered them with oilcloth to keep them dry.

On December Sundays, the homilies for the season were some of Will's favourites. Father Albert spoke of the Star, the charity of the innkeepers toward the Holy Family, and the animals in the manger speaking on the night that the Child was born.

On Saturday the 22nd, a press gang from the Yorkists swept through the town. Will was frantically pumping the bellows while Smith hammered shoes into shape. The horsemen spared him nary a glance. The Miller boy hid, escaping, but his two friends were not so lucky and seized with only the clothes on their backs and tossed up behind knights heading north. If anything, this made the bully more dangerous. On the way back after Sunday Mass, he lurked behind Will, looking for a chance to do the boy harm, but there were always too many people around.

**

As Sunday evening fell, Dick Miller stayed beneath the trees, using their shadows to cloak him while he watched Anne carry her pails from the spring house to the barn for the evening milking. Earlier, Will had gone into the loft by the upper door. *Interesting,* he thought, *a boy and a girl alone after dark in an outbuilding—they have to be up to something nasty. I can ruin them both in one swoop.*

He crept to the loft door and slid it open a crack, relieved when the hinges didn't squeak. It was dim in the room, the only light being that which reflected from the ceiling. *The girl's got to be down below, near the animal pens.* He could hear the streams of milk hitting the sides of the pail as she milked the brown cow. Lying on his stomach, he inched forward, finally reaching the edge of the loft floor and looking downward. *They're not doing* anything *at all—she's working and he's sitting with his back against the wall. Fie on them, I'll get them later.*

Then his gaze fell upon the pile of bright red in the corner of the stall. *It* moved. *Is that a goose? No, it's a devil or monster.* The dragon looked straight at him and then launched itself upward, wings spread. *Hellfire, it's a creature of the Pit.* He leapt to his feet and bolted through the loft door, stopping just long enough to slam it behind him. *I've got to tell Father about this and get him to warn the Priest.*

**

The day before Christmas dawned clear, cold, and bright. Anne milked while Will forked the manure into the wheelbarrow and dumped it onto the pile outside the byre. Finished, they both took the time to feed the dragon grain and, for once, it allowed them to get close enough to rub its feathers. The kittens were large enough that they were poking their noses into all of the corners, while Brindle-cat watched her unusual family from above, sitting on the edge of the loft.

"Just a half-day at the forge today, Anne." Will smiled. "Mass tonight will be beautiful. Is your mother baking all day?"

"Don't worry. I'll bring some nut-cakes over with your supper tonight. I also mended your vest so you won't look like a landless peasant when you sit in church. Blessings on you, Will." She closed the door behind her. Will followed a moment later, giving a last glance at the animals to make sure all was in order.

Will pumped the bellows and Henry hammered the hot bars into shape. He used a punch to make holes for the nails and then, when each shoe was done, they quenched them in the water barrel. By now, they didn't have to speak much, just watch each other's moves. The smith smiled when Will couldn't see—the boy was going to be better than him, given time. When the war is over and things settle down, he'd start looking for a good marriage for his daughters, starting with Anne. Once they were out of the house, he could finish Will's training and sell the boy the smithy—sit by the fire, no longer have to worry about being kicked in the skull. This was work for the young.

After work, Will sat in the warmth of the fire and ate his bread and cheese. There were hours of prayer today to get ready for Mass tonight. One had to be worthy to welcome the Holy Child to the world. First, though, he walked over to look in, once more, on the marvellous creature that had come to stay with them. The dragon was awake and when it saw him at the door, it stood up and walked across to him on its legs and wings, like the largest bat in Creation. "I'll have to give you a name," he said, rubbing the side of its long neck. There were feathers that had fallen off and were lying in the manger. Before he went back to his mat in the smithy, he made sure that he had picked them all up and hidden them safely in his pillow.

**

An hour before midnight, Will sat up on his pallet, pulled on his shirt and tightened his belt. On the walk, his boots crunched on the snow, for it was cold enough that his breath not only came out as steam, but lingered in the air as he passed. The townsfolk moved briskly toward the church, as above it, the Dog Star shone and the Hunter guarded the starry expanses for yet another year.

From the rear of the church, he had the ideal vantage. This was one of the nights where the noblemen and women usually came to the village church, but the Lord and his knights were not present—they must have ridden off to the impending battle, though what side they were fighting on, Will didn't really know or care.

As Mass wore on, though, Will noticed a tenseness. The Priest seemed distracted and often would glance at the benches where his Master was seated. Other men, some of them men-at-arms, were doing the same. Edward Miller could hardly stay still in his seat and his son Dick turned around every few minutes and smirked at Will. The chill running up Will's back was not from the air seeping through cracks in the wall behind him. *He knows. He found out, somehow, and he told people. This is really bad.*

The Nobles left first after Communion, giving Will time to slip forward and catch Anne's eye. She met him in the shadow of an arch.

"Dick Miller knows. I think he told his father. Look at them over there by Father Albert—there's a half-dozen whispering together."

Anne looked past his shoulder, toward the front of the chapel. "What are we going to do? They'll kill it for certain."

"Talk to your da'. Tell him anything, but get him to delay those men, even if just for a few moments. There may be something I can try that will work."

"All right." Anne moved toward Henry Smith as Will slipped through the door and into the night. "Father," she said, "Will's in trouble and needs our help."

He leaned down so that she could whisper in his ear.

**

Will ran as if all of the devils in Hell were after him. He stayed out of sight of the line of horses carrying the Manor-folk back to their home—it would take too long to make excuses if one of them stopped him to ask his business. The icy air filled his lungs, freezing him from the inside out. By the time he reached the byre and struck the lantern, he had finalised his plan. The animals were asleep in the corners, with the dragon in a pile with Brindle and her kittens. He opened the door to the sheep pen, letting them wander into the light. Brownie wanted to stay asleep, but he poked her over and over until she reluctantly stood up and stuck her head into the manger, chewing on a few sheaves of wheat she had missed earlier. Will found a spot behind the animals where he hoped no-one would see him.

**

"That boy says that there's a devil in my byre?" The smith glared at Dick. "That's why you're making such a fuss?" The cords on Henry's neck stood out in the flickering torchlight. "Don't you think I would know if such a thing were true? Father, you cannot possibly believe this."

Father Albert's voice, gritty from hours of preaching, could just barely be heard over the low rumble of conversation within the dozen men standing in a circle. "I have my doubts, Henry, but the Church must remain vigilant. Edward Miller has as much standing in the congregation as you do and if he brings this to my attention, we must investigate."

"It's Christmas night, Father. Can't this wait?"

"Let us go to your byre and look inside. That should put all questions to rest. Go and get your swords, all, and meet us between the smithy and the byre. I will walk with you, Henry—send your family home."

**

There was a great deal of confusion when the crowd re-assembled. Several of the townsmen, better trained in pike than sword, were waving their weapons around in ways that endangered each other. The Captain finally told them to sheathe them, shut up, and wait for Henry and the Priest to arrive.

When they were all together, they moved in lock-step to the door of the byre, threw it open and stopped, stunned, at the sight before them.

Sitting in the manger, moving its head from side to side staring at the torches wielded by the intruders, was the dragon, the size of a small calf. Several of the men had pulled their swords halfway from the sheath and stepped forward when Brownie, the cow, spoke to them.

"Why is it that you come to disturb our prayers on this Holy Night, children of Man? Do you not know that a manger is a sacred place, the birthplace of Our Lord?"

Edward Miller shouted at the animal—"That creature of the Devil is among you. We have come to destroy it, as we did its sire."

The ram raised its head and stared Miller in the eye. "That was its mother that you killed. She left it in this byre for safe-keeping and it has been here ever since, under our protection. Step forward and I shall butt you and knock you on your nethers."

The Captain said, "But you must know, dragons eat animals like you. How can you protect it?"

Brindle-cat took a moment off from washing her

face to answer, her voice quivering with disdain. "It has been eating rats and mice, like the rest of my babies. We work to keep your farms and homes free from vermin and what do we get—chased and tormented by evil children. Get thee hence. Leave this creature, which is just another child of God, in peace."

The dragon lifted its head and croaked, "When my wings are ready, I promise that I will fly back home and leave you alone, forever."

Father Albert looked at the animals, whose eyes reflected the fire of the torches. "The stories are true—the animals can speak tonight—and the words that they say must be so, since they come by way of Our Lord in Heaven. Let us leave them be. Henry, close your door before the poor things freeze." He turned and led the procession away, in the direction of his church.

When they were gone, Will stood up, sore from kneeling in one spot for so long. *The miracle is that that cat didn't just walk away or the sheep run out the door while I was doing all that talking for them.* He stopped for a moment to scratch the dragon beneath its chin and, closing the byre's door behind him, stepped into the cold, heading for his pallet in the smithy.

**

The old man held the hands of his two grandchildren while he finished his story. They were sleepy, for the trip up from London was hard on a child.

"They're for bed, now, da'," his daughter said. "We need to put them to bed before we walk to Mass."

"No, not yet, I want to show them. You too—you haven't been up here since the elder was born. Come out to the square with me."

Will's daughter, Margaret, just showing silver threads woven within her red hair, bundled the two young ones. "Lizzie, James, come with us outside, just for a few minutes."

The two children rubbed their eyes and waddled out of the cottage door. To the South, the village church shone with the lights of Christmas Eve—Orion's Belt and Sirius brilliant above them in the clear English night just as they had been that midnight so long ago.

They waited in silence, until the first whispers of wings came to them across the breeze. Then, wide wings flapped as England's last dragon flew above them to perch on the steeple of the church. It folded its wings, looked across the village, and then began to voice the unearthly beauty of its eight-note night-song—as if it were the largest nightingale that God had ever created.

About Tom Trumpinski

Tom Trumpinski is a stay-at-home dad and writer who retired from university teaching five years ago. He lives in the American Midwest. *The Christmas Dragon* began when a friend of his asked him to write a story with a cat and a dragon in it. He decided to make everything non-dragon as realistic as possible. For most of humanity's existence, children have had to worry about whether or not they'd have enough food, whether they'd be drafted for a war, or if one army or another would raze the only homes they have ever known. We need to make sure this stops and never starts up again.

CPSIA information can be obtained at www.ICGtesting.com
Printed in the USA
LVOW08s1113280414

383531LV00003B/148/P

9 780473 277215